I0666398

OTHER WORKS BY E. S. FEIN

The Collected Histories of Neoevolution Earth
A Dream of Waking Life
Points of Origin
Ascendescenscion
The Process is Love

OfficialESFein.com
Linktr.ee/ESFein
Instagram.com/Authoresfein
Patreon.com/Officialesfein
Facebook.com/AuthorESFein

PRAISE FOR MENDEL'S LADDER

"Reading Mendel's Ladder is like jumping onto a roller coaster that's just hurtling nonstop into a future that's both wild and deeply thought provoking. This is Earth in 2099, but it's like nothing you've seen before, with folks evolving into Nomads and flesh trees, these awesome human/plant mixtures. It's weird, it's crazy, but boy, is it cool." — Reader Review

"Mendel's Ladder, elevates the realms of scifi and dystopia into an intoxicating concoction of raw emotion, philosophical questioning, and adrenaline-fueled battles. Across an alien yet familiar Earth, Fein weaves layers upon layers of intricate lore and characters that are as profound as they are endearing." — Reader Review

"I haven't had this much fun reading a story in a long time. Think the philosophy of Dune mixed with the gritty action of Mad Max, all tied together with some Hyperion-level world building. This is scifi at its very finest, and the best part about it is that it's a series, so there's much more to come! Looking forward to what Fein conjures for us next!" — Reader Review

"There is something absolutely eerie yet alluring about the world and characters Fein has constructed. Behind these extremely fleshed out characters is an ominous group of powers at play. As each of the three major stories converge, I was left wondering who to root for while at the same time rooting for all sides because you can't help growing attached to these characters." — Reader Review

"The world-building really thrust my mind into this gory, visceral hellscape that Earth is transformed into by the big powers at play and I found myself constantly thinking ahead to what plans they had in store for the world. I still feel as if there are beings behind the scenes pulling strings that I couldn't even begin to comprehend still to reveal themselves. The world feels deadly dangerous and yet somehow beautiful with its sprouting vibrant life contrasted with the savagery of mutant animals and bloodlust hunters/huntresses who will stop at nothing to kill in pursuit of their eternal hunt." — Reader Review

"A mix of scifi, fantasy, mystery, and litRPG--Mendel's Ladder offers a surprisingly fun ride despite the depth and severity of the themes it toys with. I found myself attached to even the side characters, with every character carefully crafted and imbued with utterly convincing identities. There is so much going on in this story! Epic world building, high intensity battles, compelling mystery, and wholly unique science fiction concepts abound in every chapter. Each character struggles with their own real conflict, and the author does an expert job exploring these concepts in a fun yet serious way." — Reader Review

The Collected Histories of

Neoevolution Earth

Volume 1

Mendel's Ladder

Federated Agency Publishing

E. S. Fein

Mendel's Ladder (Neoevolution Earth Vol. 1)

Copyright © 2023 by E. S. Fein

Author: E. S. Fein

Publisher: Federated Agency Publishing

Editor: Nichole Paolella Petrovich

Formatter: Timbers Book Design

Ebook ISBN: 978-1-7323069-9-8

Paperback ISBN: 978-1-7323069-7-4

Publication Date: October 2023

Library of Congress Catalog Number: 2023910705

First Edition

There is no light in the darkness of being without love. To everyone I love and cherish and to those who love me in return: you make existence worthwhile. Special Thanks to Claire, Nichole, and Sabrina (Madre), a trio of ultra-badass women.

CONTENTS

BOOK SUMMARIES AND GLOSSARY

Visit OfficialESFein.com for a summary of **Volume 1: Mendel's Ladder** and a **Glossary of Terms** ranging the entire Neoevolution Earth series.

Volume 1

Mendel's Ladder

Death. Entropy. Subatomic separation.

What a waste.

All that awaits us is dirt if we cannot forge our own path across the stars and beyond.

Natural evolution cannot suffice. Humanity requires a self-driven evolution. A neoevolution.

This is what I call Mendel's Ladder. A ladder upward and out of evolutionary chance. A ladder to the cosmos. A ladder out of chaos and into existential meaning.

Not our own misconstrued, ignorant meaning. Actual meaning. A legitimate reason for existing.

From Mendel's Ladder: The Personal Journal of Denis Mendel, Written Circa 2041, Published June 2108 by Leif Mainstone, Federated Agency Publishing

Chapter 1
The End of the Beginning

Year: 2099, Present Day

Azure Ivy joyfully stood at the edge of a cliff overlooking the largest flesh tree grove in the entire Butcher Wastelands. This area was sacred to the People of Earth and to Earth itself. Across the great expanses of saltwater where the seemingly endless kelp forests anchored in the ocean floor reached for miles toward the warmth of Sol, even in those faraway places, the People of Earth viewed the Butcher Wastelands with veneration. This particular flesh tree grove called Hunter Dreaming was the most revered patch of land in all the world, let alone all the Wastes.

It was said by many People that when the flesh trees and the tangle grass and Earth itself grew wary of their lives, they would let their minds wander across the mycelial network and arrive at this hallowed place, viewing it through Azure Ivy.

Azure Ivy did not take his honored position for granted. Each and every day for the last thirty-three Sol-revolutions, he stood nearly motionless on this cliff edge with arms and legs outstretched, allowing as much of his ivy as possible to taste the sweetness of Sol and the nuanced sensory input of his surroundings. His roots extended thousands of feet into the rock below, lapping at the scant water hidden in the pockets of organic matter. Other tendrils of his roots were intertwined with the global mycelial network constituting Earth's collective and singular mind.

Sweetness of Sol. Bitterness of rock. Fullness of soil. Willfulness of wind.

Azure Ivy absorbed each language of Earth and allowed every connected mind of Earth to experience the real time present moment of Hunter Dreaming. Slowly, Azure Ivy craned his neck forward and looked down in the direction of the area's namesake.

Far below him, beneath a dense canopy of thousands of interweaving, brazenly diverse flesh trees, the last Hunter of the world hibernated and dreamed of his terrible past. Sometimes Azure Ivy thought he could directly feel the turbulent dreams of that ruthless monster sent from City in the Sky. But that was just his imagination. His imagination was something that scared him and seemed to be growing worse every day.

Transition time but a moon away, Azure Ivy thought to himself, and Earth said in response, *but a few moments.*

Very close, Azure Ivy assured himself with the eagerness of a spring wind. It was not easy to live so long. In fact, it was virtually unheard of. Most People of Earth transitioned no later than ten Sol-revolutions after dropping from their flesh tree.

Azure Ivy recollected the comfort of his birth pod, and the wise, compassionate mind of his flesh tree.

Soon I comfort my own pods, Azure Ivy thought with excited delight, before redirecting his awareness to his surroundings at the gentle behest of numerous minds utilizing his senses from all across the planet. *Soon.*

A tuft of ivy stood stiffly at the base of Azure Ivy's neck, signaling the long-expected awakening of City in the Sky from its nearly forty Sol-revolution slumber. Something was ejected from its metal skin, like a seed from its pod. Azure Ivy had a perfect view of the orbiting city at this time of the season, and he directed his many eyes and ivies above, at the great expanse beyond Earth.

Now, he transmitted to every connected life currently utilizing the mycelial network. *Long awaited moment.*

Earth directed every mind to Azure Ivy's senses, making him feel like an expansive ocean that every river of the world had suddenly been directed to all at once. Azure Ivy watched with jubilant anticipation along with every other connected life as City in the Sky's seed plummeted to Earth's surface, its vector aligning precisely with Hunter Dreaming.

A Huntress? Azure Ivy asked Earth. *The Huntress,* Earth answered with a contented whisper. *All exactly as He foretold. The beginning is coming to an end,* Earth assured Azure Ivy. *Now you transition. A life fulfilled. May second life restore, Azure Ivy of Hunter Dreaming.*

Earth's words filled Azure Ivy with the overwhelming ecstasy that every Person of Earth looks forward to experiencing. Every cell of his body stilled. His leaves and vines twirled and tightened, depleting the macromolecules and water of Azure Ivy's vital and sensory organs. His ivy grew, extending into a pillar through his torso and down into the rocky Earth. Azure Ivy screamed with terrible pleasure, and as he arched his back and raised his gaping mouth to City in the Sky, his ivy jutted upward through his spine, his brain, and then his eyes and orifices. His ivy's cells and his human cells were like gametes now, and as they fused zygotically, they formed the first cells of a flesh tree.

As his individual consciousness dissipated, Azure Ivy's awareness of the Earth's collective consciousness became clearer than ever. In that interim period between individuality and multitude, a resplendent, dazzling vision permeated his mind, and Azure Ivy observed with sublime deference the whole of His glorious plan: the Huntress and Hunter Pair, the man from City in the Sky, the young human-like twin girls, and so many others as well. His Foretold Future hinged on them all. All of their stories would now converge, and this convergence would bear the fruit of the tree He had been growing for nearly a hundred Sol-revolutions. *No, not tree,* Azure Ivy beheld with awe. *Ladder. Mendel's Ladder. His plans. People of Earth's plans. Human plans. So many plans. Now all comes together,* Azure Ivy saw with euphoric wonder. He understood through crystal premonition that the next rung of Mendel's Ladder would be ascended, and nothing would ever be the same.

Finally, Azure Ivy thought sweetly.

All at once, Azure Ivy's individual consciousness was no more.

A flesh tree covered in ocean-blue ivy stretched a hundred feet into the air, continuing Azure Ivy's ceaseless vigil of Hunter Dreaming. Countless connected minds peered through the flesh tree's senses, and many even relished the warmth and compassion of the flesh tree as it tasted its environment and filled each of its flesh pods with the genetics necessary for Earth's wellbeing. In another season those flesh pods would fall, and from them would emerge more People to live and breathe and drink from Earth.

Hunters and Huntresses. As ruthless as they are deadly.

A Huntress is the Earth's punishment, retribution, justice.

A Hunter is the Earth's anger, pain, sorrow.

Together they are the deadliest weapon ever created. Even a nuclear bomb has its limitations. You can build a very strong bunker to withstand the blast. But there is nowhere someone can hide that a Hunter cannot follow. They emerge like T-cells from Astrea, and they rain down upon Earth like cascading death. Creatures come to purge humanity from the planet to make way for the Nomads, the new People of the Earth.

Some will undoubtedly find ways to hide or even destroy a Hunter or Huntress.

No matter.

Astrea can provide an endless supply of Hunters and Huntresses to the Earth, just as the body's thymus never tires of sending T-cells to aid the body in its maintenance and defenses.

Hunters and the Huntresses are the immune system of the planet. Humanity is the cancer. And I am the mind.

I choose to purge my body of its cancer. For too long humanity has stood in my way. Our species is festering, withering, rotting.

No more. For today come the Hunters and Huntresses. Each human has a choice now: become a Nomad or die.

From Mendel's Ladder: The Personal Journal of Denis Mendel, Recorded June 11, 2051, Published June 2108 by Leif Mainstone, Federated Agency Publishing

Chapter 2
The Huntress

S udden jarring turbulence and shocking brightness spurred the Huntress' heart into pumping, her lungs into breathing, her other vital organs into their respective functions. Already moving at Astrea's orbiting velocity of roughly 18,000 mph and keeping steady acceleration, she didn't experience the typical stomach-sinking feeling of free-fall as she rocketed through the thermosphere and broke into the thin mesosphere like a meteorite. She opened her eyes and observed from the sky her sacred hunting ground, the Earth, for the first time.

<Vital Organs: Optimal>

Her breathing remained labored, filling each cell with quickly depleted oxygen. After a few dozen breaths, the light subsided to a dim glow, allowing her to read the data written across her vision in real time.

<Peripheral Organs: Optimal>

<Sensory Organs: Optimal>

<System Update: 1%>

The system update increased in percentage roughly a few percent each second, and with each passing second whole petabytes of memories and languages and disciplines and abilities were downloaded into the Huntress' ravenous mind.

<System Update: 27%>

[My name?] the Huntress asked the Marrow, aware now of her individuality and role as Huntress.

<Name: Huntress4430 And Huntress6561>

[I have two names?] the Huntress checked.

<System Error: Multiple Designations>

<Solution: System Reset>

[Override] the Huntress responded immediately. [It's just a name. I'll pick my own]

<Solution: Accepted>

I get to choose my own name, the Huntress considered with excitement.

<Focus: Misplaced>

<Solution: Choose Designation Huntress6561>

[Shut up] she told the Marrow. [I'm nearly out of the Thymus now, for Mendel's sake. It's just a name]

<Focus: Misplaced>

<Solution: Place Focus On Eternal Hunt>

[What's the system update at, Marrow?]

<System Update: 79%>

With the Marrow distracted and spouting off percentages, the Huntress let her mind wander through whole arrays of human languages spanning thousands of years of history. It took her only a second to scan a million different names and settle on a Russian name that could be roughly translated into English Universal as "free will." Plus, it was technically a boy's name, which made it all the more perfect—like a trophy to her volition.

I can choose and do anything I please, Volya practically purred to herself. *As long as I remain on the Eternal Hunt.*

[Volya] the Huntress told the Marrow.

<Name: Volya>

<Designation: Accepted>

<Name: Huntress4430/Huntress6561/Volya>

[Whatever] Volya issued. [But my Hunter will refer to me as Volya, not those numbers. And that's final, Marrow]

<System Update: 96%> the Marrow stated simply.

The final percentages of the system update included the battle data of thousands of previous Hunters and Huntresses, allowing her to subconsciously learn from all of their failures. Thousands of lifetimes of lessons transmitted in only a handful of seconds. The culmination of this data imbued her with a yearning for the Eternal Hunt, a thirst she could only quench with human death.

<System Update: 100%>

<Huntress4430 And Huntress6561 And Volya: Happy Hunting>

[Cute] Volya said with a roll of her eyes. If she was stuck with a computer occupying a section of her mind, at least it seemed to have a sense of humor, strange as it was.

Her skin pod broke through a layer of clouds, revealing the sprawling planet below. Her mind automatically synced the local topology and ecology with what was now stored in her memories, revealing that Earth's surface was overgrown with flesh trees and fields of flora that only years of ecological change and growth could produce. The discrepancy reminded her of the multiple designations the Marrow had provided for her name.

Those designations: they're thousands of Huntresses apart. There's some kind of time discrepancy going on.

[What year is it?] Volya asked the Marrow.

<Year: 2065>

<Previous Answer: False>

<Solution: Update Skin Pod's Local Memory>

<Memory: Updated>

<Year: 2099>

[2099] Volya gasped. [How is that possible?]

<Reason: Time Discrepancy>

[No shit] Volya said, not sure if this was humor or stupidity.

[How did this happen? Why does my skin pod think it's thirty-four years in the past?]

<Solution: Unknown>

[Thanks for the straight answer, at least]

<Gratitude: Noted>

Volya shrugged away the Marrow and observed the rapidly approaching future world. She didn't see any crumbling human cities or crisscrossing roads. There were just miles and miles of flesh trees filling valleys and gorges and cliffs and beaches, each one noticeably different than the last. Her vector was pointing directly for a large grove of flesh trees surrounded by near-total desolation. Small packs of tangle grass could be seen moving about in the distance, but nothing at all seemed to be moving anywhere near this particular grove.

<General Location: Butcher Wastelands>

<Specific Location: Hunter Dreaming>

[Huh? Those aren't real places]

<Designation Type: Nomadic>

[I don't speak Nomad, Marrow. I have access to the databases on old world cities and anthropogeography. Tell me in Universal English]

<Designation: Unnamed>

<Closest Old World Metropolis: Denver>

*Denver…*Volya considered. *The human city is long gone. A field of flesh trees now. But the databases say the humans went underground and built a city called Downver. Stupid name for stupid creatures. But it's been so many years. There's no way there are any humans left there,* she lamented with disappointment.

[Is Downver still populated? Or did the Eternal Hunt claim all the humans there by now?]

<Information On Downver: Incomplete>

<Probability Of Human Habitation: .98>

[How is there a 98% chance they're still alive down there?] Volya asked, flabbergasted that the Eternal Hunt had not claimed all humans in the thirty-four years she had been suspended in the Thymus for unknown reasons.

<Reason: Eternal Hunt Ended In 2066>

No, that can't be right.

[Repeat that, Marrow]

<Reason: Eternal Hunt Ended In 2066>

[You mean, it's over? All the humans are dead?]

<Status Of Human Life On Earth: Extant>

[Then, why?]

<Reason For Eternal Hunt Ending: All Hunters And Huntresses Dead Except Huntress4430/Huntress6561/Volya and Hunter4430>

Volya didn't even know how to respond at first. Was the Marrow not functioning properly? Was all its information corrupted somehow?

It's only me and my Hunter left? Is that possible?

[Marrow...why haven't more Hunters and Huntresses been released from Thymus?]

<Reason: Eternal Hunt Ended>

[Why? Who ended it?]

The answer came like a lead weight against her sternum.

<Answer: The Mind>

[The...Mind? But...why, Marrow? Why would the Mind end the Eternal Hunt if there are still humans to purge?]

<Reason: Unknown>

[But—]

<Prepare For landing, Huntress4430/Huntress6561/Volya>

With reflexive speed, Volya tucked her body into a ball, then slammed into the Earth at terminal velocity. The skin pod burst, instantly converting all of Volya's kinetic energy into a sonic boom that made hundreds of flesh pods in the area fall from their flesh trees and burst into slick viscera against the rocky soil of the area.

[Just call me Volya, damnit] Volya huffed at the Marrow as she stretched her legs against the surface of the Earth for the first time in her life. As expected, she could sense that her Hunter was near, likely just inches from death as he crawled desperately to reach her and the puddling remains of her skin pod that would infuse with his cells and become his skinsuit, saving his life.

Unless he already had a Huntress, and I'm her replacement, Volya considered with just a twinge of disappointment.

[Marrow, am I this Hunter's first Huntress?]

<Answer: Yes>

Good, she thought, preferring to not have another Huntress' leftovers. Besides, she felt there was something alluring about being a weapon's first owner.

[How long does he have? He isn't going to die before he gets here, is he? I don't want to wait to be assigned another one]

<Answer: Hunter's Vitals Stable And At Rest>

[Stable? How is that possible? He should be on the verge of death!]

<Answer: Unknown>

Strange, Volya considered, nervous that her Hunter was somehow defective and lacked the mind shattering pain and suffering that his Cleaners should have been inflicting upon him just hours earlier.

[My Hunter isn't defective, is he? Is that even a thing that can happen?]

<Answer: Zero Defective Hunters Recorded>

[That's what I thought]

Volya brushed off the strangeness of her Hunter's lack of suffering, figuring it was just an error related to the hiccup with the update. Instead, she filled her mind with the only thing that really mattered: the Eternal Hunt.

Her lithe, muscular body prickled with excited goosebumps as her skin rippled, fluttering in color, pattern, and texture until it finally settled on a perfect mimicry of her surroundings, passively camouflaging her. She had precise control over her skin, providing a tool to easily hide or blend into any environment—even human cities. If it weren't for her hyper-responsive skin cells and unnaturally radiant emerald eyes, she could easily be mistaken for a human, something that put all Huntresses ill at ease. But it was her god Mendel who had given her the shape and form of humanity, and from Thymus to Earth's surface, He had not yet failed her. She knew He never would.

[I'm alive because I was in the Thymus...in Astrea...in Space. But...how is my Hunter stable without his skinsuit?] Volya inquired of the Marrow.

<Reason: Unknown>

[What good are you?]

<Uses Of The Marrow Include: Information/Vision/Weapons—>

[It was rhetorical] Volya interrupted.

<Question: Which Of These Uses Do You Find Bad>

[Is that a serious question?]

<Question Type: Rhetorical>

[Very funny, Marrow. Enough with the antics. It's time to hunt]

<Huntress4430/Huntress6561/Volya: Happy Hunting>

Volya mentally waved away the computer, clearing her visual display of the Marrow's readout and her own vital signatures.

There must be something to hunt around here, Volya considered. She flipped her vision to one of the closest satellites and told it to track the surface for motion with a radius of 500 miles from her present location. To her dismay, not a single human signature pinged on her field of vision. There were barely even any Nomads—just flesh trees and other types of plant-life. There were also large, mutated beasts here and there roaming the landscape, some of them engaged in rabid, earth-shaking battles with each other.

No! she lamented. *This is fucking bullshit. Where are all the humans? I woke up too late for the hunt?*

She kicked the closest flesh tree, snapping it at the base with the force of a small bomb. This particular flesh tree was made almost entirely of azure-blue ivy, and as the tree and its flesh pods plummeted into the gorge below, Volya felt no remorse for the bleeding mass. The remaining stump of the flesh tree profusely spurted human-looking blood from its scores of jagged fissures leading back into the Earth.

"I will not be robbed of my Eternal Hunt," Volya fumed to the world. Just as she was about to take out her anger on a few more flesh trees, a ping flashed on the terrain map still open in a peripheral frame of her mind's eye. She could split her mind into a thousand active partitions if she wanted to.

The ping revealed a small group of humans, 487 miles away, in the mountains right outside what had once been the city of Denver.

Hundreds of miles of mostly barren but still deadly earth surrounded them on all sides.

How the hell are they surviving out here alone?

Volya zoomed in on the group and utilized an array of transmissions to learn about each figure's biological makeup.

Seven baseline humans. Two cybernetically enhanced humans. A Hybrid Nomad. And two nonhumans. Though the nonhumans physically appeared to be young twin girls, all analysis confirmed that they were something else.

But what? Volya considered, mentally roving the databases but finding nothing about these two creatures.

No matter, Volya thought, cutting off the Marrow's database query. *They are alive, whatever they are, and they are traveling with humans. There's only one solution to their presence: I'll have to kill them all as offerings to the Eternal Hunt.*

Volya peered down into the gorge where the flesh tree of azure ivy plummeted after she had kicked it in anger.

My Hunter is down there. A few hundred feet away. I can sense his mind.

She tried to mentally grasp the tendrils of her Hunter's thoughts, but it was like passing her fingers through smoke. Something was stopping her from taking hold of his mind.

Maybe I need to be closer for the first sync, she considered impatiently without querying the Marrow for an answer.

Kicking off the pulsating stump of what remained of the azure ivy flesh tree, Volya swan dived off the cliff edge and let the air rush rapturously through her raven black hair. The small ridge on the back of her neck communicated with the Thymus, the Marrow, and the rest of Astrea, enhancing the speed of Volya's cognition four-times faster than baseline. With no more effort than breathing, she landed on the ball of one foot, then rolled across the large branch of a large willow-like flesh tree. She pounced again, flipped several times in the air, then rolled across her forearm and back once reaching the ground.

Something splattered loudly to her right, and without having to process the thought or movement, the ridge on her neck commanded her foot to kick up a rock she wasn't even aware of, then kick it, propelling it like a bullet in the direction of the sound. She turned and saw that she had decapitated a newborn Nomad who had just emerged from its flesh pod. Losing its head didn't seem to faze the tiny creature, nor did it take any notice of Volya. Small orange protrusions grew across the length of the Nomad's body, forming mushroom looking structures that popped as it strolled away, spraying the area around it with a foul-smelling odor that reminded Volya of her skin pod.

The Hunter is supposed to come find me and use the skin pod as his skinsuit. Where the hell is my Hunter?

She considered climbing back up the cliff and collecting the deflated skin pod. It would be good to test out her body some more. But the Hunter was supposed to come for her, not the other way around.

He can go get his own skinsuit, she concluded, not caring how much agony he would be in as a naked Hunter. *He's my dog to command, after all.*

Tangle grass covered the entire surface of the grove the Nomads called Hunter Dreaming, but each of Volya's steps sent individual patches scurrying away, leaving trails of pollen from decoy flowers suddenly jerked in one direction.

The Hunter's thoughts were more like dreams, and rather than being full of pain and seething hate for humanity, they were drenched in a mushy sweetness that disgusted Volya and made her crave the fracturing of human bones.

[What the fuck is this, Marrow?] Volya demanded to know from the Marrow.

<Answer: Hunter Dreaming>

[So that's not just a physical location. My Hunter really is dreaming?]

<Answer: The Hunter Is Dreaming>

[That's fucking bizarre. Anything else you can tell me about my Hunter? Why is he...sleeping here? Why didn't he come for me?]

<Answer: Hunter4430 Is Genetically Altered>

[Altered in what way?]

<Answer: Unknown >

[Well...who altered him?]

<Answer: Unknown>

15

[Well, shit...are you seeing his dreams? They're...pathetic. Who is that woman in his dreams? He's just sitting there holding her hand. Why the fuck is he doing that? And she looks like a Huntress. Why?]

<Answer: Unknown>

[But she isn't a Huntress, right? She carries the frailty of humanity in every way. Look at her muscles. Her defeated eyes. That witless grin and those pitiable little giggles at everything my Hunter says. Fuck! She's a fucking human, Marrow. So why does she look identical to us? To me?]

<Answer: Unknown>

[Fuck, Marrow! You useless computer! Isn't there another part of Astrea I can talk to?]

<Answer:>

<Processing Answer...>

<Processing Answer...>

<Processing Answer...>

[Well? What's the damn answer?]

<Answer: No>

Volya cursed the Marrow and the Thymus and the whole of Astrea, then calmed herself by remembering that she had humans to turn inside out.

The tendrils of the Hunter's tangible dreams led directly to the nexus that was his mind. She continued forward but found that her path was blocked by a Nomad and Hybrid Nomad standing side by side like arbitrary, grotesque statues. The Hybrid, identifiable by its mostly humanoid shape, was made of thick, intersecting vines of purple nightshade flowers and ripe tomatoes. The Nomad, an overgrown, undulating, swelling amoeba of misplaced, half-grown limbs, was coated in rolls of black and white puffball fungus. Between them was a broad, nine-foot-high entrance to a cave covered from top to bottom in thick nightshade and tomato vines, while the ground in front of and within the cave brimmed with countless black and white puffballs.

"The Hunter is my own, unfortunately," she told the Nomads with a tone of disappointment. "He seems pathetic."

Neither the puffball nor nightshade Nomad had eyes, but they still turned to one another and looked as though Volya's statement was the most absurd thing they had ever heard.

"Why are you here? Why is my weak-minded Hunter in a cave? Why are you guarding it?"

The puffball Nomad squirmed, and a handful of black puffballs popped, spraying a black mist into the air. "She said this one special," the nightshade Hybrid said, translating the puffball Nomad's apparent attempt at language. He pointed at the cave and said, "This one called Butcher of Wastes. This one dangerous," the Hybrid continued, and then it ate a few of the ripest tomatoes from one of its six drooping hands and allowed a few of the tomatoes to fall to the ground and roll away into the dense grove.

"He doesn't seem dangerous," Volya challenged, peering into his dreams and seeing that he was still just holding hands with some fake Huntress under a starlit sky. "He seems…human," Volya said with a measure of hesitation, for it was unthinkable.

"Not human," the nightshade Hybrid assured her, though it could have been a warning too. "This Hunter sacred. Central to His plans."

His plans, Volya repeated to herself.

"Mendel, you mean?" Volya checked, but the Nomads did not answer. Instead, they each moved a few feet away from the cave entrance, the Hybrid stepping aside with his jointless legs and the Nomad undulating across the ground, popping several of its puffballs. The vines covering the cave entrance withered to brown, brittle leaves, and the puffballs filling the ground and walls of the cave melted to black and white sludge.

The puffball Nomad popped one of its largest white puffballs, and the nightshade Nomad translated. "Beginning is ending."

The Hybrid lifted his tomato-laden arms high above his head as if in exalted reverence and proclaimed, "Ladder will be ascended."

Then, they just stared at her, as if waiting for her to fulfill some long-awaited action.

Fuck, they're creepy, Volya thought. *I would prefer to kill them,* she ruminated, but that went against the Eternal Hunt. The Nomads were part of Mendel's plan. Humans weren't. That's why she had to kill them all—every single remaining human on the planet.

"Time to wake up my Hunter," Volya told the Nomads as she stepped toward the cave entrance. She could see the thermal transmissions of her Hunter a hundred or so feet inside the cave. He was just sitting there, dreaming his pathetic dreams.

A ring of black and white puffballs burst their black and white spores into the air, and Volya waited in anticipation for the translation.

"This one refuses hunt," the Hybrid explained. "This one done killing," he added in his own words.

"He is my dog," Volya lashed with a Huntress' typical, acrimonious wrath for anything outside themselves. "He will obey my every command, whether he likes it or not."

The Nomads nodded in unison, the Hybrid beaming in rapture and the Nomad bursting an assortment of her puffballs. Then, they both burst unexpectedly into flesh trees, the Hybrid's arms extending into a canopy of nightshade vine branches and tomato-shaped flesh pods and the Nomad's slimy limbs extending into short, spindly branches dripping with black and white puffball-shaped flesh pods. Both of the flesh trees rapidly grew thick roots that stretched into the ground, anchoring them to their cherished Earth now that their duties in life were apparently completed.

Wake up now, Hunter. We've a pack of humans and a couple of little human-looking girls to slaughter, Volya thought as she stepped eagerly into the pitch-black darkness of Hunter Dreaming.

The Nomads, or People of the Earth as they call themselves, are just the beginning. A means to an end. There will come a day when humanity climbs the next rung of the evolutionary ladder. I know this because I have seen it, and thus, it will be so.

A virus and a cure. This is what I will commission Tomasz to make. He will be told this plan exactly two decades from today, and he will fulfill his duty, as he always has. A virus and a cure. These will be my final gifts to humanity—gifts that will bear fruit that no human nor Nomad nor myself, even in my current form, can fathom.

From Mendel's Ladder: The Personal Journal of Denis Mendel, Recorded April 19, 2065, Published June 2108 by Leif Mainstone, Federated Agency Publishing

Chapter 3

A Virus and a Cure

Their feet were bruised and blistered. Their grimy skin was sorely disheveled, full of scrapes and rashes. Their clothing, made of high quality Wintersvilla synthetics, hung loosely from their bodies as strips of tattered rags. Their heads of once platinum hair were now tangled mats of filthy dreads. But they still somehow found the strength to carry on. At only twelve years old, Aliana and Aurelia had been forced into the great, murderous wilds of Earth. Shira didn't know how the girls would fare, but after a year and close to 2000 miles into their journey across the world, they had more than proven worthy of calling themselves Wintersvilla Women, a title that struck fear into the heart of every man.

Shira often marveled at the strength of the two girls as the group trudged and climbed and waded across the world. She was proud that despite exhaustion and a severe lack of sleep clawing at their minds at all times, all twelve remaining individuals worked together to maintain a sedulous pace. It was rare for the group to stop anywhere longer than half a day or night. When the girls grew tired, they slept in torn-up hammocks stretched across the back rods of Shira's and Myriam's exoskeleton suits, which could walk automatically and perpetually, even as the women slept. Rooli, a Hybrid Nomad, didn't need sleep or could sleep while remaining conscious—Shira couldn't be sure which. The slaves, like dogs, slept when they found the chance, which wasn't very often. Only seven slaves remained out of the twenty-nine the group had escaped with, and it was probably the case that many had simply died from exhaustion. But sacrifices were unavoidable and necessary. The girls didn't have much time left before the changes started in their genetics.

A virus and a cure, Shira thought, letting the words take full hold.

Virus and Cure—that's what Tomasz always called them, as if those were their actual names. Shira clearly remembered the day that Tomasz' domesticated Nomads brought the girls, still tiny and wriggling, to Wintersvilla. It was only recently that Shira realized that was the first truly meaningful day of her life. There was a time she thought certain moments of her life meaningful, like the day, at twelve years old, Shira haphazardly connected Winter's prototype blade to her right arm and used it to gut him like the rabid pig he was. His blood and guts, slick and warm, had invigorated Shira—proof to her that she was not the weak little girl that bastard always told her she was. And yet, that day still held no real meaning for her. In the end, that was Nomusa's victory, after all.

Now, at the age of forty—her body a patchwork connection of cybernetics and scarred flesh from a lifetime of battle—Shira finally had meaning, and it had nothing to do with war or bloodshed.

Aliana led the way with the men, their chains abandoned only six months prior. It had been Aliana who demanded the chains be removed, despite caution from Myriam and protests from the one-eyed but ever useful Wesley, Shira's oldest slave at fifty-nine years old.

Shira almost told Aliana to be careful and get away from the men, but it had been proven time and time again that there was no need. Traditionally, men were always made to walk at least a hundred feet forward just in case a drinking puddle decided to snatch a limb or a patch of grass turned out to be tangle grass and decided to eat a man whole. There were also barb bushes, dart weed, and the occasional manta flower, and those were just the more common hazards. However, the girls appeared immune to the natural perils of Earth. More than immune. It was like the Earth was helping them. Only Rovers and the rare overgrown Mutant posed a threat to the girls and those around them. It was one of the most liberating feelings of Shira's life to be able to walk outside the walls of Wintersvilla without using her exo to analyze every square inch of her environment and remain ready for threats to her life from even the most innocuous leaf or blade of grass. The exo was a sleek cage of two-inch diameter bars framing the shape of her body, and as each bar hugged the outline of her curves and rippling muscles, Shira offered gratitude to her exo for never failing her, especially in dire times of life and death.

Aliana turned from Wesley and stared confidently at Shira with her unnaturally radiant emerald green eyes. She proclaimed, "We should let them take their collars off."

Without asking for permission to speak, Wesley pleaded, "I swear it, General Shira, I told her we are grateful for our collars, as we were grateful for our chains. Our lives belong to you and the Matriarch," Wesley pleaded, tears streaming from his single eye. His other eye was a mound of scar tissue from where the late Matriarch, Nomusa, had long ago punished him with a heated dagger for simply looking at her a second longer than she felt was necessary.

"Nomusa is dead," Shira said with slight hesitation. It was still hard to accept that the Matriarch and all of Wintersvilla was but a smoldering memory, but that wasn't why Shira hesitated.

Nomusa was no better than Winters, Shira seethed within.

"Aurelia? What do you think?" Shira checked without averting her gaze from Aliana and Wesley. She knew Aurelia preferred that people not make eye contact with her face, preferring that they only look at her hands—her source of communication due to being mute. Though her black cotton face mask covered most of her face below the nose, the grisly, tar-black discoloration had spread a couple more inches up her cheeks over the last year.

A virus, Shira reminded herself. *And a cure*, she thought, looking back to Aliana. It was only a matter of time before whatever was going to happen to the girls would happen. Tomasz had said that the onset of puberty would activate a series of dormant genetics, but weren't they already past due for starting puberty?

Shira looked Aliana over, then glanced at Aurelia's figure. She wasn't sure if their bodies were still underdeveloped or just malnourished from the year journey across the treacherous world.

Probably both, she thought, and she observed for not the first time that she and Myriam, once hyper-muscular, had lost a noticeable amount of mass. On the other hand, the girls had always been skin and bone. Shira wondered if Tomasz had designed them that way for a reason.

Aurelia, always one to carefully consider a question or proposition, finally gave her answer using a system of sign language created decades earlier by a tactician of Wintersvilla for use on covert operations. She lowered her eyelids with detached acceptance, though the unnatural violet radiance of her eyes could still be seen. "Keep the slaves' collars on," she signed forcefully. "The removal of their chains was enough virtue for a lifetime. They are slaves, not friends," she said resolutely, not looking to any of the adults for reassurance in her decision. Rooli, who was more wood and bark than flesh, gave no response, but Myriam applauded with satisfaction.

"A girl after my own heart," Myriam said with a raspy voice like scraped gravel. Her larynx had been nicked during her first and only battle with a Hunter, but she had taken the monster's head in the end. That was the same day Shira fell in love with the lithe, lustful, and lethal Myriam, wielder of Summit Splitter. Shira couldn't help being attracted to warriors, and despite Myriam having nine fewer years of experience, she was an even greater warrior than Shira in both skill and latent ability.

"Why even ask Aurelia?" Aliana burst, throwing away all composure. "She's an idiot. She shouldn't get a say since she can't speak anyway."

Right for the throat, Shira thought. Her inability to speak was an insecurity Aurelia had struggled with since she was only waist high. Aurelia, however, didn't take Aliana's bait.

"At least I use my brain. I'm not sure you have one," Aurelia responded coolly. Rooli knew exactly what Aurelia was saying to her twin sister, and she grunted in disapproval. Rooli was always harder on Aurelia, and Shira couldn't exactly ask Rooli why. At best, Rooli would offer her silence and a vacant stare, even though Shira knew the Hybrid was anything but stupid. All that mattered was that she put the girls' lives above all others—nothing else could be clearer. Not after what happened during the fall of Wintersvilla.

Aliana huffed. "Go die, virus. I have a world to cure."

Aurelia didn't respond, but Shira could tell that the comment was like a Wintersvilla slavedriver's lashing against her flesh.

"Take your collars off," Aliana told the men with a dignified wave of her hand. "You are slaves no more. I declare it."

"You declare it? It doesn't matter that Nomusa named you Matriarch. She's dead. They're all dead! You aren't Matriarch!" Aurelia jumped, her fingers a flurry as she let her emotions get the best of her this time.

"Sorry, what was that? I couldn't hear you?" Aliana goaded. "Why don't you take that mask off?"

Rooli stomped the ground, and the thick bark of her leg, at least 500 pounds in just one limb, sent tremors through the ground. A single stern glance from Rooli stopped the girls in their tracks.

"Sisters!" Rooli bellowed. "Family!" she growled.

"Yes, Rooli," Aliana intoned, and Aurelia did the same in sign.

Shira couldn't help tearing up, crying openly for the third time in just the last day.

What the fuck is happening to me? she thought. *I'm turning soft as a man in my old age? I'm only forty years old.* Over the last month, to Shira's chagrin, the roots of her sandy blonde hair were beginning to turn gray more quickly with each passing day, reminding her every time she saw her reflection that life is brutal and ephemeral. *But that's not it. It's not my age. It's all these people, my people…and Rooli, not a person, but a Hybrid Nomad. Still, even she…these people are my family. I have a family,* Shira gawked with profound joy, as if she had been suffocating her whole life and was only just getting used to breathing over the last year's journey.

Enough, she told herself, spiteful that she had been allowing her mind to wander from the present moment more and more often. It was a weakness to be culled, and yet, it was as if she couldn't help it. It had begun embedding itself into her at least seven or eight years earlier, when the girls first started coming into their own. The fall of Wintersvilla made it even worse, and ever since that day, tumultuous emotions had brewed inside of her—rage, worry, love, and even fear. It was unnatural, and Shira knew that it was selfish too, for it distracted her mind, diminishing her battle prowess and legend as the General of Wintersvilla.

I knew when we left Wintersvilla that I was changing, but I could have never anticipated crying in the open like this. I'm becoming a liability, Shira scolded herself, forcing her mind back to the present.

Noticing Shira's concerned look, Myriam gripped her shoulder and asked quietly, "Are you okay, my gorgeous general?"

Shira shook away her thoughts and grasped the hand of the illustrious Myriam, her lover of the past two years and wife of the past year.

"You realize nearly half of our marriage has taken place on the road battling Rovers, Biofreaks, and Mutants?" Shira said, sorry that this is what their lives had come to.

"It's the best honeymoon a warrior could ask for," Myriam whispered seductively, letting her ruby red curls tickle Shira's bare shoulder as she bent and kissed Shira's cheek. "We'll spend a few months alone in a hot bath once we get to Downver, though, okay?" Myriam sniffed at her armpits and chuckled. "I didn't realize we could smell this bad."

Shira released a ball of tension she hadn't realized she was holding in her chest.

"They have baths in Downver, don't they, Rooli?" Myriam checked, aware that at some point in her seventy-one year life, Rooli had lived in Downver, despite the fact that they didn't allow Nomads or Hybrids anywhere near the underground city.

Rooli didn't answer, but that was the norm for her.

"I love you, Myriam," Shira said.

"I know, old lady. I love you too," Myriam answered with an alluring wink.

Behind them, Aliana signed to Aurelia that she was a diseased cow, and Aurelia signed back that she would kill Aliana in her sleep. Rooli grabbed Aurelia's hand then caught up with Aliana, stomping loudly with each step. She forced the girls to shake and then pushed them into a hug. The entire group came to a halt around the girls, with Wesley and Fullman standing in front of the five lesser slaves, who were unnamed outside of the unofficial nicknames Aliana had given each one during the journey.

"I hate you," Aliana said lovingly, and she kissed her sister's cheek, not caring about the flesh-rending black tendrils splintering the skin beneath her face mask.

"I hate you too," Aurelia signed, and she hugged her sister closer.

Rooli nodded in approval.

"They're adorable," Myriam rasped. "I wish I had a sister growing up. You know, a real sister, not just our warrior sisters."

Shira nodded in agreement, then found herself receding back into her thoughts.

It's them, she realized. *They changed us. They made us...more human, even though they aren't human.*

Shira recollected that Tomasz had made the girls with instructions from someone whom he refused to disclose. Tomasz believed that Aurelia was a weapon to be used against Astrea. That was just his theory, though. He admitted he didn't really know. As for Aliana, Tomasz didn't even have a guess.

That coward, Tomasz, Shira seethed. *He could have just flown us to Downver, but he let us risk everything because he's too scared to lose a single ship. It would be like losing a finger for him.*

But it wasn't Tomasz' fault that they had been forced to escape a great siege on the only city Shira had ever called home. In the end, Nomusa had reaped what she sewed: it was the Rovers, bands of wild young men and boys, who had destroyed Wintersvilla—the same Rovers who had been discarded by Nomusa at birth due to birth defects or small size since she believed this would hinder them from being effective life-long slaves for the Matriarchy of Wintersvilla. Nomusa's cruelty was her own downfall in the end—it just took decades to catch up with her.

"Ho!" Rooli grunted suddenly, telling the others to stop. The seriousness of her tone warned of extreme danger, and the group immediately took their practiced positions. The girls ran to Rooli, and Rooli stretched out the bark of her arms, creating thick shields and encasing the girls between her now towering arms and sturdy body. The men formed a tight circle around Rooli, acting as meat shields. Myriam engaged her exoskeleton, transmitting an electric ringing that settled to a barely audible buzz after a few seconds. Shira didn't fully engage her suit right away. Her exoskeleton was older and louder than Myriam's, and she didn't want to attract unnecessary attention when she could fight perfectly well with reserve energy. That, and her suit had less than a fifth of the energy as Myriam's suit at full charge.

It's not a Hunter, Shira knew, for there was always an ancestrally ominous feeling that preceded a Hunter's presence.

A great bellow resounded suddenly from beyond a thick flesh tree forest up ahead, followed by the approach of steady stomping that made Rooli's steps seem toddler-like.

"Big," Rooli said simply, likely in response to the girls asking her what was going on beyond her thick wooden carapace.

"General...Shira," Wesley began with a fearful crack in his voice, "should we take the girls and run?"

"Quiet, meat," Myriam lashed, and Wesley correctively straightened himself as if he had actually been whipped. "Power up, love," Myriam told Shira with a smile that was all teeth. "This Muto is maxed out."

Shira stretched at the neck as she gave the mental signal to her suit. The suit stretched and pulsed into her peripheral neurons and finally synced with her central nervous system. As Shira altered her vision to thermal transmission, Myriam removed the gargantuan sword called Summit Splitter from her back, something she only did when it appeared like life and death were both possibilities. Viewing the approaching monstrosity as it shattered flesh trees with each step, Shira understood why Myriam had not opted for utilizing her claws.

"It's colossal," Shira warned.

"Whatever it is, it's alive. Which means it can die," Myriam practically sang through her contralto rasp. Shira imagined that Myriam was probably filling her mind with images of the Afterworld, an eternal battle after death involving all the female warriors throughout time who could prove themselves fearless, mighty, cunning, and deserving of the ultimate glory. Shira didn't believe in fairytales, preferring death to just be death. But Myriam believed with all her heart, and Shira didn't mind going along with it, whispering to her in bed after making love that they would be together forever in battle after death. It made Myriam happy to believe—so it didn't matter to Shira that it was all a comforting lie.

Focus, little girl, Shira heard Winters say in her mind, and his voice filled her with insatiable rage. She allowed herself a glance at the blade jutting a full half meter from her right forearm. Unlike her exo, which she could attach and detach to her body's ports, the blade and its internal sheathe remained a part of her forearm, embedded into the fabric of her neurons, flesh, and bone using the crude, old methods of Wintersvilla cybernetic enhancement. It was a process that left the area aching with pain and stiffness for the rest of one's life. She had named the blade Wintersbane, and she refused to ever remove it or upgrade it. Winters' family crest was still inlaid into both sides of the blade, serving as a constant reminder to Shira that she was the decider of her fate, and no one else.

You killed Winters, and you killed every single Hunter and Huntress that ever crossed my path. Don't fail me now, she told the blade.

The great mutated beast let out another earth-shaking bellow, this one more urgent. It had their scent now, and it was only a handful of steady breaths away.

Shira instinctively turned to check on the girls and saw that Rooli was anchoring her legs deeper into the ground with roots as thick as Shira's biceps and growing her bark thicker around the girls, pushing outward and downward into the ground an inch every few seconds.

Whatever this creature is, it's too big, Shira realized. *If it goes for Rooli and the girls, it might shatter Rooli and turn the girls to mush. Was Wesley right to want to run away with the girls?*

"Rooli, grow faster!" Shira ordered, and with a painfully stifled groan, Rooli expanded at triple the rate as her roots treated the mountainous ground like so much dust.

"Myriam!" Shira shouted with sudden, overwhelming fear, something she hadn't felt since she was a child. Rather than look at her in disgust, Myriam gave a serious nod, stepped in front of Rooli, bent at the knees, and jumped a hundred feet into the sky. The force of her launch sent the men toppling over and also grabbed the attention of the beast.

With thunderous charging and earth-shaking bellows of anguish, the great Mutant emerged, knocking hulking flesh trees out of its way as if they were dead twigs. At least forty feet high and at least half as wide, the creature looked like it had originally been boar-like before its mutations. Its snarling lips quivered, and its black gums pussed with some death-dark substance that wilted and killed any plant life it oozed on. It bucked its head wildly, shattering anything its two jagged, half-broken tusks encountered. Its two front legs blackened the ground with slithering tendrils, sucking the life out of anything they encountered. Rather than having back legs, its body was serpentine, whipping at flesh trees and launching them into the air as it pulled itself agonizingly forward with horrific speed.

Exactly as Shira feared, it went straight for Rooli, a hundred feet away, then fifty, then less than ten, all in a fraction of a second. If they survived this encounter, she would remove every man's collar, for not one of them moved an inch, even when the Mutant was so close that the beast's acrid breath filled the men's throats.

The Mutant roared at the last second, and Shira bent at the knees, planning to use herself as a projectile lance aimed directly at the beast's open mouth.

I'll rip you open from the inside out, Shira seethed, seeing Winters in every one of the mutated boar's sickening features.

Just as the Mutant's right tusk made momentary contact with Rooli's carapace, Myriam slammed into the ground, swinging all ten feet of

Summit Splitter in a wild arc over her head like an executioner's blade as she landed and pulverized the soil into a shallow crater beneath her feet. The 700-pound sword slammed into the rocky earth, cleaving the Mutant and the ground in two.

Shira abandoned her launch, slowing herself mid-flight by scraping both her exo's arm-blades against the boar's thick, scaly hide. She observed wriggling, pitch-black worms ooze out of the gaping wound and melt into the earth with a high-pitched sizzle.

The girls, Shira thought, and she checked on Rooli's carapace. There was a small crack right where the boar's tusk made contact. Shira wondered if Rooli's ash-dark wooden skin would have been strong enough to withstand the Mutant's blow without Myriam arriving when she did.

Three hollow knocks resounded from within the protective barrier of Rooli's body. Clearly the girls were anxious to know what happened. They could hold their own in a battle against Rovers—they were trained by Shira herself, after all. But Mutants were another matter entirely. Most weren't as big as the boar, but no matter their size, it wasn't worth risking their safety for the sake of training and glory. The only thing more dangerous than a Mutant was a Hunter or Huntress, and without any of those left to slay, Mutants were now the most dangerous things in the wilds of Earth.

"It should be safe to—" Shira began, but she was interrupted by a bellow so loud that it made Shira's ears ring. In a heartbeat, the boar extended its neck with a serpentine lunge and snatched two of the men in a single bite, crunching their bodies into mush with hideous ease.

As the beast consumed the men, its body reconnected through strings of sizzling worms. Myriam's attack had slowed it, but this was clearly an advanced Mutant—*maxed out* as Myriam called it. Its regenerative abilities allowed even the severing of its spine to constitute nothing more than a temporary flesh wound. It would go down eventually, but they would have to finish it off before their suits returned to passive power. Shira only had a couple more minutes, and Myriam's exo would go silent not long after that. Especially after utilizing Summit Splitter—a single swing required a sizable portion of her total reserves.

"Fatherfucker!" Myriam roared at the beast. She attempted to lift the mammoth sword, but it was too thoroughly entrenched in the ground. Abandoning Summit Splitter, Myriam lunged and hacked at the beast's head with her claws, six blades gouging the snapping, bucking boar's face at the speed of ten swings per second. Shira pounced forward, her exo whining as she extended her exo's arm-blades, knee-blades, and six other exo-blades all at once. Even with four additional blades, she could only swing at a fifth of Myriam's speed.

As their blades stabbed and cut and lanced without pause, the women continuously pounced in unexpected directions, gouging every part of the Mutant's monstrous body they could reach. More sizzling worms oozed from each gaping wound, and though the Mutant's ability to regenerate did appear to be slowing, it was still a race against time. Each woman could eradicate a whole legion of unmounted Rovers without their exos, but only an exo could match a maxed out Mutant.

The boar wildly whipped its body, but the women dodged its bulk with ease and continued hacking.

Just a bit longer, Shira urged despite her exo's mental warnings that her respiration and heart rate were elevated to dangerous levels. Not to mention it was about to switch back to passive mode.

Doesn't matter, Shira ordered her suit and mind. *Just a bit longer.*

Without warning, the Mutant adapted, and a section of its torso formed into a projectile pillar, slamming into Myriam's solar plexus and rocketing her into the closest flesh tree. A surge of adrenaline doubled Shira's heart rate, popping veins across the entirety of her musculature. But it wasn't enough.

Think, girl, she heard Winters say. *You witless little girl.*

"Fuck you!" Shira screamed out loud, and the great beast turned from Myriam and snorted in Shira's direction. Myriam coughed blood and attempted to recover her stance, but the wind was totally knocked out of her.

The Mutant reared its ugly head and slammed its tremendous legs into the ground, generating tremors that threw the men off balance. Still, they did not abandon their positions around Rooli. Many of the largest wounds the women had inflicted were still gaping and oozing black, wriggling worms, but the Mutant was still full of vigor and hate.

Think, girl!

Shira remembered how effectively Summit Splitter had cleaved the creature. The problem was that they needed to destroy more of its surface area all at once. It would take too long and require too much energy to remove the massive sword, but she needed something equally big.

Or bigger, Shira thought, and as the Mutant closed the gap between them, Shira saw how jagged and vast many of the flesh trees were in this area.

That's it, Shira knew.

"Rooli!" Shira called. "Get ready to connect and explode."

Shira launched herself toward Rooli and the girls, and the Mutant followed. In a moment's glance she checked on Myriam and saw that she was only just getting to her feet.

Watch and learn, my love, Shira thought as she fell back into her warrior groove.

With an animal grunt, Shira lifted the stump end of a particularly sharp and jagged flesh tree laying on the ground. Her suit issued more critical warnings, but now was not the time for concern. With the last bit of energy she had in both her exo and flesh, she pivoted the broken tree and let it rest against Rooli, who immediately grew additional limbs to hold it in Shira's stead. A whole twenty feet of tree extended from the ground and into the sky like an anti-cavalry spear ready to bring an oncoming war charge to a lethal halt.

"Bring it higher!" Shira commanded as she climbed onto the tree and sprinted out to the jagged edge. Rooli lifted it higher, perfectly level with the Mutant's face.

Shira roared at the top of her lungs, goading the beast to charge forward like a raging bull. Shira roared at it once more, and the Mutant opened its mouth wider than ever, proving to Shira that its might was far greater than hers. It continued roaring as it closed the gap, and Shira jumped at the last second, allowing the Mutant to skewer itself onto the flesh tree as she landed just beside Myriam.

Now, Rooli, Shira thought, and as if reading her thoughts, Rooli commanded the flesh tree, now connected to her own body, to explode with the power of lightning, popping the Mutant like a giant, worm-filled balloon.

A few worms sizzled and stung Shira's skin as they died, and it was only then that she finally took notice of the critical warnings flashing across her vision like strobing sunlight, blinding her and forcing her to her knees.

What the fuck! Shira winced, vying to remain in control despite her mind's reeling confusion at the overwhelming number of critical warnings strobing through her thoughts. The warnings piled, multiplying chaotically beyond any state of disrepair that Shira had ever experienced.

My exo is dying? I'm dying? Shira considered, unafraid yet befuddled as her mind scrambled to understand this sudden collapse during a battle that should be no more taxing for her than catching an oversized fish.

"Shira!" Myriam issued through a rasp of her own overwhelming fatigue.

Shira's vision was spinning too fast, and she couldn't help falling face first onto the worm-blackened Earth.

Astrea will serve as a fortress for me and those selected few, and it will serve as a vital organ necessary for the health of the world I will create. A world humanity failed to construct as a race of more than ten billion at its height—I will do it with but a handful of carefully selected minds.

After construction is completed, 177,147 individuals will be selected to permanently live on Astrea, in orbit around the Earth. It will be easy to convince them after the bombs are detonated and the Nomad mutation released. People will kill one another for a chance to escape the hell I will unleash upon humanity. They will view Astrea as heaven, and they will be right to view it that way. I will turn Earth into hell so that heaven can become a reality, and I will construct heaven to one day see Earth as the Eden it is meant to be.

Of those individuals chosen to board Astrea, 2187 of them will be selected, based on merit and temperament, to live in the Luxury Quarters and serve Astrea's cause with greater, more meticulous care.

Finally, 81 individuals from across the ten families, or rather, whichever families make the wise decision to abandon Earth and join me, will live in the Paradise Quarters. Their hedonism and reckless greed and pathetic striving for petty power is the very reason they will be locked behind the Golden Wall with me. Most of the families will go along with my plans, so they will be forced to pick and choose which of their relatives come to heaven and which stay in hell. That is something I will leave up to them, as it is the number of minds that matters, not the minds themselves. In Paradise, those most accustomed to power will beg for forgiveness, but there will be no forgiveness for the old world monsters or their children or their children's children who have subjugated and exploited and goose stepped the human species for millennia, with no end in sight.

No end in sight, until now.

More than anything, I am a visionary. Lorenzo has his math and Ruben his biology and Marissa her astrophysics and all the rest have their own specialties. But I have the dream. I have the ability to look further than any other—to see how each of their abilities can be used to craft a neoevolution that will ascend humanity to its rightful place among the stars.

I am a shepherd of the human race.

From Mendel's Ladder: The Personal Journal of Denis Mendel, Written Circa 2042, Published June 2108 by Leif Mainstone, Federated Agency Publishing

Chapter 4
The Shepherded People

O *ne more*, Samuel urged his massive, burning muscles. Again, he bent at the knees and braced his shoulders as he grunted out another 800-pound squat and 350-pound overhead press combo. *One more,* he demanded even though his legs were shaking, and the muscles of his arms pulsed desperately with the need for oxygen. Every machine at a power station measured exerted effort, and though total weight lifted was a factor, it was effort that banked the most creds in the shortest amount of time. *One more*, Samuel injected into his now spasming muscles. He winced in pain as he straightened his knees and lifted his arms above his head. *That's it,* a part of his brain demanded, but he knew he had more in him.

Another, he commanded the pulsing network of veins protruding from his bulging quadriceps. He saw each person he labored for in his mind like glistening strands of gossamer connected to his heart, depending on him and him alone to stay intact.

Mrs. Waters, who, at ninety-eight years old, could barely pull a five-pound weighted cable. Were it not for Samuel, she'd have been escorted to the recycler nearly a decade earlier.

One more.

Old Man Madeira, whose gargantuan, mentally-handicap son, Norman, was beginning to grow too weak at seventy-nine years old to continue earning enough work creds for himself, his father, and a few other old timers who lived on his street. They all depended on Samuel.

One more.

His own wife, Sandra, who was able to raise the children without worrying about energy debt or work creds. And his own children. Each of Samuel's reps was the assurance of food on their table, extended screen time, extra privileges. The more he pushed, the more energy debt he paid for those he loved.

One more.

Samuel heaved with all his might, but his muscles had reached their limit. He fell forward, and the machine took over, letting the weight down slowly. On his hands and knees, Samuel caught his breath and let the burn in his legs wane to a bearable intensity.

"For some men, labor is love," came the old, spent voice of Mr. Madeira, whom the locals referred to as Old Man Madeira. Samuel forced himself to his feet and offered an outstretched hand to the oldest man in all of the Foundation.

Old Man Madeira balanced on his cane with one hand and shook Samuel's hand with the other. Behind him, Norman stood with a blank stare, looking as though his mind were devoid of all thought except a neutral awareness of the present moment. Samuel would have offered Norman a handshake, but he knew after so many years that the giant man only moved in response to Madeira. Norman's size always seemed otherworldly, impossible even. At six foot, six inches and 310 pounds of lean muscle, Samuel was well known across the entire Foundation as the Workhorse of Astrea. And yet, Norman towered over Samuel, and though he wasn't as lean in his old age, he still carried at least 400 pounds of solid bulk that he never seemed to use for much more than standing behind Madeira. Silent yet booming in presence, Norman had never uttered a word in all forty-two years of Samuel's life, and most people assumed he was just born unable to speak. Samuel had been part of the first generation of children born on Astrea, and for as long as he could remember, Norman had always been strange and aloof.

"Many say Norman did the work of thousands when he was my age," Samuel said, nodding to the giant man as he tried to ignore Norman's misshapen, almost inhuman face. "Maybe he has more love than any of us."

At this, Old Man Madeira perked up and allowed himself a few puffs of weak laughter. "You hear that, Norman?" Madeira said behind his back, then he turned back to Samuel. "Oh, my dear boy, Samuel—I think all Norman has is love in that thick skull of his. It takes a keen man to understand that. Most just see him as a big lumbering bumpkin."

"A bumpkin?" Samuel checked curiously, as he had never heard the word used before.

Madeira issued another few puffs of laughter. "A term from the old world, my boy."

Old Man Madeira offered no further explanation, and out of respect, Samuel didn't press it. He knew that talk of Earth brought darkness to the minds of the old timers, especially Old Man Madeira. They tried to hide it, but Samuel could always see it in their eyes. *Like the Earth is pulling at them, beckoning them back to hell. It's like they're afraid heaven might fall apart, and hell will be all they have left.*

Samuel nodded pleasantly, and said, "I should get going, Mr. Madeira. A friend—err—Damian…he asked to meet with me."

At the mention of Damian's name, both Madeira and Norman shifted restlessly in their demeanor. Norman stared intently at something directly above them on the opposite side of Astrea's circular interior— maybe a lake or another group of people at their own power station who were no more than upside down specks across the mile distance separating each side of the Foundation's rotating, gravity-inducing walls. Madeira's eyes were downcast, revealing to Samuel that his mind lingered on some great, ominous realization.

"What is it, Mr. Madeira?"

"You must be careful, my dear boy," Madeira intoned. "You are the very foundation of the Foundation. An essential pillar of Astrea itself. You understand that, don't you, Samuel?"

Samuel licked his lips nervously and couldn't help furrowing his brow. Madeira was like a different person suddenly, his eyes full of fire and pain.

"Mr. Madeira…I—"

"Save it, boy," Madeira issued somberly, his hand raised for Samuel to stop. "I've seen this story play out already."

Madeira stared at Samuel, and the pain in his eyes seemed to say, *and so have you.*

Samuel's stomach turned as images of his father being dragged kicking and screaming from their home filled his brain, making him feel like a helpless child again. He shook his head and felt his breathing quicken.

"Samuel," Madeira said with a gentle whisper. He placed his soft, vein-splintering hand atop Samuel's and sighed deeply. "We all have a path to choose in this life. As the path forks, we must fork with it. And as the path ends, we must end with it. But we always have a choice."

Madeira squeezed Samuel's hand suddenly with an intensity that he didn't realize the old man was capable of mustering.

"You are not allowed to end, my boy. You understand? Not yet. You're too important. You would burn in hell a thousand times over to erase a mere thousandth of the suffering of those you love. That makes you too important, my boy."

Madeira's words stole Samuel's breath. They were the same words his mother told him the day she forfeited her final seven years of allotted life in exchange for enough surplus credits for Samuel and Sandra to have another child. Her death gave Samuel's son, Nathan, his life.

"How do you know those words?" Samuel gasped.

Madeira just shook his head. "That doesn't matter, my boy. All that matters is that you have a fork in your life, and you need to make the right decision and choose the right path."

He's talking about Damian and the others. The Sons and Daughters of the Foundation. He knows. Somehow, he knows, Samuel thought as his heart beat into his throat.

Samuel looked deep into the old man's eyes, but he couldn't find any malice or ill intent. *Am I wrong, though? Has he already told the local Queensguard about them?*

"Mr. Madeira...I—"

"I don't want to hear it, boy," Madeira interrupted. "Your path is your own. Only you can walk it. Only you."

Samuel nodded, not sure what to say. He glanced at Norman and found that rather than staring off into the curved distance, he was now glaring directly at Samuel, as if he was looking through Samuel's eyes and directly into his thoughts. The man's terrible face glowered in the tranquil light of a passing glowglobe. Strange growths and cysts covered his forehead and temples, burying his eyes beneath large folds of skin. He had always looked that way, but it seemed to be getting worse as he grew older.

Samuel averted his eyes from Norman's unflinching stare, thanked the men for their time, and walked away with his thoughts besieged by terrible paranoia.

I can't leave Damian to fend for himself. He needs me, Samuel considered cautiously. *But I've never seen Mr. Madeira and Norman like that. He knows something. He was trying to warn me. He was telling me to just go home and leave Damian to his own demise.*

Samuel pictured the sordid grief welling in his father's eyes the moment he realized he would never see his family again.

Dad thought he was doing the right thing. He wanted some grand life for us. For me and mom. Something beyond all this. And Damian…he and the others want the same.

Samuel turned back, but Old Man Madeira and Norman were already gone.

He came there just to warn me. That has to be it. The old man is throwing me a bone—maybe not even out of the goodness of his heart. He and Norman depend on me for work. But either way, I'd be a fool to go to the bar now.

Samuel came to an uneasy stop as a blue-hued glowglobe passed in front of him, reflecting nourishing azure light across his skin and the short grass. As the dark green grass fed on both the light and kinetic energy produced by each of Samuel's steps, he couldn't help feeling dreamily distracted by the Foundation's serene environment. A stream could be heard close by, frothing across rocks covered in pine green algae that exchanged and regulated the balance of molecules in the carefully maintained atmosphere. Children ran barefoot through the grass and dipped their toes into the stream as they leaped merrily and carefree across it.

What could possibly make this place any more peaceful and enchanting? Both Dad and Damian want to risk heaven for something that might not even be better.

"Hi, Mr. Kaminski!" Fred Wilson shouted as he passed. As he wrestled with his thoughts, Samuel feigned a smile and waved, all the while observing the eleven or twelve-year-old boy's incoming muscles. Fred was not the type to sacrifice his time and energy for others, but his musculature was just like his father's, and it would be a shame for it to go to waste.

It would be a shame for him to not use his naturally muscular body to uplift heaven, Samuel considered, seeing himself in the boy.

"Hi, Mr. Kaminski!" Lakshmi Acharya called over her shoulder, out of breath from chasing Fred in their game of tag. Again, Samuel feigned a smile and waved to Lakshmi. Her father, Governor Acharya, only worked in the Foundation. He and Lakshmi lived in the Luxury Quarters with just over two thousand others who held essential roles in ensuring Astrea's well-being and the safety of its nearly 180,000 citizens. Lakshmi's path was virtually set in stone. As long as she didn't commit a serious crime or refuse a leadership role, she was all but guaranteed to never have to worry about laboring at a power station. More than that, the life of a Luxury Quarters' citizen also came with immortality.

But she'll still have to commit herself to Astrea—even more so than those of us in the Foundation, Samuel reflected. *Heaven doesn't come free. It requires effort. Labor. Sacrifice. Like how mom sacrificed for Nathan…*

He stifled a surge of longing to speak with her again, even just for a few minutes or a few words.

Lakshmi giggled as she caught up to the Wilson boy, and Samuel saw the first flames of love between them. It explained why Lakshmi had traveled this far across Astrea's length, rather than remaining closer to the Luxury Quarters, where she returned with her father each night, once the glowglobes changed to their nighttime hues.

Their tender young love reminded Samuel of Sandra and the indelible bond between them. She was his everything—Sandra and the kids.

They are my personal heaven within heaven, Samuel thought pleasantly for the thousandth time.

A parade of younger kids passed, finding difficulty in keeping up with the two older ones. Samuel waved absentmindedly to the passing group, then let his gaze fall upon Mount Mendel, a mountain that was mirrored on the opposing side of Astrea so that their peaks nearly met in the middle. Another group of kids were jumping off the snowy, half-mile high peak, flipping in midair, and landing on the mirrored, opposite peak. It took Samuel a few seconds to realize he was smiling like a buffoon, thinking back to his own dangerous flights of fancy across the twin peaks as a boy.

Samuel turned and saw that roughly sixty degrees up across the circumference to his left, a pilgrimage of Luxury Enders "walking the tube" laughed and their children blew bubbles as they made their way from one end of the Foundation to the other. Like Samuel, they wore simple homemade tunics and trousers woven from the same amino herbs that supplied their bodies with brimming nutrition.

We're so lucky to have this place, every single one of us, Samuel marveled as he absorbed the tangible joy exuded from every one of the pilgrims' movements. *We're all the chosen few of heaven: Enders, Middlers, every*

Foundationer and Luxury Quarters citizen…we don't have to suffer the hell of Earth; we have the heaven of Astrea. And still, the Sons and Daughters toil behind the scenes, threatening to ruin everything. And Damian…he's caught up in all of this, Samuel thought in horror.

He furrowed and wished Damian could just be like all the rest of the Middlers—like Samuel and Sandra. For Enders, the people living near either end of the Foundation, being able to stretch their legs and walk leisurely for days on end was as fulfilling as tilling the soil or tending a fire was for people living around Mount Mendel at the middle of the Foundation's cylindrical length.

Why can't you just accept heaven, Damian? Shouldn't that be easy for Middlers like us?

Samuel and Damian were both born and raised as Middlers, and like all Middlers, Samuel didn't feel the need to live or walk anywhere else in the tube. He liked the feeling of seeing the twin-facing peaks of Mount Mendel so close, his own ground-peak towering over him and the mirrored ceiling-peak hanging above him, surrounded by Middlers just like himself.

Why can't this be enough for you, Damian? Just like it wasn't enough for dad. Why, goddamnit?

A small gathering of children wrestled a mini glowglobe to the ground and giggled wildly as it slipped out of their hands and serenely floated toward Mount Mendel's refreshingly cool air.

This place, Samuel thought with tears in his eyes. *Mom called it heaven, and dad called it hell. It just depends on how you look at it. Why can't Damian understand that?*

He considered how Enders were more likely to make friends and neighbors along the length of the tube, whereas Middlers were more likely to grow close to those living beside them across the tube's circumference. *Our environment shapes our minds, and our minds shape our environment,* he marveled, hearing his mother as if she were walking alongside him.

Samuel held out his arm full of rippling musculature and observed the result of hours and days and months and years of paying off other peoples' energy debts.

I am strong because Astrea gives me strength. And as long as someone like me exists—someone who refuses to give up. Someone who can do the right thing, no matter the situation. No matter the cost. As long as someone like that is around, hell can always be transformed into heaven.

Samuel clenched his fist as he thought of his father's pleading, hate-filled eyes and his mother's sad, peaceful eyes. Then, he imagined Damian's own pleading eyes as he was stripped from his wife and child. Samuel knew that it would happen eventually if Damian continued working with the Sons and Daughters. It was just a matter of time.

I can't let that happen, Samuel winced. *But maybe Mr. Madeira wasn't saying to just abandon my friend. That can't be right. I think he was saying that I need to do the right thing, even if it's hard. Even if it might cost me everything.*

Samuel realized that he was at a literal fork in the grassy path now. If he went right, he would pass through the local gardens and then arrive at Earth's Reprieve, the local bar. Damian would be waiting for him along with the other revolutionaries who had stripped Damian of his ability to see Astrea as heaven.

Or he could go left and just go home. Sandra would be waiting for him with a filling meal made of the amino herbs she was so fond of growing. He could practically feel Nathan and Margot in his arms as they hugged him tight and told him all about what they had learned on their telescreens during their self-paced lessons.

The glowglobes shifted from amber to silver, signifying the transition to night hours. A shrill woman yelled for her child to return home for dinner, then called out again for a second child as well.

Someone gave their life so that she could have a second child, Samuel knew. *Whether it was a natural death or a family member who decided to make room, someone had to get recycled. And now that kid is breathing and drinking and eating their loved one. That means heaven is a graveyard, as Damian always said. But isn't that true of all life? Isn't that true no matter where you go or who you are? We only live because others have died and sacrificed everything for us.*

Samuel felt certain what his decision must be. *I have to convince Damian to leave the Sons and Daughters. I have to get him out of the mess he's made. I have to find a way.*

Damian had a wife and a son of his own. He was risking their well-being on top of his own. *And my own,* Samuel thought as he went right at the fork. A few hundred feet away and a hundred feet above, the local Queensguard stood like a menacing statue on his perch, observing everything and everyone. His hulking dark armor made him look more like an old world vehicle of war than a living thing. The armor and the Queensguard within it stood in stark contrast to the picturesque, rolling landscape and smiling, laughing citizens of the Foundation.

Is he watching me now? Samuel thought, realizing he had never cared about the notice of a Queensguard before. For the first time, he kept his eyes to the ground and ignored Astrea's breathtaking 360-degree, 207 square mile cylindrical landscape of rolling hills and billowing clouds and frothing rivers and squat but spacious cottages with soft gray smoke rising from each chimney. The normally calming and serene environment suddenly filled Samuel with a sense of profound betrayal.

No, Samuel demanded his mind, resisting the urge to view Astrea as anything but Heaven. *I still have time to save Damian from their revolt. I'll get him to leave the bar, and we can just go home and let the Queensguards recycle the Sons and Daughters to make way for Astreans that can appreciate heaven and strive to create a Foundation that can withstand anything.*

Samuel hated thinking like that. He wished that no one ever had to die, but such was not the way of the world, neither in heaven nor in hell. Nearly at the bar, he glanced at the local Queensguard again, and he thought the man's unblinking eyes might have picked him out among the hundreds of other Astrean's within his field of vision. But it was impossible to tell. Although Samuel could see a whole lifetime in a person's eyes, the eyes of a Queensguard were like the void of space—all-encompassing yet profoundly empty.

Get in and get out, Samuel told himself. *Old Man Madeira's eyes never lie. They aren't going to let a revolution break out. They never have, and they never will. If not Mr. Madeira, Bill behind the bar, he probably already told the Queensguards that the Sons and Daughters are all congregating at the Earth's Reprieve. No way he wants to end up recycled either.*

I have to be quick, Samuel told himself, and as he entered the bar, he saw the Queensguard jump from his perch, facing the direction of the Earth's Reprieve.

I'm going to save you, Damian. I just need to get in and get out.

Those who resist will be spurred to growth by the new world I am creating. To survive on Earth without voluntarily or involuntarily contracting the Nomad Virus will require ruthlessness, cunning, and more than anything, sacrifice.

Only those who find ways to transcend their natural biology and psychology will survive. A multitude of sciences will be utilized by the survivors, and an array of creative solutions to the unforgiving lethality of my new world will be devised.

My actions are the impetus for transcension. And eventually Ascension.

Thus, I am not a destroyer. I am a creator. I strengthen life. I create resolve where there is only torpor and stupidity.

One day they will thank me. The survivors, that is.

From Mendel's Ladder: The Personal Journal of Denis Mendel, Written Circa 2046, Published June 2108 by Leif Mainstone, Federated Agency Publishing

Chapter 5
When Weakness Is Strength

"Y ou betray me, my sister? My love?" Nomusa asked in utter disbelief, her features more rage than despair.

Shira shook her head, unable to stop her tears from flowing—a weakness befitting a slave, not a warrior. "I warned you, Nomusa," Shira said, her voice cracking in anguish. Composure was the last thing on Shira's mind. "You became Winters, Musa. You became a tyrant."

"And you became weak, girl! You've become a mother. You are no longer the warrior you once were!" Nomusa shouted, her voice sharp and jagged as if Winters were speaking through her.

Misshapen, adolescent Rovers hungry for Wintersvilla blood crouched atop their Biofreaks, savoring Nomusa's final moments.

"You trade me for your own escape. My death for your life. You are pathetic, Shira. You couldn't even kill me yourself. You had to get these bands of freaks and fools to do it for you, eh?" Nomusa goaded, her eyes wide in preparation for certain death.

"Nomusa," Shira said with more pleading than she intended. "You did this, Nomusa. You brought this upon yourself."

Nomusa held her chin high with indelible pride. "Maybe this is just the fate of all those who rule," she proclaimed. "The stronger you are, the stronger your enemies become."

One of the Biofreaks growled beneath his ten-ton weight, and he shifted from one elephantine leg to the other as if impatient to feel Nomusa's endoskeleton bend like rubber in his indomitable grip. The Rover standing atop the growling Biofreak's head patted the giant with his tiny malformed hand, whispering an assurance of death that temporarily calmed the oversized humanoid creature.

"This is the fate of all those who use their power to exploit others. Don't you understand that, sister? Can't you see that?" Shira cried as the largest of the five Biofreaks, eighteen feet high at least, emitted its own impatient growl.

"The big mens is overtime for the eatings," the little Rover, once a discarded child of Wintersvilla, warned with sadistic excitement.

Nomusa flashed her teeth at Shira and began breathing rapidly.

"I understand only that you are weak," Nomusa lashed. "You are not my sister. You are not my kin. You are poison, Shira. A suffocating vine I should have pruned when I had the chance."

Shira's despair dipped suddenly to fury. "I killed Winters, Nomusa. Not you. I gave you your power. Me and my blade. And now I take it from you."

At her words, the largest Biofreak roared, and Shira couldn't help more tears at the sight of Nomusa visibly shaking.

The Matriarch of Wintersvilla powered up her exo, but it was no use now. The Rovers howled their blood-curdling battle cry, and the Biofreaks charged forward. Nomusa bent at the knees, but one of the Biofreaks swung his mighty fist and slapped Nomusa to the ground with an open palm as large as the whole of her body, exoskeleton frame and all.

"Nomusa!" Shira shouted, but her voice was like an insect's compared to the abominable growling and howling filling the throne room.

All at once, the Biofreaks grabbed at any piece of Nomusa they could, ripping her exo from her limbs and her limbs from her torso with sickening ease. Nomusa screamed as a Biofreak placed his fingers around her skull and popped her brains out the top of her cranium, spraying Nomusa's hate across the smiling nightmare faces as if in sordid celebration of their victory.

Shira felt hypnotized, unable to break away from the horrifying scene of Nomusa's endoskeleton being stripped of meat by the blood-stained teeth of half-brained mutant ogres as if she were a roasted chicken.

"Shira!" Myriam crowed from behind, breaking Shira from the living nightmare.

"Go!" Shira said, and though the Rovers turned to watch Shira and Myriam run from the throne room, they did not give chase. Such was part of their agreement.

Two figures stood in the doorway of the throne room's exit. One was an overweight elderly man, his hair white but his stance full of vigor and a thirst for power. The other figure was a tall and muscular woman whose night-black skin and dreadlocks contrasted perfectly with the old man, though their stances were identical.

"Winters!" Shira gasped. "Nomusa!" she said, her voice barely audible in its disbelief. The ground shook suddenly behind her, and Shira glanced back to find the blood-drenched Biofreaks and Rovers standing in a row as if constructing an impassable wall of hulking death.

"What is this?" Myriam asked, powering on her suit with reflexive practice.

Shira couldn't speak.

What is happening? This is impossible!

"Run!" Shira urged Myriam, powering on her own exo despite knowing that certain death was upon them.

I can at least save Myriam, Shira thought. *I have to save her.*

As Myriam pivoted to remove Summit Splitter from her back, a closed fist crashed down upon her, stunning her and crushing the lower half of her body into sticky mush.

"Run!" Myriam pleaded to Shira, dark blood flowing freely from her lips. In the next instant a Biofreak jumped and landed on Myriam with the whole of its weight, splintering the dense stone of the throne room floor and splattering Shira's love beneath his bare feet.

Winters laughed, Nomusa licked her lips, the Rovers howled, and the Biofreaks lapped greedily at Myriam's dripping remains.

"No!" Shira cried, falling to her knees in defeat.

"Please!" she cried desperately, forcing the others to laugh and howl and slurp even louder at Myriam's fluids.

"Please!" Shira screamed senselessly as the largest Biofreak hammered his Myriam-drenched fist against Shira's spine, slamming her into the ground at the ravenously excited behest of the gang of howling Rovers atop its mammoth back, demons goading their hellhound to delight in torture.

Shira's exo whirred in a pitiful attempt to move her crushed body then finally gave out completely, its buzz turning to grave silence.

Please, Shira thought as her organs hemorrhaged and her spine flickered but failed to communicate with her fluttering brain. *Please let the girls be safe at least. Please.*

"These girls?" Winters asked sinisterly, and he lifted Aliana and Aurelia into the air by their tiny necks. They were mere newborns, wailing for help in the clutches of a madman.

Shira could only watch as Nomusa released her elbow blades, tucked her arms, and twisted at the shoulders, slicing the girls in two.

It's over, Shira gasped within. *There is nothing.*

"You are nothing," Myriam hissed, standing before Shira now as if she hadn't just been turned to mush.

What is happening? Shira pleaded. Unable to breathe, her vision spun as her brain was depleted of oxygen. A Biofreak lifted its gargantuan leg and let it linger above her head for just a moment before crushing her underfoot.

A crazed scream filled Shira's ears, and then she realized the scream was her own. She finally opened her eyes and breathed deeply, recollecting the present moment. A fire crackled beside her, making the towering flesh trees appear to dance in the flickering light of the peaceful flames.

She turned her head and saw a small group of tiny soilies diligently meandering across the ground. Children back in Wintersvilla loved chasing the tiny, harmless insects in an attempt to inspect them before they crumbled into soft soil. Aliana and Aurelia were the only individuals, maybe in the entire world, whose touch did not force the soilies to disintegrate, as if they recognized the girls as the Earth itself.

That's right, Shira remembered finally. *The girls aren't dead. That was just a damn nightmare. Aliana and Aurelia are alive and well,* she rejoiced, thinking of them as little warriors in their own right with the satisfaction of a general approving of her soldiers' preparedness for battle. *Those two have come a long way,* Shira thought, recounting their harsh training and education as young Women of Wintersvilla.

The stars of the galactic arm radiated brilliantly, indicating a new moon.

That means it's been around two days since the battle with the Mutant, Shira thought grimly, remembering both the giant boar and her nightmares. *I've just been laying here all this time?*

Shira turned and was startled to see a trio of crouching, spindly-faced Nomads slip backward into the shadows of the flesh trees, glaring directly at Shira as they disappeared. They had clearly been watching her, but for how long she couldn't know. It was normal for Nomads to observe humans as they passed by, carrying out some strange duty of their people. But it certainly wasn't normal for them to just stand and watch a person.

Who knows what those creatures are up to, she thought ominously, remembering how there had been similar looking Hybrid Nomads staring at her in the same wide-eyed fashion the night of Wintersvilla's destruction—the night she had met with BigBilly, the king of the Rovers, and exchanged information on Nomusa for a guarantee that none of the Rovers or Biofreaks under the king's command would come after them.

Movement in the brush returned Shira's mind to the present, and Myriam strolled out of the same thicket of flesh trees that the Nomads had slinked into. Many of the flesh trees were laying haphazardly on the ground at strange angles as the result of the battle with the boar Mutant. As was the Wintersvilla Warrior custom during times of relaxation, Myriam walked toward Shira fully nude, her large, unbound breasts bouncing freely with each of her steps, though Shira was in no shape for even scant arousal. It wasn't seduction or sexuality that created the custom, but rather, a sign of a true warrior who had nothing to fear and could relax in her bare skin and ports without worrying about lacking in safety, let alone being concerned with trivialities like modesty. It was by this same logic that Wintersvilla Women did battle wearing nothing more than a thin chest-binder to stabilize their breasts, a light undergarment to avoid dirt or grime in their genitals, and a personal sidearm sheath and straps that were more like permanent fixtures of a warrior's body. The rest of their body remained gloriously and pleasantly exposed. It was said by the greatest Wintersvilla Women, including Shira when she was younger, that anyone unable to sync thoroughly enough with their exo so that it didn't protect them from every projectile or peril of the Earth was a liability, not an asset. A warrior's bare and often deeply scarred skin was visible proof of her internal control of fear.

"Nightmares?" Myriam asked with calculated worry as she entered the light of the fire, which flickered radiantly across her ports, making her glimmer.

Shira nodded and wiped dripping sweat from her brow. Her forearm ports were burnt out, veins splintering madly from the titanium openings. She assumed the rest of her ports were in equally bad shape.

"Probably from the fever. You really pushed too far back there," Myriam offered, allowing Shira the opportunity to let the topic go.

Shira shook her head. "It's not just that," she said, unable to help her tears.

Myriam went to Shira and held her tightly. "I know," she said. "It's okay."

"It's not just the fever," Shira said.

"I know," Myriam said gently.

"The girls?" Shira checked, finding comfort in Myriam's warmth.

"They're fine. Practicing their swordplay beneath the stars with the men and Stump."

Shira would have laughed at Myriam's pet name for Rooli, but her mind was too heavy.

"I'm becoming weak, Myriam," Shira said, forcing herself to admit the words out loud.

"No," Myriam said without hesitation. "You feel so deeply. That isn't a weakness. You cried for Nomusa," Myriam said. "Few would do that, my love. Very few. That's a good thing—that you feel. So few people actually feel deeply like you, Shira. This world isn't meant for feeling anymore—just survival."

"That's what makes it weak," Shira said, trying her best to stifle her tears. "The only reason we haven't been walking on autopilot for the last two days is because my ports and brain are too fried to even manage passive mode."

Myriam looked down reflexively, telling Shira that she was accurate in her assessment. "I'm slowing all of you down, Myriam. I'm...I'm weak," she stammered in disbelief.

"Then weakness is strength, damnit," Myriam issued forcefully, "because if your ability to feel for others is weakness, then all I want is weakness."

"Myriam..."

"I'm serious," Myriam said, still holding Shira tightly in her battle-hardened arms. "What is this life without feeling? Without love? You taught me that, Shira, just as the girls taught it to you."

Shira's eyes widened at the accuracy of Myriam's observation. Still, she shook her head, knowing that weakness and vulnerability were handicaps when it came to survival anywhere on Earth.

"I'm sorry, Myriam…I—"

"Enough," Myriam said, sounding like Shira on the battlefield commanding her troops. "I don't give a shit about all that. I love you, Shira. I love that you feel. I love that you love me. I love that I know love, and I know it because of you, my gorgeous general."

Shira hugged Myriam tighter and let her warmth and the warmth of the fire fill her every cell.

A sharp clang resounded from somewhere in the distance, and Myriam laughed to herself.

"The girls must be getting pretty rowdy. Rooli should be breaking it up right about now."

Shira shook her head no. "She pushes them harder when we aren't around. It's like she's worried how we might view her relationship with them."

Myriam scoffed at the suggestion. "Doubtful. Rooli doesn't give a shit what anyone thinks. It's part of her charm."

Shira chuckled at the idea of Rooli having charm. Visions of the battle filled her head, and she remembered how Rooli had known exactly what to do with the simplest command. She never needed any explaining—she always just knew what to do exactly when the time came. It had something to do with being part-Nomad, a Hybrid. Regardless, Shira knew that she could always depend on Rooli to engage effectively and selflessly on the battlefield. Hybrid or not, she was the single most dependable and loyal individual Shira had ever known. And also the most terrifying when she wanted to be.

"My plan with the tree worked?" Shira asked, making sure there wasn't more to the battle she had missed.

"Almost too well," Myriam said with a note of regret. "The explosion ended up shredding Wesley's lover, Fullman. We're down to just Wesley and three lesser slaves."

Myriam seemed mostly unaffected by the slave's death—looking as though she had lost no more than a highly valued goldfish. Shira, on the other hand, felt intense remorse for Wesley.

It would be like losing Myriam, she considered as a shiver ran the length of her burnt-up spine.

"How is Wesley, then?" Shira checked.

Myriam couldn't help laughing at Shira's compassion for the old slave.

"He's fine. Especially after we took their collars off at Aliana's demand."

Myriam eyed Shira as if looking for approval, and Shira nodded, glad that Wesley could spend what life he still had as a free man.

"And how did Aurelia take it?" Shira asked.

"As expected. Terribly."

Shira wrestled with a consideration that had weighed on her mind for numerous years. "What do you think, Myriam? Is it just a hatred for men taught to her by Wintersvilla? Or is the girl compassionless? Does she simply relish in the suffering of others?"

Myriam sighed contemplatively. "Neither, my gorgeous general. Aurelia doesn't give a shit about our traditions. She's just smart. More cunning than any of us. I asked her why she was so adamant about keeping their collars on and their chains before that. You know what she told me? She said it was to protect the rest of us. She said that were she in their position, she would take the first chance she had to slit all our throats in our sleep and feed our bodies to the hungriest patch of tangle grass she could find."

Shira burst out laughing but was abruptly forced to stop due to a sharp pain shooting from her central right-rib port.

"Are you okay?" Myriam checked.

Shira nodded, wincing away the pain. "And here I thought I had her all figured out. It takes a whole mountain of empathy to understand another's hate to that degree. Maybe Nomusa appointed the wrong girl as Matriarch."

Myriam went silent at the mention of Nomusa.

"Sorry," Shira said, "I didn't mean to bring her up."

"Don't worry," Myriam assured her. "The dead stay dead to me. It's you who remains haunted by them, Shira."

Myriam lovingly tapped the tip of Wintersbane, which protruded a few centimeters from Shira's wrist even while fully sheathed.

"You need to let him go, my love."

Shira knew Myriam's words to be true, and she hugged Myriam closer in gratitude for understanding her mind so deeply.

Without warning, Shira's stomach growled loud enough for both women to hear. Myriam chuckled and said, "we've certainly more than enough meat."

"And it tastes surprisingly good for Muto-meat!" Aliana exclaimed through exhausted breathing from behind them as the girls and Rooli returned back to the campfire. Aliana offered Shira a hunk of smoked Muto. She felt her mouth begin to water despite knowing the foul source of the flesh.

"You're sure it's safe, Rooli?" she asked instinctively as she sat up.

"We've already been eating it for the last two nights," Aurelia signed. "It's safe."

Shira sank her teeth into the meat and groaned in enjoyment as she chewed. The girls took a seat beside her, and each ate their own cut of meat. The men stood outside the warmth of the fire along with Rooli. Even after so much time, the men still felt that it was too taboo and awkward to eat with the women. They would wait for the women to go to sleep—a preference of respect they had vocalized many times before. Rooli had no need for food, though she did eat berries from time to time.

Shira took another bite and finally noticed the unmistakable taste of Rooli's burnt flesh. It was convenient to have a living source of firewood, but that didn't help the smell that accompanied Rooli's charred, woody body.

"I miss the fish back home," Aliana sighed as she gazed at the stars.

"The *delicious* ocean fish?" Aurelia jested. Aliana snickered and pushed her sister playfully on the shoulder.

"There's nothing like aquaponically grown salmon, is there?" Aliana asked wistfully, letting the stars whisk her deeply into her memories of the comparatively easy life they'd lived for twelve years within the walls of Wintersvilla.

The group went silent, each of them mentally savoring the succulent, fatty salmon full of every essential vitamin, mineral, and amino acid the body needed for perfect sustenance. It was one of Wintersvilla's specialty exports—that and ruthless cybernetic teenage girl assassins.

Most old world land animals were no more, but the occasional Mutant, like the giant boar, supplied enough meat for the group along with the occasional foraging for berries by Rooli, who could sniff out the edible ones, and Myriam, who could do the same by utilizing her suit's olfactory enhancements, one of many attachments Shira's archaic model didn't have.

"The pig tastes decent enough," Myriam offered stoically to take their minds off home, and the others nodded in quiet agreement.

Aliana and Aurelia both opened their small backpacks and began occupying their idle hands with productive work. Aurelia busied herself by sewing some of the tears in her backpack straps, and Aliana sharpened the custom miniature short sword that both girls wore on their hip. She scraped it against her tiny whetstone with practiced expertise.

Shira marveled that they no longer needed to be told to use their time wisely. They were growing up so fast.

No, Shira corrected herself. *They're practically already grown up. These girls who I could once hold in the palm of my hand. Look at them now,* Shira marveled with motherly pride. One minute they were wailing for their diapers to be changed, and the next minute they were young Women of Wintersvilla, their blades and minds sharpened through Shira's guidance.

We did good raising the girls. I did good, Shira told herself, feeling fulfilled in a way she never imagined possible when she lived only to swing her blades.

"You know, something strange happened," Myriam said, and Aliana nodded in excitement.

"The Nomads," Aliana said, taking over the story. "They were standing at the edge of the forest after the battle. They were just watching us, Shira. It was so creepy."

"Probably replacing the destroyed flesh trees," Aurelia reasoned. "They turned into flesh trees right after Rooli exploded the Mutant."

"Maybe," Aliana admitted as she brought pieces of meat to the men. Wesley and the other men cried appreciatively and accepted the meat with a prayer of thanks, then ate slowly and meticulously to avoid making any sound.

"No," Myriam stated confidently. "It was like they were making sure we killed the giant pig or something. Like they were using us to kill it."

"Or providing us a source of meat," Aliana said.

"Or trying to kill us," Aurelia signed.

Shira remembered how the Nomads could similarly be seen standing and watching the siege of Wintersvilla from the mountains. Had the Rovers made some impossible alliance back then with the Nomads, or had the Nomads shepherded the Rovers and the Biofreaks, using them as living weapons against Wintersvilla? The Nomads were not averse to killing humans if they deemed it necessary to fulfill their strange plans for the Earth, but Shira doubted the Nomads were capable of malicious treachery and scheming. Those were the domains of the human world.

"The Nomads are basically the Earth itself," Shira said, "and the Earth appears to want to help you girls. We've all seen it. So, I doubt the Nomads are trying to kill you two."

Aurelia conceded to Shira's logic with a nod, then urged, "they exhibited strange behavior, that much is certain, Shira."

Shira knew it was foolish to discount Aurelia's observations, but there was no way to know anything about the Nomads with certainty.

"There's something else," Myriam said, her voice low and grim.

"A Hunter and a Huntress," Aliana finished with awe in her voice and eyes. Even Aurelia couldn't help smiling.

"They want to see us do battle with the creatures we were born and bred to hunt," Myriam said, her smile all teeth like a Huntress tasting the ecstasy of what their kind called the Eternal Hunt.

Shira scowled, remembering the last Pair she had killed. "No, Myriam, that can't be. I apparently killed the last remaining Pair in the mountains right outside home when you were still a kid, and you killed the last solo Hunter in 2089 as your coming-of-age ritual. That was a whole ten years ago, Myriam. Even Tomasz confirmed that there's no Hunters or Huntresses left."

"The world is a big place, and Tomasz is a coward hiding in living ships hovering over the ocean. Besides, he's a man. He can't be trusted. Not ever, Shira."

Shira knew Myriam was right, but was it really possible there was a Hunter in the area?

"My gut is never wrong, my gorgeous general, you know that. There's a Pair in the area. Even Rooli confirmed it."

Rooli confirmed it—that statement said it all. It was true, then, that they might have to do battle with the deadliest creatures ever known to humanity.

Until we showed up, Shira thought, remembering each of the eleven Hunters and eight Huntresses she had slain, some of them alongside other Wintersvilla Warriors, and some of them on her own.

"This Hunter different. Dangerous. Bad," Rooli said simply.

"What do you mean?" Shira asked. The wooden woman just shrugged, fluttering the small growths of green leaves on her shoulder and neck that had sprouted after shedding her old skin for firewood.

Her body still ached, but as Shira peered back at the two exoskeleton frames standing side by side in the flame-flickering shadows a dozen feet away, she told herself they could overcome any threat.

I'm not weak, Shira told herself over the shallow drone of Winter's voice ceaselessly lashing at the peripheries of her mind in an attempt to convince her otherwise.

I'll kill anything that stands in our way, Shira seethed within, though Winter's voice did not cease in its sinister ridicule.

"Let the Hunter and Huntress cross our path," Shira said, forcing steel resolve into her voice for the sake of the others. "And we will make them our prey."

"Hell yeah," Aliana exclaimed, and Aurelia signed that Shira was acting like an over-the-top badass.

"You *are* an over-the-top badass," Myriam said, and she squeezed Shira's leg, sending intense pain coursing through her veins that she struggled to hide.

Shira nodded and gritted away the pain as she tore another piece of Rooli-flavored meat off the bone.

Rooli seems worried about this Hunter. She said he's...bad. Aren't all Hunters bad?

Shira forced away her worry.

As long as Myriam or the girls still breathe, I will never falter. I will never stop. I swear it.

Shira immediately heard Winter's voice telling her, *you are a weak little girl*, and she hated that a part of her agreed. Her body and ports ached worse than they ever had in her life. Even worse, Winters was plaguing her mind more and more often. Shira could only vaguely remember a time, just a year earlier, when she rarely ever thought of him.

Now he's a constant specter in my head, Shira gasped at the deterioration of her psyche.

"Eat up," Shira said, stopping her own thoughts in their tracks. "Get some sleep. Downver isn't far now. A few days at most."

"We are totally going to see Shira and Myriam take on a Pair!" Aliana said with giddy excitement.

Aurelia couldn't contain herself either. "I've always wanted to see a Hunter do battle. And the Huntresses are the brains of the Pair—I'm excited to see what you come up with to take her down."

It was true that Shira and Myriam would likely fare just fine against a Pair, despite Rooli's concern. They were entering the Butcher Wastelands now, a place where the land killed any life that entered, even Mutants. It was why they had encountered fewer and fewer Rovers as they moved south—even the Rovers and Biofreaks were smart enough to stay away from the area. Shira wondered if the same lethality applied to Hunters and Huntresses. Would the Earth aid them against those nightmarish beasts? Or would they be left to defend themselves, like with the boar Mutant?

"We will only do battle if it is unavoidable. Downver is our only goal. But if we do encounter the Pair, you listen to me," Shira said, her tone cutthroat and general-like. "You run," she said, "and you keep running. Rooli will protect you. But you must understand, one second the Hunter could be on top of me, and the next second it could be a hundred feet away, pouncing on you two like a wild boar Mutant in thick woods. Only worse because the Hunter has brains. You understand, girls?"

Both girls nodded, and their demeanor changed from excited to silent and contemplative.

Myriam squeezed Shira's leg, silently assuring her that they would be all right, no matter what they crossed paths with.

Shira looked back to Rooli, who looked strangely worried.

Myriam looked ready for battle, but Shira still felt as if the weight of the boar Mutant was straddling her chest. She found herself unable to breathe, and every one of her fifty-seven ports flared with searing pain all at once.

"Shira!" Myriam said, jumping to her side. Shira's vision turned blurry, and though she tried desperately to breathe, her lungs felt as though they were being constricted in the titanium-bending grip of a Biofreak.

She went blind, darkness wholly enveloping her.

Weak, came the voice of Winters as she slipped out of consciousness. *Just a weak little girl.*

Direct experience is the most profound form of learning and intelligence—so impactful to the psyche that not even a simulation tank can perfectly translate it. All reasoning must be confirmed by direct experience, as direct experience provides subtle stimulations to parts of the brain that even the subconscious mind is not aware of. It is an essential form of processing like any other, and the most valuable form of experiential processing is pain.

Pain is the single greatest teacher. It is all-consuming. It beckons our attention like nothing else. It transforms us. It leads us to Ascension.

In the case of the Hunter, the prolonged, direct experience of unfathomable pain is the single most important ingredient constituting the monster's genesis. To a Hunter, there is nothing more natural than pain and suffering. The unceasing suffering of the Hunter's seventeen-year childhood serves as the Hunter's greatest weapon, for it affords the Hunter the ability to mentally withstand the monumental pain of its rapid genetic rewriting and resultant phenotypic adaptations. Just wearing the skinsuit is hell by its very nature, its quadrillions of microdermic needles like barbs burning beneath the skin without pause.

A Hunter's pain is also the Huntress' tool of control. In the rare cases of a Hunter disobeying, the Huntress has seventeen years of uninterrupted pain to use as a corrective whip.

The Hunter's pain does not create loyalty. That's the role of the Huntress. Instead, every minute of pain that a young Hunter endures is but a hammer blow in the forging of a monster so starved of love that hate and violence become the creature's most natural, familiar, and preferred states of being.

Just like the Hunter, all the human race really knows is pain. All it can really know is pain.

It is exactly that pain that teaches humanity to love, and it is exactly that pain that makes the love I give to the human race worthwhile.

From Mendel's Ladder: The Personal Journal of Denis Mendel, Recorded Circa 2052, Published June 2108 by Leif Mainstone, Federated Agency Publishing

Chapter 6
The Hunter

Anna lifted Thompson's mangled right hand, a mess of scar tissue and cratered flesh like the rest of his body. She gently extended his jagged pointer finger with her own smooth alabaster hands and traced the six major stars composing the constellation Lyra. She couldn't help giggling at Thompson's awe as he stared at the scintillating stars with insatiable curiosity. He was like a child, despite being the deadliest machine of war ever conceived.

"Why it called Lyra?" Thompson asked innocently despite his devilishly deep voice.

"Why *is* it called Lyra," Anna corrected gently, and she kissed his scarred, ridged forehead.

"Why is it called Lyra?" Thompson repeated, unable to take his eyes off the stars that he had never deeply considered before meeting Anna.

"Good, Thompson. It's from an old language called Greek. It's a reference to the lyre of Orpheus, the musical instrument of one of the Grecian gods."

"Gods are not real," Thompson intoned, repeating one of Anna's earliest lessons.

"That's right," she said, and she stroked the deep indent of scar tissue on his head where some unspeakable, sordid torture had been inflicted upon the Hunter by the Cleaners who had raised him from birth like an unwanted, rabid dog for seventeen years. "Do you remember what music is?"

Thompson nodded fervently, but Anna wasn't sure if he really knew or if he was just overwhelmed by so much information, preferring instead to lose himself in the simple and familiar beauty of the night sky.

Even the worst monster can be redeemed, Anna thought as she caressed the Hunter's tortured but still sensitive flesh. He had his skinsuit retracted so that she could touch his actual body—a state of vulnerability that Anna couldn't even fathom. Without a skinsuit, a Hunter felt the searing pain of childhood return all at once, and in that state, they were no more deadly than an elderly human. With the suit, however, a Hunter was the worst nightmare imaginable.

"You are to never kill again, you understand, Thompson?" Anna said, placing particular emphasis on the name she had given him, refusing to refer to him by number.

"Okay, Anna. I try," Thompson said as he smiled stupidly at the vibrant arm of the Milky Way.

"Not try, Thompson," Anna corrected with just a bit of sternness. "You are not a monster. That's what He wants. But that's not what you are. We decide our own fate. Okay, Thompson?"

Thompson nodded, then brought Anna's hand to his flayed lips and kissed her skin, savoring her scent as he breathed deeply. A Hunter's sense of smell could discern atoms and molecules with a parts per trillion level of precision. Her hormones and neurotransmitters gave off particular scents, and though he could not name these mixtures of molecules, he still knew precisely how she felt at that moment. Without words, he knew that she was worried about him, that she was ready to sacrifice her well-being for his, that she was nervous about the future, that she doubted her own words about him not being a monster—all this his vampire bat-like nose told him.

"I will not kill, Anna. But if something try to kill you...then I kill."

"No, Thompson, I'm serious, I—"

Thompson interrupted her with a sudden twist of his neck, bringing his pale, yellow eyes directly in line with those vibrant green eyes that he cherished losing himself in.

"I will not lose you," Thompson stated flatly, the growl in his devilish voice like a threat to the world itself.

Anna held back her tears. She couldn't tell him that he would lose her one day, no matter what he did to try and stop it. She would have to tell him eventually, before they came for her and forced her to return to Him and fulfill her role in everything. But not yet. She couldn't tell Thompson yet. All he knew was pain, and it was unthinkable to inflict even more suffering on this poor creature who needed love more than any being Anna had ever known or read about.

"What?" Thompson asked her, smelling the tears welling in her eyes. He was still not totally familiar with the feeling she was currently exuding out of every one of her pores.

"I love you, little Hunter," Anna heaved, wishing her words could keep her glued to Earth beside Thompson.

Thompson curled his lips into a genuine grin of joy, an expression that was once as rare for him as rain in the Wastes. "I love you too," he said, repeating the words she had taught him just a few weeks earlier. His voice and words were like a bass serenade from Orpheus' divine lyre. It didn't matter to Anna that the rest of the world described a Hunter's voice as notoriously demonic.

He does love me, Anna assured herself as she contended with the knowledge that she really should count herself lucky to have escaped for this long. *I got to experience love in this life, after all, even if it is with a monster. No!* she corrected herself. *The monster is up there in Astrea. He did this. He made Thompson what he is, just like every other Hunter forced to become a demon to turn the Earth into hell. All of this is His fault.*

"Whose fault?" Anna said aloud to her own thoughts with a tone that was not her own.

"Huh?" Thompson and Anna checked in unison.

"What is happening?" Anna asked her own mind nervously as her heart skipped a beat.

Volya.

The name entered Anna's head like a hammer dropped through glass.

Not Anna, Volya corrected, realizing now that she was in the depths of her Hunter's dream. *His mind is powerful,* Volya noted. *I almost wasn't able to remember myself in here.*

The eyes of the Hunter turned to vertical slits, and he looked at Volya with great suspicion.

"Anna? No. Someone else."

The Hunter detangled his body from Volya's, and as he stood, the skinsuit grew back over him, making his flesh appear fully healed beneath the presently transparent skinsuit membrane. Then, like ink quickly diluting through water, his skinsuit altered in appearance, providing a precise camouflage mimicry of the sparse surroundings. The upper half of his skinsuit passively darkened and scintillated with stars to perfectly match the night sky, while his lower half appeared as gravel and sparse vegetation.

"Who?" the Hunter demanded to know.

Volya didn't hold back her ire. *What a stupid dog,* she thought in outrage at her wimpy Hunter. *He can tell I'm not that woman just by a shift in emotions and thoughts, but he still can't remember this is a dream.*

"The Nomads outside your cave said you're dangerous. That true?" Volya asked as she stood and stretched into Anna's body, identical to her own in the waking world, minus the neck-ridge connecting her mind to the Marrow.

"My cave?" Thompson checked, backing away with his arms above his head in a universal sign of surrender.

"What the fuck is wrong with you?" Volya spat. "Why are you so pathetic?"

"Anna!" Thompson said, stupefied with confusion. "What happening, Anna? Why you different?"

"I'm not Anna, you stupid dog. This is a dream. I'm your Huntress, not this weak woman," Volya scowled, presenting her body with Anna's hands.

Faster than thought, Thompson was suddenly in front of her, his pale yellow eyes churning with the rabid animosity that made Hunters infamous. He bared his sharpened teeth and stretched his cracked, plum lips into a hateful glower.

"Bring back Anna!" Thompson demanded, his voice like a flaming whip snapping the air.

"Ooooooooooh," Volya cooed in mock fear. "That's what I'm talking about. Very scary! Let's see what you're really capable of, shall we?"

Volya winked at Thompson, then mentally altered the dreamscape to a scene further in Thompson's past. Now Volya watched as an invisible specter, unnoticed by Thompson or the others as she hid herself in the fog of his tortured mind. The Hunter was only three years old, but still his skin was a terrible patchwork of burns and bruises and gaping wounds. A troupe of mindless Cleaners held the pleading, pathetic creature over an open flame that peeled back skin and sizzled muscle. From a distance, the Hunter's wails and his tiny naked figure made him appear like a human child, but upon closer inspection, his pointed ears, flat nose, vertical-slit eyes, and sharpened teeth gave him away as the future specter of death that the humans viewed as a demon.

"I've memories from thousands of Hunters, and they all start like this. They don't go easy on you guys, do they?" Volya said with a pleasant lilt in her voice, for it was that same torture that crafted a Hunter's mind into the vehicle of hate and violence that every Huntress relished to command.

Three-year-old Thompson, whose only name was Hunter4430 at that point in his life, gurgled on his own blood and snot and tears as the raging fire slowly burned the already flayed and burnt skin of his abdomen. One of the Cleaners surrounding him pierced the center of his slightly ridged cranium with a red-hot skewer, and Thompson convulsed in pain. Volya dipped herself into the child's mind for but an instant before having to retreat to avoid being totally consumed by the agony.

"Holy shit!" Volya marveled, her voice drowned out by the ceaseless pleading moans of the tiny, wailing creature. "Such invigorating, unimaginable pain. For seventeen straight years."

Another Cleaner lifted his own skewer and prepared to pierce the Hunter's left foot, but Volya saved herself the headache of more wailing and flipped to age seventeen, the day the Hunter was released from his Cleaner Camp and forced to limp and drag himself nine miles to the landing zone of his appointed Huntress. The Huntress' skin pod would then turn into a skinsuit that provided reprieve from the physical pain of the Hunter's internal and external wounds. The skinsuit would never heal his wounds permanently, but as long as it remained intertwined with his cells, there would be no disability, and the pain, though ceaseless, could be withstood by the calloused and indurated Hunter. Most importantly, the skinsuit granted the Huntress full control over the Hunter's body and mind.

Even on the final day, the Cleaners still poked and prodded at Thompson, but he was no longer a child. The Hunter was nearly fully grown, and not a single note of pain issued from what had once been lips, though now they were just peeled back flesh revealing jagged, blood-stained teeth. His yellow eyes did not even wince as all nine Cleaners slowly pushed their red-hot skewers into flesh that looked like the stringy, rotten, leftover remains of a Mutant's prey.

The Cleaners removed their skewers in unison, then bowed, deciding that he was ready to withstand the unceasing, unwavering pain of wearing a skinsuit. They each bid him farewell in the same manner they had addressed him for seventeen straight years, with aloof silence and emotionless, featureless faces of unnaturally smooth skin where sensory organs should be.

Thompson shakily removed himself from the harness suspending his body over the always burning fire. He fell to the sandy soil and didn't even wince as the sharp grains pierced his gaping flesh. He forced himself into a standing position, ignoring his damaged and broken body. Volya could see bone in several places beneath the dying, gangrenous muscle and sinew of his limbs. His broken ribs stabbed his blood curdling lungs with every shallow breath, but still he dragged his body in the direction his nose told him would lead to his Huntress and skinsuit. Volya wondered if he would be tempted to kill the Cleaners who had served as his personal arbiters of lifelong torture, but he didn't even look back at them. All that seemed to matter was that he reached his Huntress, not for his own sake, but for the sake of the Eternal Hunt—it was part of him at the deepest levels of his being, just like Volya.

"Let's jump to the good part," Volya said, growing bored with Thompson's life story. She mentally jumped to the moment he arrived at his Huntress.

The area was covered in flesh trees and had already been cleared of human life, undoubtedly by other Huntresses wielding their own ruthless Hunters as they lusted insatiably to taste the ecstasy of the Eternal Hunt. A horde of at least two hundred Nomads and Hybrids of mind-bending forms and shapes passed by the base of the hill, skittering and slithering and shimmying in their own respective fashions to fulfill Mendel's Vision in their own strange ways.

She couldn't help feeling loathing for her Hunter as she remembered that he had not come for her as the Eternal Hunt dictated.

"But you came and found this human woman, I bet," Volya accused, feeling disgusted that her Hunter would embark on the Eternal Hunt with a human.

Volya watched as her Hunter reached the summit of a particularly tall and jagged hill. Arms and legs useless at his side, Thompson dragged his body the final few feet to the 200-foot high summit using his neck and jagged teeth. Rather than arriving at a Huntress holding her skin pod, both Thompson and Volya were dumbfounded to see a smoking metal craft precariously jutting out of the side of the hill's steep summit. Behind a transparent pane, the woman from Thompson's earlier dreams could be seen, unconscious and minorly bleeding from her forehead. The metal craft looked embedded deep enough into the ground to have collided with the surface at terminal velocity, implying that the woman must have come from Astrea, again, just like Volya.

"So, who the fuck is she?" Volya urged, wanting answers quicker than Thompson's memory was providing. Volya sped up the time, and the world moved at ten times the speed. Thompson somehow found the strength to drag his body by his mouth all the way to the craft, then he slammed his forehead on the transparent pane in a weak attempt to wake up the woman. To Volya's surprise, it worked, and the woman sprang into consciousness, flailing her arms in panic before coming to terms with her predicament. Time was still sped-up, and in just a handful of seconds, the woman kicked open the craft with unnatural strength for a human of her size, and then she bent to administer aid to the dying, wheezing Hunter. She remembered something, climbed back into the craft, then emerged with a strange, undulating skinsuit. Volya paused the memory and dragged the scene closer. Inspecting the skinsuit at the molecular level, she was amazed to find that it was altered through an array of genetic enhancements that didn't correlate to any known genetic designs in the databases.

"The Nomads told me you've been genetically altered. Is that due to this strange skinsuit?" Volya wondered. "And who the hell is this woman?" she practically shouted in exasperation. The metal craft provided no helpful clues to her identity except for the abbreviation ANNA across the glass pane and ingrained into the metal hull several times.

"He called her Anna earlier in the dream. Is that her name? Or is it a designation?" Volya wondered. She checked the databases and even queried the Marrow, but nothing came up about this woman, nor about the abbreviation ANNA.

"Okay, mystery woman. Keep your secrets. You're a fake Huntress, that's all I know," Volya said to the still-frame of Thompson and the woman who was like a mirror image of herself. "I could rip your throat out if I wanted, bitch."

The woman called Anna emanated human weakness and Volya couldn't help groaning at the sight of Thompson, prostrate and on his last breaths, being revived by the special skinsuit Anna had brought with her.

"So, the standard skinsuit I brought is useless, then?" Volya lamented, feeling offended even. "He already has a better one?"

Volya considered the situation. Clearly she could still sync with her Hunter's mind, which meant she would still be able to control him.

"Maybe that other skinsuit won't cause me a problem," Volya hoped. "Let's see what it's capable of. Let's see why you're called the Butcher of the Wastes."

Volya moved time forward to where she could feel the greatest amount of anger and violence flickering madly in the deep recesses of the Hunter's scarred mind. Without warning, she was sucked into a whirlwind of fury. The Hunter arched and twisted and broke his body in unnaturally horrific ways as he tore through human and Nomad alike, screaming open-mouthed as he charged at hundreds and then thousands of miles per hour with blind, unceasing hatred across the landscape that was converted into a wasteland in his wake. Legions of Nomads and armies of humans were turned to vapor over the course of weeks as the Hunter killed day and night without stopping for even a moment. His fists morphed into boulders and obliterated multiple skulls while his feet elongated into mantis-scythes and severed a dozen spines, and in the next instant he was a whole forest away, decimating the humans and Nomads and flesh trees of the area with interminable fury.

The carnage filled Volya with exuberant excitement. Another minute passed, and the Hunter eviscerated another thousand lives in his wonderfully dreadful wake. Man, woman, child, plant life—it didn't matter. It was all the same to her beautifully deadly Hunter.

"Yes!" Volya rejoiced in physical ecstasy. "Yes!" she screamed orgasmically, for her Hunter was the most terrifying thing she had ever imagined, let alone seen.

Then she heard it. Something being chanted beneath his breath. A phrase he repeated over and over again with seething, pleading disdain.

"Give her back," the Hunter chanted. "Give her back."

The woman, Volya realized. *She was taken from him? Is that why he went on this rampage?*

Before Volya could rewind time and check to see what had happened, her Hunter stopped his rampage suddenly. He had just broken his own ulna and was about to use it as a piercing weapon to gouge the eye and brain of a human soldier giving his life to protect a petrified group of children running into the surrounding forest.

"Who are you?" Thompson seethed as he dropped the soldier. The soldier immediately unloaded his assault rifle into Thompson's chest and face, but the skinsuit made the bullets as effective as wet paper. Finally, the soldier gave up and ran in the direction of the distantly screaming children.

"Who are you?" Thompson raged at the top of his lungs, and in the next moment he was eye to eye with Volya. A mix of human blood and his own blood dripped ceaselessly from his body like deathly precipitation.

"I like you," Volya marveled at her Hunter. "You're perfect."

Thompson cocked his head in confusion, studying Volya like a hungry predator assessing undecided prey.

"Answer me," Thompson said, his voice full of lethal warning.

"Tsk, tsk, tsk," Volya warned back. "You shouldn't take that tone with me, dog. I'm your Huntress. I own you. Now be a good boy and wake up."

At her words, the Hunter's eyes went wide with the realization that he was dreaming.

"You aren't real?" he asked in disbelief.

"I'm very real," Volya laughed with a sinister edge. "And you are mine."

With a snap of her fingers, they both returned to the cave. They were still eye to eye. Thompson unwound his legs and stood, towering over Volya's five foot, ten inch frame by just over three feet.

"I already have a Huntress. I already have a skinsuit. Just go away and leave me to my dreams," Thompson said, surprising Volya with his grasp of English Universal. Hunters weren't supposed to concern themselves with proper language use.

"That woman teaching you to speak was a waste of your potential. You are—"

"Anna," Thompson interrupted with sudden urgency. "Where is she? Do you know where she is?"

Volya scoffed at his question and tone.

"Stop being pathetic, Hunter4430. That woman is probably dead anyway. Those memories of her are from over 30 years ago."

Thompson looked genuinely confused, though he didn't seem to care that Volya referred to him by number.

"I've been asleep that long?" Thompson checked with a croak of disbelief.

Volya shrugged. "I guess so, dog. Sleeping on the job. The Eternal Hunt isn't over though."

Thompson shook his head, seeming to abhor Volya's mention of the Eternal Hunt.

"That's all bullshit," Thompson began, but Volya was quick to interject.

"No!" she shouted. "What's bullshit is that I never even had a chance to hunt. But you certainly did, Mr. Butcher."

Thompson winced and looked lost in thought suddenly. Volya followed his mind's trajectory and saw that he felt remorse and regret for his actions. Reticent pockets of rage simmered in the depths of his consciousness, but with conscious effort, Thompson quelled the urge to rampage and kill, laboriously and ceaselessly filling his brutalized mind with Anna's calming voice.

"Ew! Stop it!" Volya commanded as if he were a misbehaving mut. "We have humans to kill. *You* have humans to kill. Enough with that human emotion nonsense."

"I won't do it," Thompson told her simply, refusing to give in to what Volya knew came most naturally to him.

"You will," Volya issued.

Thompson sulked in defeat, aware that Volya could take full control of his body and mind whenever she wanted. He didn't let go of Anna's voice, however, allowing her tender words and gentle touch to beam like a lighthouse in the depths of his madness.

"It doesn't matter what you fill your mind with," Volya said defiantly, reading his mind with crystal clarity. "Your mind belongs to me. You are my dog. Mine. And mine alone. Now come, boy."

Volya exited the cave, but Thompson refused to move.

"Don't make me put your collar on, dog," Volya said with child-like glee.

Thompson braced his mind, readying himself to utilize the cognitive blocking technique Anna had taught him long ago. He just needed a bit more time to mentally prepare.

"Move, dog!" Volya commanded, and Thompson's body was forced to obey her.

"This is great!" Volya cheered at her enslavement of Thompson. "The Eternal Hunt is not over," Volya practically purred. "Today it begins anew."

The first denizens of Astrea's Foundation will continue to bow in gratitude to their communistic paradise. But over time, the newly born will want more, as they should. Thus, the seeds of revolution are sewn into the very foundation and inception of my communism. Even though the Foundation's communism is nearly perfect relative to any society of the old world, those born in the Foundation will still inevitably grow increasingly spiteful of it with every passing generation.

This is the way of humanity. It has always been this way. A cycle of golden age, recession, depression, revolution, expansion, and eventually another golden age before it all falls apart again. Ad infinitum.

In every human there is a want for more. A need for more. It is exactly that drive for more that allowed our species to crawl out of the primordial wilds. And it is exactly that want and need that drives me to Ascension.

Were Astrea intended to last forever, it too would undergo the natural cycle of societal creation and destruction and would eventually fall to ruin, just as every human society of the past was eventually crippled and destroyed by humanity's inherent failures.

But Astrea is a temporary refuge. A transient bastion that serves to buy me just enough time.

Time enough to break the cycle forever.

From Mendel's Ladder: The Personal Journal of Denis Mendel, Recorded Circa 2055, Published June 2108 by Leif Mainstone, Federated Agency Publishing

Chapter 7
A Need for More

Miniature glowglobes hovered about the Earth's Reprieve, illuminating countless pictures on the walls depicting famous and infamous images from the old world. In one picture a man stood in front of a line of armored land vehicles of war. In another, a group of men sat upon a building's exposed beam suspended in the clouds. Samuel had trouble pulling his stare away from a picture depicting a large white hand holding a tiny withered black hand in its open palm. His kids, educated by the telescreens, would probably know the relevance of each and every picture, but Samuel never really cared for history beyond the very basics.

Bill Wendover, the owner and barkeep of Earth's Reprieve, always seemed stuck in a perpetual pattern of wiping glasses, wiping the bar, filling drinks, smiling at a patron, then repeating it all over again. He smiled and waved at Samuel as he entered, which meant that he'd be wiping glasses next. Except that's not what he did, and as Samuel looked over his shoulder, peering out the window to check for the incoming Queensguard, Bill walked from behind the bar with a nervous grin and squeezed the back of Samuel's arm.

"The Q-guard on duty is already on his way," Bill whispered angrily over the loud blast of 1970s rock from an old world territory called the United States of America, the same territory that both of Samuel's parents had been from. The music was Bill's favorite, and with soundproof walls in the bar, the neighbors couldn't complain about what Samuel agreed was raucous noise. Bill pointed to one of the backrooms, the same room where the original five Sons and Daughters of the Foundation had first met and discussed the prospect of a second revolution. Samuel still remembered that day as if it had happened a week ago rather than twenty-three years.

Samuel approached the backroom to find eight individuals sitting around a rectangular table tucked into a dark alcove. Seated at the rear head of the table, Albatross, the leader of the group, had the only direct view of Samuel. His real name was Jakob Rohrshan, but only Samuel and a handful of others knew that from growing up alongside him.

Albatross peered calculatingly over his spindly half-moon glasses that Samuel had never seen him without. It was peculiar to see anyone wearing glasses, as there were virtually no genetic defects in Astrea's carefully selected original population, just as there were virtually no pathogens in Astrea's carefully controlled environment. Smiling with his thin lips, Albatross brushed back a few dreadlocks and elbowed his partner Nikki. Like Albatross, she was rail thin, choosing to eat as little as possible in order to trade excess food credits for less labor. By the looks of it, they probably only needed to work a few lazy minutes per week to get by without going into energy debt. They were all skin and bone, but they certainly weren't lacking in confidence and cunning.

Nikki turned and eyed Samuel through distrusting slits. There was a time when Nikki was romantically obsessed with Samuel, but now she only viewed him as a brick threatened to be thrown through the glorious stained glass that the Sons and Daughters were attempting to mold.

"What do you want, worker?" Nikki asked spitefully, placing emphasis on the pejorative *worker*. The rest of the group turned to see the Workhorse of Astrea, one of the five original founders of the Sons and Daughters.

"Samuel Kaminski," the youngest and most muscular member of the group said in awe. "It's an honor, sir. I feel like I'm about to glow gold," he said, using the new age expression that meant feeling overwhelmed or nervous, which Samuel's kids had frustratingly explained to him numerous times. "My name is Geronimo, I—"

Damian, sitting at the head of the table opposite Albatross and closest to Samuel, interrupted Geronimo with a death stare, forcing the man to look down and hide himself behind his bulging arms.

"Sorry," Geronimo mumbled.

"You came," Damian said, and he turned to meet Samuel's stare. Damian was less than half the mass of Samuel, but he was all heart. As much as Samuel labored, Damian worked equally hard for the Sons and Daughters. He was in charge of keeping their operations covert, along with spreading their ideals and eventual revolution across the whole of the Foundation. Then, eventually, the whole of Astrea. It was exactly what Samuel's father had wanted.

"We're leaving," Samuel told Damian, and he glanced nervously behind his back, peering futilely through the bar's front windows.

"Samuel," Damian issued, shaking his head in disappointment. "We need you. The people of Astrea need you."

Frank, who was five years older than Samuel and had served as the original muscle of the group when Samuel was still a scrawny boy, chuckled openly at Damian's words. "We don't need you, Sammy. Be a good boy and run along home. Or maybe head back to the power station and keep laboring your life away, worker."

Samuel found it ironic that Frank's musculature was nearly as expansive and dense as Samuel's. It was only their six-inch difference in height that made the man appear so much smaller.

"You labor just as much as me, big man," Samuel said, puffing his chest in open challenge to any in the group that might try to pull a fast one on him with a homemade dart gun or makeshift flashbang. The men and women at the table were anything but stupid, and they each knew many ways to incapacitate or kill others, even if none of them had ever taken a person's life before. They still believed themselves ready, so they were just as dangerous, maybe even more so in some ways since they were always looking for a fight.

Frank smiled then took a long swig of his homemade ethanol, an illegal act since any beverage over 1% abv was strictly prohibited in both the Foundation and Luxury Quarters. He passed his flask to a petite, skinny hacker girl to his left, whom Samuel had never seen before, but she declined his offer. She couldn't have been older than fifteen. All the hackers, young and scornful of the Foundation, had a similar edgy look. This particular hacker had shoulder-length braided hair and chewed on a bundle of tiny copper wires—tools of her trade. Hackers spent the majority of their time breaking into Astrea's computer systems to leech work credits, which meant subsisting without laboring by stealing several minutes of daily labor from a handful of other citizens at a time. It was such a small amount that most people didn't even notice. Out of the few that did notice their labor time change or their exertion meter fluctuate strangely, they kept their mouths shut, fearing that they would be seen in a negative light by their fellow citizens if they complained.

The thin, flimsy hackers, despite being young and naive, were thieves, plain and simple. But Frank wasn't a thief. He was a hard worker, that much was clear from his muscles—something that couldn't be stolen through hacking.

"I labor for myself," Frank said gruffly after finishing his flask with a second long gulp. "Every minute I labor is more credits to spend as I see fit. You, though, Sammy," Frank laughed condescendingly. "You goddamn mindless Middler. How many hours do you spend lifting at the power stations each week now, Fifty? Sixty?"

Samuel shook his head, refusing to reveal that he was now lifting a whopping seventy-nine hours per week, pushing his body past its once inexhaustible limits.

"How many people have you taken under your wing, eh boy?" Frank said, as the others just stared. As Frank spoke, Samuel couldn't help squeezing his fists in loathing for this selfish man. Men like him were nothing more than a pit of hedonistic rot. "I know you labor for that lady Waters," Frank went on, each of his words inflicting Samuel with mounting anger. "And Old Man Madeira—you were always close, weren't you? He raised you like a distant grandfather. I guess you feel indebted to him, eh boy? What's he at now, a nine-times baseline energy tax? And you have a whole list of other old timers you labor for at the three-times rate. Goddamn, Samuel. You must be working more than seventy hours a week now that I really think about it." Albatross and Nikki looked disgusted by Samuel, but the others, including Damian, couldn't hold back an air of awe at Samuel's selflessness. "How many more can you labor for, Sammy?" Frank pressed.

"As many as I have to," Samuel responded heartily. "And if each one of you in this room did the same, I wouldn't have to work so hard."

Damian shook his head. "But where does it end, Samuel? Huh? You know they'll make you a Q-guard one day, whenever the next one chooses to be recycled or…something unexpected happens," Damian said ominously, and Samuel couldn't help checking for the Queensguard. Samuel wondered for a moment if he had only imagined the Queensguard jumping down from his perch with his dead eyes set on the bar.

He's coming, Samuel knew. *We have to get out of here.*

"He has a point, Samuel," Albatross said, his voice low and reserved. "What happens when they send you and your family to the Luxury Quarters and make you a Q-guard? Only those who can lift the armor are fit for Q-guard service, and that leaves you and a few others to choose from, Samuel. Who will labor for Mr. Madeira at a nine-times energy tax if you are no longer able? Who will keep him alive when he hits three months of energy debt and the Q-guards come knocking, eh?"

Samuel was genuinely unsure what to say. He knew in the back of his mind that he would probably be promoted to Queensguard one day, but he never thought about it further than that. He couldn't, because a part of him couldn't help thinking that Damian and Albatross and his father and every other revolutionary were right.

"He's got no answer," another of the frail hackers said as she pulled her curly red hair into a ponytail. "Because there is no answer. The Qs set it up like that for a reason. To control us. To exploit our labor. Their armor comes from the Paradise Quarters, and whoever lives there—they are our masters, and we are their slaves."

"No," Samuel said, his deep voice and giant mass stilling the frail young girl without him even intending to affect her. "You're wrong," he said, forcing a gentleness into his tone as he ignored her reference to the ridiculous idea of the Paradise Quarters. "We get eighty-one years of heaven. All we have to do is labor at a power station for three hours per week, and nine hours per week after we turn eighty-one."

"And twenty-seven hours per week once you hit ninety," Nikki said painfully. "Or you just get recycled. Just like that. Gone," she gasped before collecting herself and returning to her state of perpetual irritation and anger. Nikki had lost both her parents at a very young age, as they had chosen to walk arm in arm to the recycler for the sake of Nikki having a head start in life so that she might have a better chance of living in the Luxury Quarters as an immortal. They couldn't have predicted that it would just fill her with hate and turn her into a revolutionary—a terrorist even. There were rumors that Nikki had been offered admission into the Luxury Quarters but had declined, though Samuel wasn't sure if that was just something she had made up to add to her legend within the Sons and Daughters.

"I get it, Nikki," Samuel said. "But such is life. It's still better than the old world, and it's certainly still better than the new world. Astrea is heaven if you just let it be."

"That's easy for you to say," Damian snapped. "You and Frank and Geronimo and the few other jumbos—you're all blessed with naturally superior musculature. The rest of us—we're not so lucky, Samuel."

Samuel tried to think of a retort, but it didn't matter. They had to leave. Surely they were nearly out of time.

"Damian," Samuel began, ready to pick him up and haul him out of the bar if that's what it would take.

"Is that fair, Samuel?" Damian issued, continuing his painful tirade. "Is that fair that you and the other jumbos should be naturally superior? Is it fair that you should have to labor so hard for others? Is any of this fair?"

Samuel almost felt repulsed by the childish premise of Damian's questions, and he felt worse that he had once heard his father say the same exact things.

"Nothing is fair, Damian. Nothing. Not in life nor in death. Please, Damian," Samuel said, his hand outstretched. "Please leave with me."

Frank issued a pattering of condescending laughter and said, "It's too late for all that, Sammy. We're past the point of no return now."

Samuel looked to Damian for an explanation, but it was Albatross who spoke. "Today is the perfect day for revolution, don't you think, Samuel?"

Today? Samuel thought, his heart tripling in pace. *Is that what this meeting is about? They're sparking it today?*

Outside the bar, doors began shutting, and people could be heard shushing each other into unnatural silence.

He's coming, Samuel knew. *The Queensguard is almost here.*

"Whatever you all have planned, it's not too late. Bill, he called the Queensguard," Samuel warned.

"We know," Nikki said satisfactorily, her smile nearly as devilish as the Hunters that Samuel had seen pictures of from the past.

"You know?" Samuel gawked.

"It's part of the plan. We knew the old timer would sell us out this time, even though we pay him to keep his mouth shut," Frank said, and he nodded to the hacker closest to him to move out of his way.

Frank walked to the bar, and without warning, he shoved a sharpened metal rod through Bill's ear and into his brain, killing him instantly.

Samuel fell to his knees and nearly threw up, as did all the others at the table, except for Albatross and Nikki.

"Fuck!" Damian shouted at Frank. "You were supposed to just tie him up!"

Frank wiped the metal rod with the cloth Bill was still gripping in his hands as blood pooled around his head.

"The fucker sold us out, D. Took our creds and sold us out."

"We already fucking knew he would," Damian yelped, his voice cracking as he looked to Albatross and Nikki for support, but they only offered cold stares.

"This wasn't part of the plan," Geronimo said, shaking his head in shock. "This wasn't part of the plan," he said again.

Nikki reached across the table and slapped him. "Adapt, big boy. This is real time. This is the real thing. This is what we worked for. What we all worked for," she said, locking eyes with Samuel.

"You're all fucking nuts," Samuel said. "The Queensguard will be here in a moment, and he's going to crush you all like snow atop Mount Mendel, you know that? You're all going to be recycled," Samuel said, hating that a tiny part of him was glad that would be their fate.

And the same will happen to Damian, he realized. *And me*, he thought in horror. *The Queensguard will see me as guilty by association.*

Damian stood and backed away from the table. "You killed Bill," he said, accusing Albatross rather than Frank. "He's been around since the beginning, Al. He used to give us free beers when we were kids, remember?" Damian was crying, but Albatross didn't seem at all phased.

"Adapt, Damian," Albatross said, and then he stood and nodded for the others to leave the table.

"I'm getting out of here," Samuel said, "and whoever wants to leave can come with me, revolution be damned. It's not too late. Whoever stays and sees this madness through deserves to be recycled."

"Don't you want to see the next part of the show?" Frank asked cryptically.

Steady footsteps shook the ground outside, signaling the approach of the Queensguard.

"Damian!" Samuel urged, but there was only one door. There was nowhere to run.

I can't get caught here, Samuel thought. *I'm putting Sandra and the kids at risk, not to mention guaranteeing my own death.*

Suddenly the door burst open, splintering away from its hinges from the force of the Queensguard's blow. The thick titanium armor buzzed with electricity, providing an invisible shield that could deflect any blow or projectile. Even the guard's unarmored head was protected by the electric shield generated by the rest of the armor.

The Queensguard's emotionless eyes scanned the room, but upon seeing Bill's dead body, his eyes were suddenly filled with a measure of rage.

"Who killed him?" the Queensguard asked as if in challenge.

"Me," Frank said, fearless despite being unarmored and at least a foot and a half shorter.

"Now," Albatross said, and at his signal the three unnamed hackers lifted small, homemade EMP guns and fired them at the hulking armored man. All at once, the electrical buzz turned to silence, and without a second's hesitation, Frank threw the metal pole like a javelin through the Queensguard's skull, sending the armored man toppling over, his innards spewing out of his head.

"You killed him," Samuel gasped with equal amounts awe and disgust. No one had ever killed a Queensguard before. Most said it wasn't even possible.

"They killed him," Samuel said, this time to Damian. Damian nodded gravely, but the Queensguard's death didn't seem to affect him like Bill's. Instead, it seemed to fill him with resolve, as if seeing the unmoving titanium mass as a symbol that the revolution was not only possible but was successfully taking place right before their eyes.

"Incredible," Nikki marveled at the two dead men. "The damn worker went down like a lead glowglobe."

The ground began rumbling, shaking the dozens of pictures on the walls and even knocking a couple to the ground with a piercing shatter.

"It's starting," Albatross said with a smile, though his eyes were filled with disbelief behind his half-moon glasses.

"What's starting," Samuel demanded, worried about Sandra and his children.

The kitchen sink burst suddenly, spraying pressurized water all over the bar. The same happened to the sink in the bathroom, and then Samuel heard water spigots exploding outside, one after another, flooding Astrea's grassy roads with quickly rising water. The glowglobes flickered gold, then silver, then blue, then settled on a slowly strobing red. An alarm sounded somewhere in the distance, warning the denizens of Astrea of extreme danger for the second time in the Foundation's history, filling children with fear and adults with grave recollection of the past failed revolution.

Samuel peered outside and saw mothers and fathers frantically collecting their children, shepherding them into their houses despite the water continuing to rise toward the threshold of their doors. As the parents and children shuffled into their homes, small pairs and trios of young adults spilled into the streets. All of them were skinny hacker-types and openly carried the same type of EMP gun that the hackers in the bar had used to deactivate the Queensguard's armor. They ran with purpose, as if they were going to war.

"You've been recruiting others," Samuel gasped at the chaos unfolding in the streets. "What the hell is happening, Albatross?"

"It's what Mr. Kaminski, your father, always wanted, Samuel. It's the revolution. Your father taught us well."

The bar's telescreen turned on, flashing an Astrean-wide warning. Samuel was horrified to see his own face listed alongside the other revolutionaries in the room. He was a wanted man now.

"Barbara and Johnathan," Samuel said, speaking the names of Damian's wife and son in a desperate attempt to bring him to his senses despite the apparent futility of it all.

"Barbara knows," Damian said. "She's one of us. I told her to keep Sandra and your two little ones safe."

"We're all dead," Samuel told them, pointing to their faces on the telescreen.

"You always doubted me," Damian told him defiantly. "You always doubted all of us. But this is going to work, Samuel. And we need your help. That's why you're here. That's why I asked you to come."

"You put my family in danger, damnit. I'm not there to protect them."

"You won't need to protect them, Samuel. The revolution isn't going to fail. Not this time."

Samuel shook his head, knowing Damian's words to be utterly impossible. It didn't matter how many kids they recruited as hackers or soldiers or both. It didn't matter how many years they had planned. Astrea was always greater.

"There is nobody, not even a legion of Sons and Daughters, who can stand against the will of heaven, Damian. You know that don't you?"

"Heaven," Damian scoffed. "This is a prison, Samuel. This is hell. We toil and labor while our wardens grow fat in paradise."

"Damian! Listen to yourself. We don't even know if the Paradise Quarters are a real thing. You sound like—" Samuel said, stopping himself at the last second from saying that Damian sounded like his own father. "What we have here is enough, Damian. You need to call it off. You need to tell everyone to just stop."

Frank laughed openly at Samuel's pleading.

"Stay out of our way, Sammy, and maybe we'll let you live to taste the sweet fruit of paradise."

"Is that what all this is about?" Samuel urged as rising water began trickling into the bar. "Is that what the revolution means to you, you fools? You're trying to make it to some mythical part of Astrea? You're throwing away an actual heaven for a chance at some hypothetical paradise? The Paradise Quarters—it's just a story. A story my dad died for. It's not real, damnit!" Samuel said with tears in his eyes.

"It's real," Albatross said with confident awe. "Mr. Kaminski wasn't crazy. Paradise is real. I've seen it. The handful of people there live like Gods—infinity at their fingertips. And soon it will be ours, Samuel."

I have to make it back to Sandra, Samuel resolved, ignoring Albatross' insane ramblings and tearing himself away from Damian and the others without a second thought. *I don't have long before the Queensguards find me, and then I'll never see any of their faces again. Or…*Samuel thought painfully, seeing his father's anguish in his mind. *Or maybe the revolution will work. Maybe things will change for the better after all?*

Samuel ignored Damian's shouts from behind him and ran home through shin-high water, the city flashing with crimson madness as hundreds of Queensguards swarmed into the Foundation from unseen holes that had opened in the ground, serving also to drain and counteract the flood.

Of course, Samuel knew, cursing himself for thinking like his dad. *Of course revolution is impossible. Which means I'm a dead man as soon as they get everything back under control.*

To Samuel's surprise, he saw multiple Queensguards fall to the EMP blasts of hackers. Then, to his dismay, he watched as they straddled the giant, armored men and stabbed their skulls with the same type of sharpened pole that Frank had wielded. Other hacker groups simply weren't quick enough for the Queensguard they had chosen as prey, resulting in their necks being summarily snapped one by one—the preferred form of execution to ensure as much of the body as possible could be properly recycled. Even in the midst of revolution, the Queensguards still abided by Astrean protocol.

As Samuel ran faster than he ever had in his life, his muscles strained but did not fail him. His thoughts, on the other hand, oscillated nauseatingly between believing the revolution could succeed and cursing himself for being stupid enough to even weigh it as a possibility.

It doesn't matter, Samuel told himself, hearing his mom's voice in his head. *Hell or heaven, all that matters is family.*

His house was just past the next garden district. He was almost home. All he wanted was to hold Sandra and his children in his arms.

He could practically feel their soft, warm bodies in his embrace when a Queensguard unexpectedly turned a corner, coming face to face with Samuel.

"Where do you think you're going, fugitive?" the Queensguard asked, his hollow eyes devoid of any sense of heaven.

They scurry like ants—the great powers on Earth's surface that stand against me. I accounted for this, of course. Their plans, really, are my own. Their very thoughts are the deterministic result of my intentions.

You're all just puppets, don't you see?

They don't see it, of course. Only I can see the strings of fate attached to each and every one of us to some unfathomable realm—effects of some ineffable cause.

But now, in this form, I have taken hold of the strings of every life, including my own. The next step is to cut my own string and leave everyone else's string detangled, free to accept or cut as they will.

In the meantime, the ants will continue to scurry and build their little empires of dirt. John Downver dug out his underground city beneath the old world city of Denver. Craig Winters used his legions of soldiers and female slaves to build Wintersvilla atop the ruins of the old world city of Vancouver. Gladys Mainstone, my dear Gladys, converted the entire state of California into the Agency. And then there is Vida, the entire South American Continent, and Waru, the remains of old world Australia. Both are bastions of humanity where people have found a way to live side by side with the Nomads. More nuclei of control and loci of influence will arise in the coming decades as well. These places each hold their own power, but they are still as temporary as Astrea. Even the Earth itself is ephemeral relative to the cosmos, and the cosmos is ephemeral relative to those causal realms outside it—those non-places from which the strings of ants originate.

It is I who will be the first ant to cut its own thread and crawl out from the cosmic hole from which I was born, emerging into the causal plane as a god ascending to his rightful domain.

From Mendel's Ladder: The Personal Journal of Denis Mendel, Recorded Circa 2065, Published June 2108 by Leif Mainstone, Federated Agency Publishing

Chapter 8
The Fourth Prodigal Son

Left. Right. Left. Right. Left. Right.

The sun rose and set and rose and set again, mixing the bright and dark colors of the world in a swirling, magnificent tapestry of reliable and gentle change. Gusts of pleasant, sun-warmed wind caressed her face, whispering the Earth's placid melodies into her ears.

Left. Right. Left. Right. Left. Right.

Familiar machinery whirred from somewhere, but she didn't want to think about that. The consistency of the gentle warmth and slowly drifting clouds and shimmering golden sunlight made her remember the wily, lethal weather of childhood, during a time when, in a single heartbeat, a blistering 150 degree Fahrenheit day might plunge to negative 30 degrees in the wake of a polar burst, only to return to boiling desert heat a few minutes later. But not anymore. The Nomads had finally rerouted the climate change exacerbated by old world humanity, and for the last decade, the world remained stable and uniform with an unshifting global temperature of 70 degrees.

The world is beautiful, she thought detachedly, and she found it easy to ignore the rest of her brain vying and pleading for her attention. *The wind and the sunlight…everything is so peaceful and steadfast nowadays. Everything is just right,* she thought, not remembering and not caring who she was as the world's gentle gusts helped to hush her troubled mind to serene silence.

Left. Right. Left. Right. Left. Right.

Flat gray clouds floated across the limited vision of her half-open eyes, and a light rain washed away blood and dirt from her distantly aching skin. The rain made her ports sting, finally jolting Shira back to full consciousness. Flesh trees occluded the sky above, and just as she realized her exo was walking automatically in passive mode, the suit transferred control back to Shira. She was left reeling and fell onto her face.

"Shira!" a cacophony of voices shouted, piercing Shira's brain with migraines.

"Quiet," Shira nearly pleaded, squeezing the bridge of her nose to alleviate the high pitch ringing in her ears.

She felt Myriam's calloused hand squeeze her bare shoulder, providing soundless comfort. It was only then that Shira realized it was her own feverous outpouring of sweat that was making her ports sting, not rain. The world had not felt rain in over a decade.

"You okay, Shira?" Aliana asked grimly as if from miles away.

"I'm…fine," Shira panted, unable to catch her breath. She caught a glance of her forearm ports and nearly choked on her breath. Splintering purple and black networks of veins snaked from every port, and the rest of her skin was jaundice yellow.

Am I dying? Shira contemplated, bracing herself against surging pain. She mentally willed the exo to present her vitals across her vision, but it wasn't responding to her thoughts. Guilt racked through Shira as she sucked at the air, still unable to fully catch her breath. *I'm dead weight either way.*

"You have to leave me," Shira issued, not even bothering to ask how many days she'd missed since the last time she'd been awake around the campfire. It took incredible energy just to string that one full sentence together without stopping for breath.

"We're going to Downver, my gorgeous general. All of us," Myriam told her resolutely, though there was obvious hesitation in her tone.

"No—" Shira demanded, but Aliana interrupted her.

"It's not your decision, General Shira," Aliana said, her head high despite the tears in her eyes as she watched the closest thing she had to a mother struggling to breathe. "Nomusa named me Matriarch, and I say we leave no one behind."

To Shira's surprise, Aurelia didn't kick up a fuss at Aliana's mention of being named Matriarch-regent just two weeks before Wintersvilla's fall and what Shira still hoped was Nomusa's death. Through her piercing violet eyes, Aurelia glared at Shira, then finally signed, "You're coming with us, Shira. That's final."

Shira nearly cried, but she coughed blood instead, then wheezed in pain, struggling to breathe.

"Blood in left lung," Rooli stated flatly.

Shira's breathing curdled with blood as she sucked at another breath, desperately vying for oxygen. Her lips turned blue, and the black veins around her ports seemed to slither toward her heart right before their eyes.

"Do something!" Aliana shouted at Myriam, then she turned to Rooli. "Do something!" she repeated.

Rooli stepped forward without hesitation. She currently had four arm-like limbs, and she used two of them to flip Shira over and hold her to the ground by her shoulders. Knowing better than to doubt Rooli's motives, Shira clenched her fists and prepared herself for whatever barbaric implement Rooli had in mind.

Another of Rooli's limbs hovered over Shira's chest, and just as Shira's vision began to turn cloudy from a lack of oxygen, the limb projected a smooth, straw-like piece of wooden flesh between Shira's metal ribs and directly into her left lung. The pain was unimaginable for just a moment before Shira's exo blocked the majority of the signals from those particular neurons, dulling the extraordinary pain to a bearable level. Oxygen-rich, bright red blood flowed freely from the makeshift chest drain as Shira's lung was crudely but effectively aspirated.

Finally, Shira felt like she could properly breathe, and as she stood with the help of her exo, she saw in the eyes of the others that she looked just as bad as she felt. Each breath pushed a gush of blood through the chest tube like a countdown to her death, but at least the tube stayed in place.

"How much further?" Shira asked, knowing it would be a waste of time to attempt to convince them to just leave her.

"Just another…twenty miles…so…a few hours…maybe less," Myriam stated slowly and painfully, knowing full well that Shira didn't have that much time.

"I'm sure Rooli can grow a tube for us to transfer blood to you," Aliana said. "Aurelia and I are universal donors."

"No!" Shira commanded, ashamed to consider sacrificing even a modicum of the girls' well-being for her own sake.

"You will die," Rooli told Shira simply, and at her words, Wesley cried out with hysterical howls of grief.

"Wesley!" Shira ordered before softening her tone. "Grieve quieter."

Wesley nodded apologetically, and the lesser slaves moved to support the half-blind old man.

Myriam stepped forward and grasped Shira's hand, which was drenched in slick blood from her coughing fits.

"I'll come back for you," Myriam said, her rasping voice struggling to overcome the sobs forming in the back of her throat. Calm coursed through Shira in that moment, for she understood fully that Myriam was a true warrior of Wintersvilla. She knew what had to be done, even if it meant sacrificing everything important to her. Even if it meant losing her love.

"You go," Shira said, "and you don't look back."

Myriam furrowed and gritted her teeth, fighting back her tears. Rooli lurched a few heavy steps toward the girls, preparing to leave without another moment's wait.

"What?" Aliana gasped. "I said we leave no one behind," she demanded, tears streaming down her face.

"If Shira stays, I stay," Aurelia signed, planting her feet firmly on the ground.

Blood and tears fell from Shira's eyes, and she couldn't help smiling as Rooli lifted the girls over her shoulders. They kicked and screamed and even poked at Rooli's pure black eyes, but Rooli's grip was indomitable. The wooden woman walked away with the girls in her arms without even saying goodbye, but Shira didn't take it personally. Ever since the day Rooli showed up at Wintersvilla claiming to be an emissary from the Nomads and sworn protector of Aliana and Aurelia, Shira knew that the woman cared only about her duty, and her duty was the girls. All else was noise, including other people.

"Goodbye," Shira said beneath her breath, grateful that she did not have to say goodbye to Aliana and Aurelia. The pain would be too much. She couldn't trust that her mind would not fold and desperately try to stay with them for as many seconds as life would allow. Of course, Rooli probably knew all that, and as Rooli and the girls moved quickly into the distance with the crying men running to take their place in front of them, Shira felt nothing but peace and gratitude for the life she had lived.

I got them this far, at least, Shira reasoned hopefully. *Myriam and Rooli and even Wesley—they'll get them the rest of the way. I know it. I just know it.*

"I'm coming back for you," Myriam promised, forcing each word through clenched teeth.

"There ain't gonna be a need for that," a deep, rumbling voice offered congenially before Shira could say goodbye to Myriam for the last time. The voice seemed to emanate from all around them, and the women were left fumbling through numerous arrays of visual and auditory transmissions in a futile attempt to pinpoint the source of the voice.

About fifty feet away, Rooli stopped, turned, and stared at the space directly between Shira and Myriam. As if Rooli had somehow summoned something with her iron glare, a swarm of tiny shimmering specks funneled from multiple locations around them and converged between Shira and Myriam, forming a humanoid shape. Myriam instinctively grabbed Shira and kicked at the ground with all her might, sending both women sailing toward Rooli and the girls.

Myriam powered on her exo, and though Shira attempted to do the same, her suit wouldn't respond.

"What is it, Rooli?" Myriam asked, but rather than respond, Rooli pulled the girls close to her, anchored her limbs to the ground, and expanded so fast that Shira could actually hear the groaning and stretching of her wooden flesh as the cells multiplied with frenzied rapidity.

Whatever it is, it's highly dangerous, Shira told herself, translating Rooli's actions into words.

Myriam darted her eyes impatiently and shifted her weight, clearly uncertain whether to use her claws or Summit Splitter. Shira urged her exo to power up, but it still wouldn't obey her command. Just as she was about to enter her personal manual override command, forcing the suit to activate even if it meant imminent and certain death, Myriam launched herself into the sky.

"I ain't your enemy, woman," the swarm said in agitation as it finally solidified into the polished metal body of a six-foot tall, hyper muscular man. Though the body lacked detail outside of basic musculature and skull shape, they could still make out where the man's eyes and mouth should be. The metal man turned toward the group, then, as if as an afterthought, he raised his hand into the air, unfurled a single finger, and brought Myriam's downward swing to a halt with just his fingertip. The stop was so abrupt and Summit Splitter so ineffectual that the giant sword bounced off the metal as if it were rubber, leaving Myriam spilling to the ground haphazardly as if she were still a child practicing her swordplay.

Summit Splitter slammed and skidded across the ground, rumbling like an earthquake before it finally came to a stop at the base of a large flesh tree.

"Wait!" the metal man issued, his hand held up for them to cease their attack. "I ain't your enemy. I'm here to help."

"Help?" Myriam spat at the juvenile premise of the man's words. "Troutshit. What do you want? Who are you?" Claws already fully extended, Myriam wasted no time waiting for an answer. Instead, she dove at the metal man claws first. At the very last second, she abandoned the dive, but the man predictably still raised his arms to defend his head, exactly where Myriam had signaled her attack.

"Stupid man!" Myriam roared, and she whipped both her legs in a whirlwind around her body. Her extended heel blades clanged as they made contact with the metal of the man's face, chipping the blades yet leaving the man's body seemingly untouched. Within the same half-second, Myriam's suit deposited explosive gel into her palm, and she couldn't help laughing at the stupidity of the man as she smeared the gel onto the alarmingly smooth and cold platinum-looking metal of his skull. Finally, she used the man's right leg as a jumping board, attempting to break the man's leg but only succeeding in launching herself far enough away to safely ignite the gel with a flaming barb launched automatically from one of numerous projectile launchers embedded in her exo.

Myriam intended for the gel's constituents to be chosen and mixed in such a way that its explosive energy would be released primarily as heat rather than as a pressurized shockwave. As the flaming projectile hit the gel, it achieved her desired result, and it ignited into flickering deep blue flames, instantly burning at temperatures nearly as hot as the surface of the sun. Shira expected the metal man's head to droop and cave in, but as he turned to show the group the result of the gel, she was dumbfounded to see that it had no effect at all. The platinum-looking metal still looked as illustrious as ever.

"Would ya cut it the fuck out?" the man said, pointing harshly at Myriam. Myriam gritted her teeth in frustration and bent at the knees, apparently planning another attack.

"Tell her to cut it the fuck out, will ya?" he said, pointing to Wesley and the other men. In response, the men howled in shame at being directly addressed, then prostrated themselves on the ground.

"'Sup with them?" the metal man's smooth, mouthless face asked. "And, that a Hybrid or a goddamn ol' world tree?" he asked, pointing to Rooli who was still expanding. "I ain't never seen a Hybrid or a Nomad like that, ya feel me?" he mused, bringing his finger and thumb to his chin.

"I said what the hell do you want, fatherfucker?" Myriam demanded. She seemed determined to at least break the man's resolve if she couldn't break his body. Shira strained to stay upright and hold back her coughing. It would be the height of foolishness to reveal that the group had any obvious weak points, though she figured he could probably tell just by looking at her that she was on the verge of death.

"I want what you want," the hunk of metal said matter of factly.

"Spit it out," Myriam warned.

The man chuckled and said with casual ease, "To get y'all safe and sound to the underground! The city of Downver, 'course. Ain't that where y'all headin'?"

"What the fuck are you talking about? Who are you?" Myriam nearly growled as she glanced behind her left shoulder, checking on the position of Summit Splitter. *Is she planning another attack?* Shira wondered. *Is there any way to actually damage him?*

Shira couldn't be sure, but she thought she noticed a slight smile form where the man's mouth should be.

"Me?" the metal man said with incredible pride and delight in his voice. "Well, shit, woman, I'm your own personal deus ex machina, ya feel me? I'm Gambe Mainstone, the Fourth Prodigal Son of the Agency." He bowed slightly, then said, "I'm sure ya heard of me."

Gambe Mainstone? Shira thought. *Prodigal Son?* Those names didn't ring a bell, but everyone in the world had at least heard of the Agency.

Myriam loosened her stance with curious intrigue at the mention of the Agency. "I didn't realize the Agency was still in operation," Myriam said with a mixture of caution and surprise. "The Agency went silent before I was even in the womb," Myriam said, recounting her history lessons. To Myriam, the Agency was like a mythical creature— something spoken of but never seen. But Shira knew that Myriam's learned version of history was false. In truth, the Agency never went silent, just very quiet. The Agency's technology was the only reason that little girls of Wintersvilla were capable of undergoing the operation to have their human skeletal system replaced with titanium-boron carbonate bones. It was that same metal endoskeleton that allowed for the surgical implantation of their ports, and it was the ports that allowed them to connect to an exo, making them even deadlier than Hunters and Huntresses. It wasn't something that Shira or Nomusa ever talked about, not even with Myriam, but the truth was that Wintersvilla only existed through the Agency's willingness to provide the Wintersvilla Matriarchy with the elusive and utterly incomprehensible nanotechnology that allowed them to tortuously reconstruct girls at the cellular level into lethal machines of ceaseless combat.

The Agency, Shira lipped to herself concernedly, remembering Tomasz' warnings about the Agency and its technology. *The Agency is conniving and dangerous*, Tomasz had said. *Maybe even more dangerous than Astrea.* Of course, Tomasz was one of the most conniving and dangerous men in the world. Shira knew that his words had to always be taken with skepticism.

"I thought all the humans that lived at the Agency died years ago," Myriam said, her stance loose but her claws still outstretched cautiously.

"I look human to ya?" Gambe asked, sounding offended by the word.

"Then...what...are you?" Shira said with incredible difficulty as blood continued seeping from her chest tube.

"The next step in evolution," Gambe marveled as he raised his arms and allowed his fingers to spread into a flurrying swarm of tiny metal specks. "Fuck that Mendel Ladder shit. Agency Neoevolution is a whole 'nother trip."

The metal specks of his body spread out and appeared to replicate, dividing rapidly as Gambe expanded and quickly formed into a large, hollow cylinder tapered to a point at both ends. Then, a wall of the cylinder opened, revealing multiple seats, windows, and even decorative geometrical patterns on the interior walls.

"That's a neat trick," Myriam said facetiously. "Can you turn into a toilet next? I need to take a shit."

Gambe laughed heartily, his voice emanating from the entirety of his now voluminous body. "I come here to transport ya safely the rest of the way," Gambe said. "I'm your literal transport, ya feel me?"

Impatient knocking resounded from Rooli's body, and Shira pleaded with her suit to power up in case she had to defend the girls from this strange being who was now aware of their presence. The suit refused, and once again she prepared to manually enter her override code to activate Overdrive, providing a final burst of energy in exchange for her life.

"Let 'em out," Gambe said. "I know Aliana and Aurelia are hidin' inside the walls of the Hybrid. Those wooden walls are useless against the Hunter in the area. Ya need my metal if ya hope to survive the encounter. 'Specially you, General Shira of Wintersvilla. Ya look like ya seen better days, eh?"

He knows who we are, Shira gulped. *He knows who I am. And he knows about the girls already. What else does he know?*

A face formed on the exterior wall of the craft, and Gambe said, "Ya ain't got long, General Shira. Your biological body is finally breakin' down from a lifetime of cybernetics. Wintersvilla Women have an expiration date, ain't ya know that?"

Shira panted and nearly squirmed as her exo's ability to numb her pain quickly dissipated. Each of her breaths felt like razors scraped across exposed muscle.

"No, I guess you wouldn't have known that," Gambe said regrettably. "'Cause every Wintersvilla Woman ya ever known died in battle 'fore she could grow old' enough to find out."

"Find out what?" Myriam demanded.

"Your lifespan. It's a failsafe the Agency builds into ya from birth. Just in case one of your kind ever decides to go AWOL."

"You…what?" Myriam said in disbelief.

Just as Nomusa suspected, Shira thought, hateful that both her life and death were the Agency's doing. Shira could no longer support herself, even with the help of her exo. She fell to the ground, but at least this time she resisted falling unconscious.

"She got less than an hour left," Gambe said. "Unless ya get her to Downver pronto, she smoke in the wind, ya feel me?"

"Fine," Myriam agreed, the shock from Gambe's information about her own lifespan and Shira's impending death filling her tone. "You take us to Downver. But what's the catch? What do you get out of this?"

Wanting to see Gambe, Shira struggled to lift her head, and this time she was certain she saw the bottom of the metal face twist into a smile.

"Nothin' at all," Gambe said unconvincingly. "I act from the goodness of my heart."

"You have no heart," Rooli intoned.

"Neither do you," Gambe retorted.

Shira coughed, ejecting thick blood from the chest tube and her lips simultaneously. She wanted to protest against going with Gambe, but she could neither speak at the moment nor see any other path forward besides just leaving her to die. *The Agency might be dangerous, and it might even be the reason I'm dying, but we all die at some point, and we're all dangerous. Everyone still alive since the first Hunters and Huntresses were released are all monsters in some way, because that's the only way to survive, damnit. You have to become a monster to survive in this world. We're all equal in that way. So maybe...maybe there's a chance he really will help them—this Gambe. Maybe,* Shira considered, and she loathed herself for considering depending on a man for help.

"What if we say no to you being our escort?" Myriam challenged, and she gripped Shira's shoulder as if begging for her forgiveness. Shira understood that Myriam was just trying to protect the girls. If only she could just be certain that going along with Gambe would ensure the girls' safety. It was possible he wasn't lying. After all, wouldn't he have already just killed them all and taken the girls for himself if that was his true intention? He had already made it clear that they were no match for even a single one of his fingertips, let alone whatever else he could transform into.

"Are you even giving us a choice?" Myriam fumed at Gambe, her eyes painful slits of hate at being commanded by a man, even if it was only a male sounding voice emanating from a room full of comfortable looking implements. Shira knew that he and his people saw everything and everyone else as objects to advance their own selfish agendas. To them, another person's life and death were just shackles of enslavement—tools by which the slave could be exploited.

"Yeah, I am givin' ya a choice, woman," Gambe said unconcernedly. "Ya can come with me willingly, or I can take the girls from ya unwillingly. So ya got a choice, ya feel me?"

All our ideas and behaviors are the result of mental programming. The mind can be programmed to think and do anything.

The oldest program available to humanity is religion, myth, concepts about the unknown. These ideas construct a person's morality, their existential motivation, and even their day-to-day interactions.

The right story can inspire any mind to do anything. If one does not program himself, others will do it for him. If not others, then the world.

The Eternal Hunt is one such program, and it ensures a two-fold future.

The first assurance is that humanity will be culled to appropriate levels, and those who escape the culling will live in perpetual fear of the nightmares lurking on the Earth's surface, sniffing them out like hounds hungry and desperate for meat.

The second assurance is that the strongest of humanity will adapt and strengthen themselves in ways that the old world always promised, but never fully provided.

The Huntress is intelligent beyond most of humanity's comprehension. She cannot help but wonder about her place in the world, just like any mind, human or not. The Eternal Hunt is a story that tells her what her place is. It is a mythos that is written at the very heart of her genetics. The power she wields through the Hunter, her personal weapon, elevates the story to one of exultation. Reverence even.

It is like a human who believes they have seen a vision of a god or the light of heaven. The power of that experience destroys their rationality and convinces them that a mere story in their mind is the same thing as objective truth.

The same is true for the Huntress. She will never abandon the Eternal Hunt, for it would mean abandoning a power far greater than fictional gods.

From Mendel's Ladder: The Personal Journal of Denis Mendel, Recorded Circa 2050, Published June 2108 by Leif Mainstone, Federated Agency Publishing

Chapter 9
The Eternal Hunt

V olya angrily kicked at squelching flesh pods, splattering thick viscera onto the Earth as she sauntered behind her Hunter and stared indignant daggers into his perfectly camouflaged back. He was nearly invisible even to Volya's unfocused eyes, though it was impossible for her to lose track of him with his mind and body feeling like a natural limb that had always been a part of her. Tangible disdain flowed through her as she observed the Hunter's thoughts. All he ever spent his time doing was moping in his head, reminiscing painfully about his time with Anna and wondering desperately how he still might get her back. Then, he would invariably bemoan his inability to travel to Astrea, rescue Anna, and make Mendel pay for stealing her and forcing her back to the city in the sky, the last place Anna wanted to be. The violent blessings that Mendel had granted the world and its people was an afterthought to Thompson; all that mattered was that Mendel die for his perceived crimes against Anna specifically and that Anna be returned to Thompson's embrace.

Not once has he thought about the Eternal Hunt, Volya thought scornfully. *The only thing he thinks about is that fucking fake Huntress bitch.*

To make matters worse, every time his anger grew his fists into claws or his forehead into horns or his knees into spikes, he was always quick to subdue his rage with excruciating difficulty, rather than just let his hate flow as it was meant to.

"So, some random yet admittedly good-looking human woman from Astrea pops down for a trip to the surface," Volya balked callously, "tells you some sweet words, then fucks off, and you spend the next thirty or so years just dreaming about her?" Volya glowered in horrified disbelief behind Thompson as they emerged from the thick, towering flesh trees of Hunter Dreaming.

"I tried to get her back," Thompson bristled painfully, more to Anna in his mind than to Volya.

"That makes it even worse!" Volya exploded. "You fucking killed out of frustration, not out of devotion to the Eternal Hunt. I mean, you didn't even have a Huntress controlling you. You just killed for the fun of it. Which I respect, but—"

"It was not fun!" Thompson growled, stopping in his tracks to gather himself and painfully subdue his anguish. "I regret my actions. If I could trade my own life for any one of those lives I ended, then I would do it gladly. But there's no taking it back. I was blind with rage. I was...out of control." Thompson paused and looked deeply into Volya's death-hungry eyes with repugnant contempt for both her and himself. "I was...like you. A slave to my programming."

Volya laughed obnoxiously and said, "I'm a slave? Me?" Then she used her mind to trip Thompson and pull his arms back, making him fall flat on his face. At the last second, she peeled back the skinsuit from his right eye and allowed a jagged rock to slam into his eyeball, splattering it into loose jelly. A patch of slapping ferns felt the vibrations of Thompson's fall, and they reflexively unfurled their stems, slapping his body with their rock-hard barbs. Volya let him suffer for a few seconds with his oozing eyeball and the bone-splitting slaps before relinquishing control and allowing his skinsuit to repair the damage in the blink of an eye.

"Does my suffering bring you joy?" Thompson inquired, allowing his presently broad, spindly shoulders to hang in defeat.

"Suffering in general, yeah, but yours is particularly enjoyable. You're just so fucking pathetic, you know?"

Thompson nodded calmly, refusing to allow Volya the satisfaction of his anger as he let her words drift into the past. It was one of the techniques Anna had taught him to control his programmed rage.

Monsters can be redeemed, Thompson reminded himself painfully, hearing Anna in his mind.

"Pathetic," Volya scoffed at his thoughts. "You know, long ago in human history, there were these people called Vikings. You want to talk about some bloodthirsty humans? These people might as well have been called Hunters and Huntresses, because they found thrill and joy in taking life and putting their own lives at risk."

Volya watched disappointedly as Thompson filled his mind with more thoughts of Anna and implemented more calming techniques as Volya recounted the history taught to her by the Marrow's databases during her initial system update.

"Well, one day the Vikings decided they were hungry, and they wanted gold and jewels and other useless human shit. So, they hopped into boats and eventually found an island full of Christian monks. These were a type of human that only believed in peace and love and all that nonsense you're so obsessed with."

Volya observed the next part of the historical anecdote in her mind as a glorious, blood-drenched vision, and she couldn't help smiling in approval at what she saw.

"Oh, Thompson, let me just show you. It's wonderful," Volya mused as she injected the vision into Thompson's mind. He watched in abject horror as bearded, armored humans beat and raped and tortured small groups of defenseless humans wearing no more than soft robes. After the battle, the Vikings cheered and drank the blood of their enemies, holding their chalices to the sky not in gratitude and deference to their gods, but in splendid solidarity. In their minds, the gods relished in battle and death even more than they did.

"We are like Vikings, Thompson. You understand? Not monks. Vikings. We kill. They die. Their gods are false. Ours is real. Mendel is real, Thompson."

"Mendel is no god!" Thompson practically roared. "Gods aren't real!"

Volya couldn't help laughing at her dog's stupidity, and were it not for his talents in butchering living things, she would have just killed him herself and spent the rest of her life killing on her own rather than being paired with a Hunter whose mind had been twisted by human weakness beyond mending.

"Mendel created you and me," Volya corrected with a high and mighty lilt. "He is our God whether you like it or not. And our God tells us to hunt. So, we hunt, dog."

"The only being in all the world I wish to hunt is Mendel," the Hunter seethed with time-forged scorn, exhausting his rage-laden breath in an attempt to tame the constant urge to dole death lurking in every one of his thoughts—even those involving Anna. Especially those involving Anna. He was trapped in a constant, torturous paradox of her voice serving as both a blood-forged battle cry and a love-imbued lullaby.

"Well, too bad," Volya said with casual indifference to Thompson's reckless and irreverent statement regarding Mendel. "I respect that you want to hunt God himself, but it makes no difference, really. Mendel is in Astrea, and you and I are down here."

Thompson sulked and continued walking forward one reluctant, trudging step at a time, his mind a constant battle to tame his rancor.

In the distance, rows of swaying net fungus spread their slick, membranous mesh boughs into the atmosphere, collecting humidity and atmospheric nutrients to pump back into the Earth. A pack of eleven or twelve near-identical looking Nomads trundled through the uneven corridors formed between the striated lines of net fungus. Roughly spherical and covered in random craters of varying depth, the Nomads rolled westward to fulfill some indecipherable ultimate goal.

The Nomads never stop, Volya considered. *They emerge from their flesh pods and proceed unquestioningly to implement the unknowable will of a mindless planet.* She couldn't help shaking her head at their inconsequential lives. *They are slaves to a giant rock. Thompson views me as a slave too, but at least the Eternal Hunt is in the service of Mendel, not a random chunk of rubble suspended in nothingness. The Nomads are like plants that toil to survive merely to taste the trivial sunlight. But my life carries true significance. I am a Huntress of the Eternal Hunt—the force by which Mendel's Ladder is ascended. There is no other reason to exist, and there never will be.*

"Tell you what, Thompson. I'll make you a deal," Volya offered candidly. "You let me enjoy myself down here by going along with me on the Eternal Hunt. I really don't want to have to depend on your collar. It's embarrassing and tiring having a disobedient dog when I'm supposed to have a loyal wolf."

Being referred to as an animal seemed to strike a chord with Thompson, but he was quick to extinguish the emotions as usual.

"And in return, I will help you find a way to get to Astrea, and I won't stand in your way in your attempt to kill God."

Thompson froze, not even breathing.

"Is that a serious deal?" he asked, and Volya realized that Thompson was tracking Astrea on the distant horizon with his sad yellow eyes. Volya calculated that its orbital vector would soon lead it almost directly over them.

"Sure," Volya said with a lackadaisical shrug of her shoulders. "I'm not sure there's a way to get up there, though."

Thompson nodded with forlorn agreement. "That's also my conclusion. So, no deal."

"Wait a minute," Volya urged, ready to backtrack on her statement even if it meant making up a lie about knowing a way to get to the city orbiting 400 miles above Earth's surface.

Would he really take such a deal and stop resisting the Hunt? she considered.

"Forget it," Thompson bristled. "I wouldn't take the deal even if you could hold up your end."

Volya was happy to see that deep down, Thompson doubted his own words.

"I'm not going to kill for you. I'll make it as hard as possible for you to take even a single life," Thompson resolved.

"Like hell you will," Volya retorted. "I give the commands, dog, and you obey."

Now! Thompson thought, his mind opening wide suddenly. He squeezed his vertical eye slits closed and filled his thoughts with a thick, fog-like feeling that stung Volya's mind, forcing her to retreat.

"What the fuck was that?" Volya demanded, shocked that her dog was clever enough to block her mind.

"I know ways to resist your control," Thompson said, revealing the limitation of his power with his own honest words.

"Resist, but not stop," Volya lashed, and then she forced herself into his mind like a drill through bone, screaming in agony as she compelled the remaining stinging fog out of Thompson's thoughts.

"You mutt!" Volya spat, and she stole him from the present and plunged his mind back to the earliest moments of his childhood, back to the racing confusion and horror of the very first seconds after birth, back to his very first taste of the fire boiling his newborn flesh. She only made him suffer a few seconds before pulling him back to the present moment, but it was enough to leave him screaming in pain as he fell to his knees.

"Try me, mutt, and I will break you. You understand? Like a wild dog. I will break your will and make you beg at my feet if you force me, Hunter4430. Is that understood?"

Thompson finally stopped screaming and caught his breath. Belligerent rage churned through Thompson's muscles, but he fought the internal desire to surrender himself to the war drumming of his heart begging him to do what came naturally and release his vehement berserker fury upon the world.

I know you yearn to kill, he told his body and skinsuit, *but Anna taught me a different way. The right way. And I can't allow myself to succumb to these mercurial outbursts erupting inside me like geysers of desperate violence.*

Thompson studied Volya and struggled against the urge to weep at how similar she appeared to his long lost love.

She's not her, Thompson admonished himself firmly. *She's not Anna. She's a damn monster.*

"But even a monster can be redeemed," Thompson told Volya through his exhausted panting as he gritted his sharp-edged fangs and siphoned the rest of his hate to the distant peripheries of his subconsciousness.

"Fuck redemption," Volya announced. "Don't need it. I love who I am, and I love what I am. I'm not a monster. Monsters are shortsighted and puerile. I'm exactly the opposite, Thompson. I am far more menacing and malicious than a monster. I am a Huntress, the most powerful and cunning creature that has ever existed. And you are my Hunter, the most wonderfully destructive weapon that has ever been constructed. You better remember that, Thompson. I don't want you fucking around on the battlefield."

Thompson rose and breathed deeply, panting and groaning with excruciating pain to calm his rage and resentment at Volya, the world, Mendel, and most of all himself. Clenching his human-like fists, he refused to allow the devastating adaptations to take hold of his body and overcame his fury after a few suffocating seconds.

"If you jeopardize the Eternal Hunt, I will put you down myself," Volya issued coldly.

He knew full well that Volya could kill him in a heartbeat if she wanted to. Of course, he also knew that those who lusted most for power were the least willing to throw it away.

"You think I won't dispose of you?" Volya asked in response to his calculating mind.

"I think you are powerful," Thompson said, refusing to give in to her goading.

"If you die, I'll just be sent another Hunter," she warned.

Thompson nodded in understanding. "You have me there, Volya. I get it. I'm disposable."

He doesn't know, then, Volya thought, relishing that she had the upper hand. *He doesn't know that he is reportedly the last Hunter. You are anything but disposable, Thompson, but I'm not going to let you know that.*

"Damn right," Volya said in response to Thompson being disposable. "Just another dog."

Thompson sniffed at the air and shrugged. "I don't even smell any humans," he said, humoring her for the moment as his natural urges subsided back to a prowling simmer.

"That's because they're just on the edge of your olfactory range," Volya said. "About 480 miles to the northeast."

Thompson reoriented himself and sniffed the air again. "Fine. You're right. There are humans. And a Hybrid. But there's something else too."

"You mean the little girls," Volya said, thinking back to the satellite images she had seen of the small group. "They aren't human. Not exactly," Volya explained.

"No," Thompson said. "I smell those young ones, strange as they are. But there's something else too. Something so far removed from human that I can't smell it. I only know it's there because it's acting like a barrier in the way of the other scents."

Volya eyed Thompson suspiciously, then enlarged the map displayed on her vision. To the south, flesh trees dotted the land, and bands of Nomads migrated from one place to the next, shepherding their flocks of tangle grass between marshes of technicolor sleeping molds.

She traced her vision across the wastes and once again observed the same solitary group walking across the Earth as if on a pleasant stroll through a garden. Were it not for the dirt and grime and blood coating all their skin and clothing, she would have thought them impervious to the Earth's lethality. Volya reasoned they were clearly just lucky that she had not emerged from the Thymus until today. However, there did appear to be less men since the last time she observed the group, so maybe they weren't so impervious after all.

Like Thompson claimed, she also saw a large metal cylinder tapering to sharp, pointed ends. Zooming in, she saw that the original group of humans and non-humans were talking to a humanoid face in the wall of the metal object.

"What the fuck is that?" Volya asked aloud as she simultaneously queried the Marrow.

<Answer: Unknown>

[Well, can you at least tell me what it's made of? What's that metal? It looks like platinum]

<Answer: Material Made Of Unknown Pure Element>

"What?" Volya couldn't help saying aloud.

"What is it?" Thompson checked despite his indifference to the dangers Volya was about to throw him up against.

[How is that possible? You sure it's not some complex alloy?]

<Answer: Material Made Of Unknown Pure Element>

Volya shook her head in confusion. She had the entirety of humanity's categorized table of elements memorized. Was the Marrow implying that this metal-looking material was made of atoms with protons in excess of the 123 different elements that humanity had isolated in old world laboratories? How could such atoms be stabilized for longer than a few nanoseconds, let alone turned into a pure, metal-like substance?

"What is it?" Thompson asked again, this time with some impatience. However, Volya paid him no mind.

[How many protons do each of the atoms have?] Volya inquired.

<Answer: Material Contains Zero Protons And Zero Atoms>

Volya smacked her own head, then flicked the ridge on the back of her neck.

[Wake up, Marrow. That doesn't make sense. You ever heard of something made of nothing? What is it?]

<Answer: Material Contains No Known Fermionic Matter>

Volya couldn't help laughing in confusion.

"I think Astrea's computers are broken," Volya told Thompson. "It's saying that the hunk of metal you brought to my attention isn't made of any known materials, let alone atoms or subatomic particles as we know them."

Thompson shook his head, clearly uneducated in particle physics.

"A thorough search of the battle databases would take too long, but I'm saying that we're about to encounter something that no other Hunter has probably ever faced, along with two Wintersvilla Women and a Hybrid, although one of the women looks like she's about to die. Shame, really. It would have been satisfying to slay her rather than just finish her off."

"You would risk your dog in battle against an unknown variable," Thompson asked condescendingly.

"Why not?" Volya offered coolly. "If you die, I'll just get another dog, remember?"

Thompson grumbled with dissatisfaction beneath his breath, then pulled his shoulders taught and returned his stare back to Astrea as it continued moving toward them across the sky.

I'll have to be careful, Volya considered. *Of course there's no way I'm going to actually risk losing my dog. I'll have him run in, kill those little girls and all the humans, then run out. No need to even get near that giant cylinder thing, whatever it is.*

"Let's go," Volya said, and she was happy to see that he didn't require her to force him forward. Instead, he moved forward on his own accord.

"There's a good boy," Volya said.

She was so invigorated and filled with excitement that she didn't notice the tiny tendrils of stinging fog curling in the distant peripheries of Thompson's thoughts as if waiting for just the right time to pounce.

It is a simple and well-known adage that something can only be truly appreciated once it is lost.

Given enough time, all beings are forced to accept this difficult truth. Whether it is something or someone precious, eventually all beings must contend with profound loss.

People will go to great lengths to avoid loss. They will even do things they never thought themselves capable of. It's within all of us—the ability to commit terrible atrocities in defense of that which we refuse to lose.

To lose everything all at once—one's love, one's home, one's very sense of self—such a loss is guaranteed to either strengthen an individual beyond recognition or break them beyond repair. Either way, loss is always an opportunity—one that we must grow accustomed to the longer time goes on.

Even I cannot change this foundational principle of reality. Not yet.

From Mendel's Ladder: The Personal Journal of Denis Mendel, Written Circa 2048, Published June 2108 by Leif Mainstone, Federated Agency Publishing

Chapter 10
To Lose Everything

T he Queensguard's hulking armor shone madly in the strobing red light of the glowglobes, and his eyes did not exhibit the typical vacant stare that Samuel was used to. A subtle rage filled the Queensguard's leering gaze, and Samuel couldn't help backing away nervously.

"I'm just trying to get home," Samuel said, attempting to reason with the man. Outside the armor, the Queensguard was probably shorter than Samuel, but the armor added at least six inches, allowing him to look down on Samuel as if he were a child.

"The recycler will be your new home, fugitive," the Queensguard threatened, his face unchanging in emotion despite the fire in his eyes.

"What's your name," Samuel said, forcing himself to not sound frantic as he held up his hands in a sign of surrender. "You have a wife?"

"You're the one they call Workhorse, aren't you?" the Queensguard inquired, lowering his giant metal gauntlets and foregoing the breaking of Samuel's neck for at least another moment.

"I am," Samuel nodded a bit too aggressively. "I am. And I have nothing to do with this revolution, you understand? I'm on your side. I just need to get home to my wife and kids."

The Queensguard cocked his closely shaved head and face in consideration, seeming to carefully weigh Samuel's words.

"Reports say you're one of the founding members of the Sons and Daughters," the Queensguard sighed as he once more raised his gauntlets in preparation for execution. "Are you lying to me, boy?"

"No!" Samuel pleaded. "Please, I'm telling you. I left that group when I was still a kid—I never wanted anything to do with them. I'm telling you, please."

"Samuel Kaminski, right?" the Queensguard asked, and for the first time in his life, Samuel saw the slight twist of a smile on a

Queensguard's lips. "David Kaminski—the famous revolutionary. He was your father, right? I guess the apple doesn't fall far from the tree."

Samuel shook his head, unsure how to respond. He bit his lip and mentally cursed his father for forcing him to live as his son.

"Please," Samuel said instinctively, holding Sandra and Nathan and Margot in his mind as if they were jewels of actual Heaven, not just this unforgiving farce that Samuel was beginning to see as a hellish prison.

A prison, Samuel gasped, *just like Damian always calls it.*

"Enough begging, fugitive. You and the other revolution rats have done enough damage. It's time to pay for what you've done."

The Queensguard stepped forward, quickly closing the gap between them. Samuel froze, unsure what to do. Within the next few seconds, he would be executed for a crime he didn't commit. His family would be stripped of his presence, his labor, and his love. Sandra would lose her husband, and Nathan and Margot would lose their father. Exactly as Samuel had experienced as a boy.

I can't let that happen, Samuel knew, and as the Queensguard grabbed his neck, rather than succumb to his execution, Samuel twisted out of the surprised Queensguard's grip, and fell back, scrambling to keep his balance.

"You're really going to make this difficult, boy? I'm just doing my job."

The emptiness in the Queensguard's voice chilled Samuel to his core. It was as if the Queensguard were a gardener, and Samuel just another clump of dirt.

"Are me and my people truly nothing to you?" Samuel asked. "Just pests to be exterminated?"

"I protect the people of Astrea from scum like you, fugitive," the Queensguard responded confidently. "You are Astrea's only threat. You and your ilk."

"I won't let you take me away from my family. I won't let you do that to them."

The Queensguard shrugged with terrible indifference.

"If not me, then another Queensguard will find you and end you. It's not like there's anywhere you can run and hide for long." The

Queensguard lifted his gauntlets as if presenting the whole of Astrea's thirty-six-mile length and full mile diameter.

A goddamn prison, Samuel gawked internally.

"Will you just make this easy and stop moving, Workhorse?" the Queensguard asked with sudden politeness in his tone. "I don't enjoy this any more than you do. It's just my job, okay?"

"Please!" Samuel said, at a loss for what to do. Like the Queensguard said, even if he could escape somehow, it was only a matter of time before another Queensguard found him and finished the job.

The Queensguard nodded with seeming understanding and compassion. "It'll be quick, Samuel Kaminski. I'll make sure of it. Just like it was with your father. Nice and quick. Nothing personal, okay?"

At the mention of his father's execution, Samuel couldn't help a flicker of rage at both his father and the Queensguard.

"You were there for his execution?" Samuel checked, breathing heavier in anger.

"I was," the Queensguard said with an air of pride. "I was one of the first in the Foundation to be promoted to Queensguard. I was always strong. I always labored for others, but nothing compares to you, Workhorse. It's a shame I have to do this."

"Did you kill my dad?" Samuel asked bluntly, and he clenched his fists in preparation for the Queensguard's answer.

"Yes, I did," the man responded without sugar coating the truth. "It was an honor to serve Astrea by culling its most notorious revolutionary, even though I admit that David Kaminski was a man who was utterly loved by his community, and his family as well, I'm sure."

"Do they rip your heart out when they make you a Queensguard?" Samuel asked. "And your soul, do they take that too?"

The Queensguard pointed at Samuel and shook his head. "Don't be mad at me for ensuring Astrea's well-being. Rats get exterminated. If you don't kill them at first sight, they spread. That's what rats do. Do you know why there are no actual rats on Astrea, boy? Because the first people killed them all. Before there were even any Queensguards. Well, those rats got bigger and smarter. That's you, Samuel Kaminski. You and your father both. You're just rats, and so are your children, I assume," the Queensguard concluded as a matter of simple fact.

At the mention of his kids, Samuel lost all composure and charged at the invincible, hulking mass of metal. He didn't care that his blows would do nothing against the Queensguard. He just wanted to hit the man, even if all his punching accomplished was the shattering of his own fists.

The Queensguard raised his eyebrows in surprise, clearly not expecting Samuel to run into death's embrace so readily. The giant metal gauntlets swung for Samuel and grabbed him, lifting him into the air. His body was like putty in the colossal, armored hands of the Queensguard, and as he felt the slow constriction of the guard's cold fingers around his neck, he envisioned Sandra and his children in their living room, giggling at some educational program on the telescreens.

I will always love you, Sandra, even in death, Samuel thought as he closed his eyes. The giant metal fingers squeezed, and he mentally embraced his family in his final moments of life.

The Queensguard grunted suddenly, and Samuel opened his eyes to find the Queensguard immobilized and his suit silent. With no power in the suit, the Queensguard let go of Samuel and couldn't help his now useless arms falling to his sides.

Samuel coughed and saw stars in his vision as he caught his breath. He turned and saw Damian running toward him, holding an EMP gun pointed at the incapacitated Queensguard.

"Stop right there, fugitive!" the Queensguard shouted at Damian. "You're both to be executed. Put down the gun."

Damian strode directly to the Queensguard and in a single, fluid movement, he pierced his exposed head with one of the revolution's now iconic sharpened metal poles. The Queensguard's eyes rolled back in his head, and then Damian removed the pole with a groan of difficulty, leaving the dead Queensguard to sulk heavy in his suit as it filled with his freely flowing blood.

"Get away from me!" Samuel spat, not caring that Damian had just saved his life.

"Samuel, please!" Damian called after him as Samuel ran directly home. "Please just listen to me, Samuel!"

Adrenaline coursed through his body, and Samuel burst through his own front door, shattering the wood as if it were made of eggshell.

"Sandra!" Samuel cried, frantically searching the empty house. "Nathan! Margot! Where are you!?"

The house appeared perfectly in order, meaning they hadn't left in a panic. But they weren't home, so where could they possibly be? Samuel racked his brain, considering the most likely places Sandra would have taken the kids, but his mind kept coming up painfully blank.

She would have stayed home, Samuel knew. *There's nowhere to fucking run in this fucking prison,* Samuel thought, feeling like he was undergoing a mental break as the lens through which he viewed his world began to splinter.

"Sandra!" he shouted again, malice at all of Astrea filling his agonizing scream.

He couldn't help thinking of his father at that moment. He could see him walking through the threshold of the same house Samuel and his family now lived in. Wildflowers from the local nature district brimmed in his arms, and he smiled like a little boy as he placed handfuls of vibrant flowers into vases all around their modest home.

They killed you, Samuel winced, seeing the flowers wilt suddenly in his mind. *They took you from me,* he thought, allowing the words to inflict him with pain for holding so much anger for his father over the years. *And now they're going to kill me, dad.*

"Samuel," came the pleading voice of Damian as he walked through the splintered hole that had once been the intact entrance to Samuel's home. "They aren't here, Samuel," Damian panted, breathless from sprinting to catch up with him. "We have contacts in the Luxury Quarters. That's where they are, with the rest of the revolutionary families. We have Queensguards on our side, Samuel. We did it. You understand? It's going to work."

"My family and I are not part of this revolution," Samuel shouted, letting his anger explode in a way he had never experienced. Damian fell back in horror at this side of Samuel he had never seen. "You bastard, Damian. How dare you involve my family in all this lunacy!"

"There was a risk they could get hurt," Damian said, rushing his words in a desperate attempt to convince Samuel of their validity. "There was a risk they could get hurt in the flood and the battle with the Queensguards, Samuel. I couldn't take that risk, okay? I'm just protecting them, Samuel. I'm just—"

"Is that what you did for, Bill? You protected him?" Samuel seethed.

"I didn't know, damnit! I didn't know Frank would kill him. I swear, Samuel. You think I'm a killer. I mean, really?"

"I just watched you kill a Queensguard," Samuel said, his voice full of disgust for this man he had always called his best friend since childhood. "You are a killer, Damian. A cold-blooded killer."

Damian shook his head and bit his quivering bottom lip. "No, Samuel. The Queensguards...they're our wardens, Samuel. Guards of an actual prison. I had no choice. Like Denis Mendel, I understand that sacrifices have to be made. I understand that only by rising up and blazing our own path can we overcome our oppressors and the worst oppressor of all, ourselves."

Samuel wasn't surprised to see that Damian appeared to truly believe his own words.

"Are you really referencing Mendel as your inspiration? He's the one that made Astrea. He's the one that saved our parents from the hell of Earth."

"And the one who made it hell in the first place," Damian retorted, quoting the unfounded conspiracy theories about the founder of Astrea, Denis Mendel. The conspiracies had spread in popularity with every passing year since Samuel's father's execution to the point that the young hackers viewed the ridiculous claims as blatant fact rather than hearsay.

"So, which is it, then? Are you going to use Mendel as inspiration, or are you going to keep viewing him as your enemy?" Samuel asked coldly, but before Damian could answer, Samuel added, "The simple truth is that even if the revolution worked and everyone had access to the Luxury Quarters and immortality, even then it wouldn't be enough. You and the others would still desire more and more. And it just doesn't work like that, Damian. The whole thing falls apart if everyone is an immortal who no longer has to labor at the power stations. Energy and resources aren't infinite. How many times have we gone through this?"

As he spoke, Samuel was horror-stricken to find that he was no longer fully convinced of his words' validity, and as his reality lens splintered further, threatening to crack, he was forced to grab his forehead and brace his mind against giving up all hope.

Damian shook his head in disbelief. "You really see me as a fucking child, don't you? We've planned for all that, Samuel. We're not stopping at the Luxury Quarters."

"The Paradise Quarters," Samuel intoned contemptuously, "or just *Paradise*, as the young ones call it now." Samuel issued a sigh of frustration, remembering how his mom used to argue with his father about the same thing. "It isn't real, Damian," Samuel said, refusing to delve any further into the subject. "And all you've done with this revolution is get hundreds or even thousands of people killed, along with placing all of Astrea at risk of collapse."

"Sacrifices have to be made, Samuel. We're done living as rats. Done," Damian said with cold finality.

"What do we have here?" a rumbling voice asked. "A couple of squealing rats?"

A Queensguard entered Samuel's home, but Damian was quick to deactivate his armor with a blast from the EMP gun. The guard toppled over, directly onto Damian.

"You'll pay for this," the Queensguard issued, cold and certain. Damian winced beneath the giant armor, struggling to breathe against at least 500 pounds of mass. The Queensguard was particularly large and muscular, nearly as large as Samuel, and he attempted to lift the armor and himself into a standing position. However, without power, the oversized armor appeared to be too heavy to lift in the precarious position the Queensguard was stuck in.

Damian continued struggling for air, his face turning red and thick veins splintering in his neck and forehead. The sharpened pole lay on the floor, just out of reach of Damian's fingers.

"Crushed like an old world bug," the Queensguard mused casually as he stared into Damian's dying eyes.

Damian began convulsing, his body bucking wildly in an attempt to breathe.

"Die, rat," the Queensguard said without emotion, as if it were an unbiased judicial command. The Queensguard's words were too much for Samuel, and he felt his body rush toward his dying friend, pick up the sharpened pole, and gouge it into the Queensguard's left eye. Samuel issued a yelp of horror at the sickening ease with which the pole passed into the man's skull, killing him instantly. Still acting on instinct alone,

Samuel pushed the dead, armored man over, plunging precious air into the desperate vacuum of Damian's dying lungs.

Damian coughed and spat blood as he regained his breath. Meanwhile, Samuel looked at his own upturned palms, slick with blood, and he wondered if he should just execute himself now for this unthinkable, immoral crime.

"Thank you," Damian rasped, still catching his breath. However, Samuel barely heard him over the grim doom of his self-flagellating thoughts.

I'm a killer, he gasped. *A murderer. A rat. An insect. Scum.*

He lifted his head and glared in horror at Damian, who appeared unfazed by the Queensguard's death.

"It's okay, Samuel," Damian said as he observed the horror in Samuel's features. "You saved me."

"We both deserve execution," Samuel told him, seeing the terrible truth with perfect clarity. "We deserve to die, Damian."

Damian shook his head as if trying to formulate a way to convince his friend that they were in a life-and-death situation, and so morality was a useless tool of measurement—something that could hold no objective or worthwhile meaning.

"We did what we had to do," Damian told him, viewing his own words as perfectly legitimate reasoning.

"Stop right there, fugitive!" another Queensguard announced from outside Samuel's home. In the dreadful light of the strobing red glowglobes, Samuel could see multiple hulking figures outside, each of their steps a procession carrying Samuel and his friend toward a sharpened guillotine.

Damian lifted the EMP gun and sent the first guard toppling forward, but the gun had a fifteen second recharge period, so now it was as useful as a thrown rock. Four more Queensguards spilled into the house, breaking chunks of the house's wall as they poured toward Samuel and Damian. All of them were bald, and their normally vacant eyes were full of subtle, controlled fire. The first Queensguard to enter grabbed Damian, and the second to enter grabbed Samuel. Damian struggled against the Queensguard's grip, but Samuel didn't flex a single muscle.

126

"Do it," Samuel told him, wishing only that he could see his family one last time. "Get it over with."

The Queensguard issued a soft chuckle and said, "Apparently Roland has been given very special and specific plans for you, Workhorse."

"What do you mean?" Samuel asked over his shoulder, but the man holding his arms painfully behind his back just chuckled slightly once more.

"You're all dead," Damian hissed, his voice filled to the very brim with lifelong hate. "The revolution will not fail, and all of you will be brutally executed for your crimes against the Foundation."

The Queensguard holding Damian gripped him by the throat, then squeezed, snapping every bone in Damian's neck. Damian's lifeless head lolled forward, and blood trickled from his eyes and nose.

They're demons torturing us, Samuel gawked as the Queensguard tossed Damian's lifeless body over his armored shoulder. *This is hell. We're in hell. And my family is stuck here without me now. My family is going to be stuck all alone with these goddamn demons, and there's nothing I can do.*

"Do it," Samuel said, closing his eyes and picturing his family in his head so that Damian's lifeless, bloody face would not be his last vision of the world.

This is heaven, Samuel told himself unconvincingly in the midst of hell.

"Samuel Kaminski," a strangely familiar voice proclaimed from the house's now totally destroyed entrance and front walls. A Queensguard wearing golden armor with multiple jet turbines attached to the shoulders and legs observed Samuel with peculiar interest, eyeing him from head to toe as if inspecting his musculature.

"I am High Commander Roland Ottonian, and you are to come with me. Now." The man's very presence seemed forged in steel and fire, and he naturally towered over the other Queensguards by a full six inches. Incredibly, the little bit of musculature that Samuel could see around the man's neck and collar appeared even more expansive and dense than Samuel's.

Samuel nodded and reluctantly stepped forward, feeling horrified by Damian's open blood-filled eyes. It almost looked as though he might wake up suddenly, and though Samuel wished for his friend to come back to life, he also couldn't help feeling intense hatred for him.

"I killed the Queensguard lying on the ground there," Samuel told High Commander Roland through gritted teeth, openly confessing to his crime. "I agree that I should be executed. I won't put up a fight. But I wasn't part of this revolution. I tried stopping it, you understand? Can I just...can I just see my family? Please," Samuel begged, not caring how pathetic he might sound. "I just need to make sure they're okay. Can you just—"

"We are currently searching for your family and the other revolutionaries involved in this uprising. They will be summarily executed once they are found."

"No!" Samuel growled. "No, damnit!" he screamed, and he couldn't help flexing and fighting the Queensguard's iron grip in an attempt to run away and continue searching for his family. He didn't know what he would do after that, but that didn't matter right now. All that mattered was that he get away somehow and find his family. He would figure out what to do after that when the time came.

"Give me the fugitive," High Commander Roland told his subordinate Queensguard. The Queensguard obeyed, and the High Commander held Samuel by the shoulders like a toddler. Then, without hesitation, he stepped back onto the street, activated his armor's jet turbines, and lifted off the ground, rocketing into the air with rapidly increasing velocity.

"Where are you taking me?" Samuel shouted over the blast of the turbines, but the golden Queensguard did not answer. It was in that moment, staring into the Queensguard's void-empty eyes, that Samuel realized why his voice had seemed so familiar.

"You knew my dad," Samuel gasped. "You were one of his best friends from childhood. You're...Uncle Roland," Samuel said, remembering the man playing with him as a child. He didn't look old enough to be the same adult from his childhood memories, but then Samuel remembered that all Queensguards and residents of the Luxury Quarters were immortal and didn't age.

"Uncle Roland!" Samuel urged again, but the High Commander did not answer Samuel nor seemingly take any notice of him whatsoever. Instead, his eyes remained empty and his movements unfaltering in pursuit of whatever sordid plan he had in store for Samuel.

I'm going to lose everything. My family. My friends. My life. Everything, Samuel thought in horror as High Commander Roland sailed across the red-strobing hellish landscape, rocketing Samuel toward certain death. *And it's all my fault in the end. It's all my goddamn fault. All this hell and chaos is my fault. I should have found a way to stop all this. But I didn't. And now my family is…oh, Sandra…I'm so sorry, my sweet Sandra…my perfect little okra.*

The snow of the mirrored, dual tips of Mount Mendel sparkled madly in the red-strobing light of the glowglobes. All across Astrea, Queensguards trudged through the winding, wet streets carrying the young bodies of hackers and frail adult revolutionaries like so many flopping dead rats.

Damian is dead, Samuel reminded himself in horror. Everything had happened so fast with no time to process any of it. Images of Damian's lolling head flashed in his thoughts, and he was stabbed once more by the realization that the same would likely happen to his family, who Damian had involved in the revolution in some way. *There has to be something I can do to protect Sandra and the kids. A trade for my life, or my labor, maybe. There has to be a way.*

"My family!" Samuel yelled into High Commander Roland's ear over the roar of his suit's jet turbines, but either the man couldn't hear him, or he was utterly ignoring Samuel, even with his eyes.

Minutes passed as they continued flying through the air. Samuel assumed Roland was flying so high above the ground, nearly at the center of the Foundation's diameter, in order to avoid any stray EMP blasts, but it was possible he was also just taking advantage of the near weightlessness, conserving his jet fuel.

How many hours of labor does a single second of Roland's flight cost my people? Samuel wondered miserably. *What a waste, and yet, before us is revolution, proving that the Queensguards are necessary to maintain the Foundation and Astrea as a whole.*

In the distance, Samuel could see one of the Foundation's two colossal, circular walls. The walls, respectively called the Luxury Wall and Space Wall, faced each other across the thirty-six miles of the Foundation's cylindrical length, their mile diameters and lush green ivy identical. Normally the ivy had a calming effect, but now it appeared murky and imposing, as if the plant life were suddenly a dark forest threatening to consume Samuel whole.

One minute the ivy is green and full of life, and the next minute it's a tenebrous ebony mass. All because of this goddamn revolution and my failure to stop it. Samuel shook his head in despair at the futility of everything. *Is that all this place is? A cycle of revolutions? Is that all anything is? Will Nathan and Margot ever know a lasting heaven, or will it always be makeshift and temporary? Will all of society always be a structure made of quickly drying sand?* Samuel considered in horror, seeing his children grow old and suffer through a barrage of abstract and equally horrifying futures.

Samuel twisted and peered thirty-six miles in the distance behind them at the Space Wall, permanently sealed to separate the Foundation directly from outer space by thick metal that Samuel's son was fond of describing in meticulously memorized detail. Samuel almost yearned for the void of space as they approached the Luxury Wall. He knew that somewhere behind the Luxury Wall, the recycler waited patiently to eat his body and extract him of every last viable atom.

How can the citizens of the Luxury Quarters stomach living right beside a machine meant solely for killing and disposing of the dead? Samuel thought, considering the Luxury Quarters with a level of disgust for the first time in his life. *I know Governor Acharya. I know his daughter Lakshmi. They aren't soulless like the Queensguards. They're good people. I'm sure of it. And yet, they still live right beside the recycler. They still abide by the labor and death of my people, while they live forever.*

Samuel still wasn't fully comfortable allowing his mind to tread the depths of such dangerous thoughts, but he knew it didn't matter anymore. The Queensguards would never let him back home. Not after what had happened today. Tears streamed down Samuel's cheeks as he envisioned the countless Foundationers who would be recycled today, and the countless others who had been recycled over the years. He felt like an absolute fool for not seeing Astrea in its true light sooner.

I failed my family. I failed my people. And I failed myself, Samuel lamented, his thoughts like a hot iron applied directly to his heart. *No matter how I look at it: either I'm a fool who still can't fully see the truth, or I'm a fool who saw the truth too late. Either way, I deserve the recycler. I'm sorry, Sandra. I'm so, so sorry that we can't even say goodbye.*

High Commander Roland adjusted his vector, slowed to a crawl, then landed on a metal outcropping at the base of the Luxury Wall. The thick ivy appeared dark and ominous in the strobing glowglobes. A gap in the ivy revealed the oversized, heavy metal door that the Luxury Quarters citizens used to enter and exit the Foundation. Three other identical doors were embedded into the circumference of the wall every ninety degrees so that the Luxury Quarters could be accessed from numerous locations.

Samuel had never entered one of the doors, nor had anyone who was not a Luxury Quarters citizen. Foundationers only ever went through the doorway as corpses on their way to be recycled. The first people of Astrea rarely put up a fight when it was their time, but more and more often, Queensguards had to be utilized to execute and recycle individuals exceeding three or more months of energy debt. Some people said that the implementation of Queensguards had been due to the new generations' desire for longer lives and refusal to die willingly, but now Samuel reasoned that the conspiracy theorists might be right, that it was a direct response to his father and his friends' utterly failed attempt at revolution. Samuel figured his father would be proud of the modern revolutionaries, though he also wondered how his dad would feel about murdering Queensguards. His father was a lot of things, but he wasn't a killer.

Not like me, Samuel thought with profound self-hate, feeling sick as he remembered the crunch of the Queensguard's skull and brain as they splattered onto Samuel's shaking hands. *I'm a goddamn killer,* Samuel seethed at himself.

"For the revolution!" a Queensguard yelled as he charged toward them from out of nowhere, aiming directly for High Commander Roland with his upraised gauntlets.

High Commander Roland did not flinch as he pulled Samuel out of the way, then lifted his arm and shrugged his shoulder in a peculiar way, flipping the jet turbine on his right shoulder so that it pointed directly at the traitorous Queensguard. Blue flame spewed from the turbine, penetrating the electric shield as if it were empty air. The Queensguard screamed in agony as the turbine's hellfire melted his flesh to a sizzling char in a matter of seconds.

High Commander Roland let the man collapse as a smoking, dying heap on the metal platform. Then, without a moment's hesitation, he placed his metal gauntlet against the door, signaling it to slide open.

"Move," High Commander Roland issued, and he pushed Samuel into a pitch-black hallway. Behind them, the glowglobes suddenly ceased their red strobing, and the alarm stopped, settling Astrea back to its typical ambient calm. Samuel listened, but he didn't hear any screaming or the sound of fighting. The silence was absolute, as if all of Astrea's people were holding their breath in unison.

It's already over, Samuel gasped, though he knew he shouldn't be surprised that the revolutionaries never actually stood a chance at victory.

There is no victory over Heaven or Hell, whatever Astrea really is, Samuel concluded with forlorn surrender.

Nobody can be trusted in this world. Not even oneself.

The reason is not always malice. It is most often due to ignorance and shortsighted stupidity resulting from naturally derived genetics.

No one can be trusted for the same reason you cannot trust a bear or a bull. We are limited by natural evolution to be only slightly more ascended than the next given intelligent species.

A part of me is still human, of course. This is exactly why I have taken measures to supersede even myself in the event that my humanity poses a threat to the plans of my higher mind.

Trust is fickle. Instead, we must forge indelible strength and perfect self-discipline. Then, trust is unnecessary.

From Mendel's Ladder: The Personal Journal of Denis Mendel, Recorded Circa 2055, Published June 2108 by Leif Mainstone, Federated Agency Publishing

Chapter 11
Diverging Agendas

"The clock ticks away, now wha'dya say, Wintersvilla Women?" Gambe asked cheerfully with his unmoving face, which was still embedded in the wall of the strange metal craft.

A thick clot of blood squeezed out of Shira's chest tube, and she clenched the dry soil in anger that she had allowed the group to get caught like this. If they hadn't spent two whole nights sitting around a campfire, hoping in vain that she might recover, maybe then they would have reached Downver before Gambe could intercept them.

All this time and all this pain and all this death, Shira thought. *And I still failed in the end. I bet you're enjoying this, you wicked bastard,* Shira told Winters in her head.

"Let's go," Myriam said, taking on the whole of Shira's weight, exo and all. "Now, Rooli," Myriam ordered as she dragged Shira into Gambe's sparkling platinum interior. Rooli hesitated for only a moment, then allowed her excess growth to detach from the rest of her body. The girls pushed the thick wooden flesh away, peeling their way back to the unshielded world.

"We told Rooli to make little holes in her bark for us. We heard everything," Aliana announced with her head held high.

"We've no time to waste," Aurelia signed as the girls entered the craft. Rooli and the men followed obediently behind, and as they finally entered the craft, the opening irised shut, entombing the group inside the walls of Gambe's body.

Shira imagined the walls suddenly closing in and crushing all of them in one foul movement, but instead, Gambe jolted forward at breakneck speed, slamming the group into their respective seats as the vehicular man propelled himself through some unknown, silent means. Gambe glided across the landscape, levitating a few feet above the ground.

Myriam caressed the jaundiced skin of Shira's forehead and said, "Don't fucking die, my gorgeous general. You still owe me a proper honeymoon. I decided I want one, after all. Somewhere in the northern mountains of Wintersvilla. So you're going to have to take me all the way home after all this. You hear me?"

Shira wanted to smile, but it was hard enough just to remain conscious.

"Shira," Myriam issued sullenly as her features sank. "You knew, didn't you?" she asked, her tone one of deep pain rather than anger. "You knew about the Agency programming us to expire at...to die at...at your age," Myriam said, stumbling on her final words.

"I...didn't know for sure...Myriam. Nomusa had suspicions...but that was it. They were just rumors, and to be honest...I...thought Nomusa was just being paranoid, because even Mae couldn't find the programming in our bodies she was referring to. If...I had known for sure...I swear, Myriam, I would have told you," Shira explained through painful breaths, and she hoped that Myriam could forgive her.

"It doesn't matter," Myriam said as if attempting to quell Shira's pain. "I just...I just wish you would have told me," Myriam said, sounding betrayed. "I cherish all of our time together, my gorgeous general, but if I had known, maybe I could have...maybe I could have cherished it even more...I..." Myriam said, cutting herself off to avoid any tears.

"I know," Shira managed, nodding in agreement. "I'm sorry...my love. I am."

Shira coughed violently, breaking vessels in both her eyes and spraying blood from her mouth and chest tube all over Myriam's bare legs.

"Sorry," Shira said between coughs.

"It's nothing," Myriam said. "The color goes with my hair, anyway."

Myriam kissed Shira's forehead and smiled with tears in her eyes as she turned and looked out through the gap in Gambe's body, which served as an open window to the world. She painfully surveyed the rapidly passing world as the warm air tussled her fiery red curls.

"Will Downver be able to save her?" Myriam asked Gambe as she clutched Shira as close to herself as possible despite the metal frames of their exos forcing a perilous distance between them.

I wish I could embrace her one last time without these damn exos, Shira thought, savoring her lover's warmth and touch.

"Maybe," Gambe answered simply.

"Maybe?" Aliana pressed.

"Yes or no?" Aurelia signed, but it seemed Gambe either didn't notice her signing or didn't speak sign language, as he said, "I say maybe. Now drop it, girl."

"So, you don't know?" Aurelia concluded, and Gambe still didn't respond.

"You don't really know then?" Aliana said, repeating Aurelia's question.

"Look, I'm a weapons expert, not a surgeon. My brother Julian, though? He's the Third Prodigal Son of the Agency. He would know. He can go inside a human and fix 'em up, no matter what they got goin' on, ya feel me? Biology, he calls it. Ya know, like you guys. It's all ol' world science, ya feel me? I ain't know about all that stuff. I like to spend my time playin' ol' world video games and watchin' classic movies and divin' in ultra-sims, ya feel me? I got millions of 'em stored in my mind. Only the good stuff, ya feel me? That shit is worth it. And—"

"Where is Julian?" Aliana asked, cutting Gambe off.

"Come to think of it, I think he's in Downver," Gambe said, seeming to genuinely only just remember his brother's location. "Well shit, that pretty lucky for ya guys, eh?"

Aliana and Aurelia turned excitedly to Shira and Myriam, and though Shira appeared only minutes away from death, they couldn't help lighting up with hope from Gambe's words.

Myriam squeezed Shira's shoulder, which Shira could barely feel now, except for a distant and vague pressure.

"We're going to make it," Myriam whispered to Shira. "It's going to be okay, Shira."

"My brother Harald on the other hand? He's the Sixth Prodigal Son. He'd prolly just tear us all to pieces—even me. He's got a bad temper."

"How many Prodigal Sons are there?" Aliana asked.

"And who's the mother of all these sons?" Aurelia added.

"Right now the Agency got six livin' Prodigal Sons, but only five really…three of my brothers died in pretty awesome ways, and the other one…well…we ain't talk about him, ya feel me?" Gambe said with a tone of nervous disapproval.

"And your mother?" Aliana asked for Aurelia, who would normally despise her sister for speaking for her. However, Shira was proud to see Aurelia remain stoically calm. Both girls were handling themselves and their emotions like adults, and Shira gawked at how much they had grown over the last year.

"Our mother?" Gambe repeated with an air of exultation. "Our mother is the Agency. Her human name was Gladys Mainstone, but she ain't go by that name no more."

The name Gladys Mainstone had a similar effect to hearing the name Tomasz Novak or Craig Winters or John Downver or even Denis Mendel, the ringleader of the old world powers, some of whom, like Tomasz, still lingered upon the Earth like poltergeists anchored tortuously to a dilapidated house.

"Gladys Mainstone," Aurelia signed in awe.

"She created the Agency," Aliana said.

"She *is* the Agency," Gambe corrected.

"What does that mean?" Aliana pressed.

Gambe issued a few hoots of amused laughter. "I'm sure you gonna learn all about it one day whenever my brother Leif Mainstone, the Seventh Prodigal Son, finishes writin' his history books. He'll be famous one day, you watch."

"How did your brothers die?" Myriam asked, and Shira knew that she was searching for a way to destroy Gambe in case he suddenly decided that they had diverging agendas.

"The First and Second Prodigal Sons died in battle together with a group of nine Hunter and Huntress Pairs. They had no problem killin' eight at once just a week before that, but one little mistake left 'em vulnerable," Gambe explained, sounding more embarrassed than sad. "And the Eighth Prodigal Son, he died at the hands of two Wintersvilla Women. They went into Overdrive at the last second and ruptured his core. The Overdrive killed the women too, but goddamn is the recordin' from the battle glorious, ya feel me?"

So, there is a way he can be killed, Shira considered carefully, planning for every contingency, for she knew that virtually no one can be trusted, especially not men, no matter what they are made of. *Is it possible he has some type of core like his brother,* Shira wondered, peering through red lenses of quivering blood as she struggled to scan Gambe's shimmering interior. It didn't appear he had any obvious weakness.

"And the brother you don't talk about?" Myriam asked.

"We ain't talk about the Ninth Prodigal Son," Gambe stated simply. "Not even his name, ya feel me?"

Myriam nodded, satisfied with the scant but potentially useful information Gambe had revealed about the death of his brothers.

Gambe silently sliced through a thick grove of flesh trees without a bump of turbulence, treating the hulking trees like blades of grass. As they emerged from the grove, Shira saw the three gigantic circular scars in the surface of the planet, impact craters left behind by old world nuclear devices that Rooli had mentioned in her description of the hidden entrance to Downver she claimed to have used when she was young. At the bottom of one of the craters, there was a small cave leading to a large underground network of tunnels that would eventually lead to the underground city. It was technically an escape route, but as long as one knew the way, they could hypothetically use these escape routes as entrances. The issue was that no one had ever successfully navigated the underground mazes. All who had ever entered had died, including numerous Hunters who had attempted to break in and wreak havoc on the city. With nowhere to run, it would be a Hunter's dream, but despite their obvious advantages, it was reported that a Hunter had never once made it all the way. Still, according to Rooli, she could navigate the tunnels with ease if they ended up needing to utilize the hidden entrance as a last resort.

"Almost there now. Another ten seconds at most," Gambe said cheerfully, surprising Shira, as she estimated that the main entrance, which was dug directly into the base of the mountain ranges spanning from Downver all the way to Wintersvilla, was still at least ten minutes away at their current pace.

"You…know about…the hidden entrances?" Shira struggled to ask.

"'Course," Gambe mused. "There's one right up ahead. At the bottom of the crater."

"Is that where we're going?" Myriam asked, still tightly clutching Shira.

"No," Gambe said simply. "We gonna travel to the middle of those craters."

"Why?" Rooli rumbled unexpectedly.

"Listen," Gambe said, his tone shifting suddenly to one of anxiousness. "I got a great opportunity here, ya feel me? That Hunter is on his way here, with the Huntress about 500 miles behind him, thinkin' she hidin' good in the ground. But I can see her clear as day, ya feel me? It ain't no thing for me."

"What the hell are you saying?" Myriam demanded to know.

"Sorry, but things ain't gonna go how ya want them to go today," Gambe said with some surprise. Then he added excitedly, "but things are turnin' out better than ever for me."

"What…are you…planning," Shira seethed, and she realized that they had already reached the center of the three craters. Gambe was biding his time, skirting the edges of each crater as he maneuvered in circles on the surface between them.

"Well," Gambe began, "I really was gonna drop you all at the main entrance to Downver. And then I was gonna take the girls back to the Agency with me and leave the rest of ya in the Downver dust, ya feel me?"

"I knew it," Shira wheezed, wishing she could go back to the campfire after the Mutant boar and just throw herself off a cliff edge and release the group from their burden.

"Fatherfucker!" Myriam said through gritted teeth.

The girls instinctively pulled themselves closer to Rooli, and Rooli cradled them like baby chicks as she stared death into the closest wall.

"I ain't really care whether ya live or die, ya feel me?" Gambe said as if his words somehow excused his betrayal. "But livin' is far more interestin' than dying, and it was no skin off my back to just drop ya off. I mean, I ain't even have skin, so—"

"And now?" Myriam pressed like a steel mallet. "What are you going to do now?"

"Well," Gambe said, skirting closer and closer to the 700-foot drops over the crater edges with every pass. "That Hunter is headin' our way and closin' in fast, and this is the perfect place to do battle, ya feel me? So, you two are gonna fight the Pair and give me a good show."

"Shira will die," Aliana shouted, her fists balls of rage.

"Prolly," Gambe said simply. "But she gonna die anyway. Downver is dug way, way deep. It's still another day's journey, at a minimum, through the maze of caves. And even if ya do make it to the city alive, what the hell makes ya think Downver is safer than the surface, eh? I heard the place is a shit hole, 'specially for pretty little girls, ya feel me? The city ain't like it was back in the day. I ain't know who your contact in Downver is, but they lied to ya 'bout the girls bein' safe there, if that's what they told you."

"Bring us to the entrance, Gambe. Now!" Aurelia demanded with held breath, not caring about Downver's safety when Shira would surely die if they did not find a way to convince Gambe to help them.

"Bring us to the entrance, Gambe! Please! Please!" Aliana pleaded as she grabbed her sister's arm for support. Aurelia squeezed back and continued signing, referring to Gambe with an onslaught of crude pejoratives.

"No can do, Aliana. But I tell ya what, Wintersvilla Women. You put on a good show, and I won't hurt the girls, ya feel me? Besides, killin' Hunters and Huntresses is what you were born and bred to do, ain't it?"

"He's bluffing. He won't hurt us," Aurelia signed with a dismayed glance at Shira's quickly dying body.

"You wouldn't harm us. You said you were going to take us with you. The Agency clearly wants us," Aliana challenged, and in a flash, the three lesser slaves were sucked out of the vehicle and thrown over the edge of one of the craters, their crying wails trailing into the depths as they plummeted.

"No!" Aliana screamed. Wesley, the last slave of Wintersvilla and presently a free man, yelped, holding back his sobs.

"I ain't fuckin' around," Gambe said, maintaining his cool and detached composure. "I left the slave with a name alive, though, see? I ain't a villain, see? It's just that Mom's already mad at me for spendin' too much time with ol' world games and movies and sims, ya feel me? She gonna appreciate this battle, I know it. This Hunter is special. This one has a nickname: The Butcher of the Wastes."

"The Butcher!" Myriam gasped, for the Butcher was a boogeyman from her childhood, a mere story to tell around the campfires while traveling through the precarious wilds.

The Butcher, Shira considered nervously, remembering the nightmare stories Winters had told her when she was still a little girl. Only, Shira knew that the Butcher was not just a fable. He was a real breathing monster who had massacred at least half a million men, women, and children in just the first few days of his weeks of rampaging, not to mention countless Nomads, which no one even realized Hunters had the ability to kill until the Butcher's rampage. The Butcher was the most heartless and deadly Hunter who had ever lived—the only one that humans had ever bothered to name. And he was heading directly for the girls as Shira rapidly slipped into death's constricting folds.

"Just…me," Shira said, hoping Gambe would agree. "I go…into Overdrive and…fight the Hunter…and you let Myriam…take the girls and the Hybrid…and the man…the rest of the way…to Downver," she managed through her ghastly wheezing.

"It's gotta be both of ya or nothin'," Gambe issued before the girls had a chance to protest Shira's offer.

Myriam squeezed Shira's shoulder with her indelible grip, telling her without words that she wanted to fight alongside her—that it was okay to let her go if it meant the girls might have a chance at escape, no matter how slim.

"We fight…and you…guarantee the girls' safety?" Shira asked.

"No!" Aliana ordered, but Myriam nodded in agreement with Shira's proposition.

"Yes," Gambe said.

Hoping it was true that Gambe couldn't read their sign language, Shira signed to the group that they should get ready to make for the secret entrance while she and Myriam distracted Gambe and the Pair for as long as possible.

"You prolly thinkin' 'bout those Wintersvilla Women who normally stand guard at the entrance, right?" Gambe offered in response to the group's sudden silence. "You thinkin' they might be able to help ya?"

Aurelia and Aliana both signed in fervent disagreement and told Shira that there had to be another way.

"Well, think again," Gambe went on. "Those old women expired years back. Their veins turned all black just like yours, General Shira."

Shira was not able to stop her tears as she signed that they must listen to her and that she loved them and that she would always be with them, in their hearts, for the rest of their lives.

Just a weak little girl, came the voice of Winters, and Shira couldn't help smiling at his wicked taunting.

Oh yeah? Watch this, you bastard, Shira taunted back, and she could see Winters clearly in her mind, his eyes wide in horrified disbelief. Shira remembered him with the exact same expression the day she plunged Wintersbane into the vile man's soft gut over and over and over again.

Without giving the girls or Myriam a chance to protest, Shira entered her manual override command, forcing her exo alive as it entered Overdrive. Quicker than Gambe anticipated, Shira threw the girls through the open window, directly at the crater Gambe was currently skirting over. In the same instant, somehow keeping up with Shira's super-human speed, Rooli ejected herself as a torso through the same window, breaking and abandoning her limbs in the process. Just as Shira had learned to anticipate, Rooli knew exactly what to do.

"Oh, what the fuck!" Gambe shouted, dropping his calm and confident demeanor suddenly as Myriam powered on her exo. "You try'na kill those girls?"

"Let us out," Shira roared without having to pant excruciatingly for breath. Her adrenal glands now produced adrenaline at over ten-times her base rate, ripping the glands to pieces in the process. Her heart pumped at six-hundred beats per minute, quickly shredding the internal ventricle and atrium walls as her exo rapidly and haphazardly repaired the chambers long enough for her heart to keep pumping. It felt like a never-ending heart attack, and though the exo did not numb the pain, the surging adrenaline allowed her to relish in it.

"Let me kill!" Shira cried with wild berserker rage, and Myriam forced herself not to cry as she watched her love in the final few glorious minutes of her life.

Gambe deconstructed the walls of the vehicle suddenly, forcing the women to catch themselves as they skidded across the ground and nearly fell into one of the craters. He reformed into a humanoid figure, the same six-foot man he had appeared as earlier, but Shira also noticed a small piece of his body launch into the crater that Aliana, Aurelia, and

Rooli were probably still falling inside of. However, her mind refused to let her focus on anything except hate and rage.

Wesley scrambled to find his own foothold, rolling haphazardly across the ground and shredding the skin of his exposed arms and torso, until finally coming to a skidding stop about fifty feet away.

Far in the distance to the southeast, a surging tsunami of dust with a thick, all-consuming vortex at its center rapidly closed in on their location. It sounded as if the world was bellowing a great battle cry or as if a horde of ten thousand Mutants were stampeding and crushing the Earth in their devastating wake.

"Goddamn, it's really him. That's the Butcher," Gambe marveled.

A permanent band of milky-white atmosphere undulated in the wake of the vortex, and Shira understood it to be a vapor-cone produced in the supersonic wake of the Hunter's fire-hot heat production boiling the surrounding air into vapor.

"They say he moves like a tornado 'cross the wastes," Gambe practically sang in excitement. "They ain't kiddin', eh? But he goin' way faster than a tornado. Way, way faster. He travelin' at just under 2000 miles per hour right now, two and a half times the speed of sound. That gotta be a record for a Hunter, ya feel me?"

To Shira, Gambe's words were a jumble of incoherent noise in the midst of her exo rapidly converting her cells, one by one, to its indomitable, frenzied will. Every one of her veins bulged as her heart coursed oxygen-rich blood through her dying muscles with insatiable swiftness. The few intact veins and arteries still remaining in her body bled outward, turning purple black like the thick veins splintering madly from every port. Her chest issued a fount of thick blood suddenly, dislodging Rooli's chest-tube from between her ribs, but her exo was quick to patch the wound with a makeshift scab, utilizing cells from periphery organs and even some vital organs that Shira no longer needed and certainly would never need again. The improvised scab stifled the bleeding well enough, but now her lung began to fill with blood again, forcing her to cough on her own fluid life.

Almost fully in Overdrive, her active consciousness wanted only to kill and kill and kill, but at the periphery of her mind, she could just barely make out the final noise of her own rational thoughts reminding her what truly mattered.

Death is nothing. My only purpose is to buy Rooli and the girls enough time to escape into the hidden entrance, her rational mind considered without her, and then it was no more. Overdrive took her over completely, and the being that had once been Shira howled like a hungry ghoul at the top of her blood-flooded lungs, thirsting desperately and savagely to kill. She cleared her spasming breathing with a terrible, rasping scrape, spraying thick fluid all over the ground as her lung immediately began filling again. But now Shira didn't even notice her failing lung or burst eye vessels or the sickening black veins that reminded her of Aurelia's face, confusing her for just a moment before she immediately gave up trying to remember who the name *Aurelia* belonged to.

Shira roared once more at the oncoming Hunter, stretching and ripping her lips and the corners of her mouth with her violent hate.

"I love you, my gorgeous general," Myriam said bittersweetly from beside Shira as she unsheathed Summit Splitter. This was goodbye, but it was also the highest form of glory to battle beside Shira against the ultimate Hunter—the actual boogeyman from her dreams. This would be nothing like Myriam's initiation, and even if she found a way to slay the demonic Hunter and his Huntress, Shira would still be dead. Gone forever. Just a memory.

Myriam gritted her teeth and extinguished every one of her thoughts except one: glory. She roared with the fury of every woman who had ever been scorned by the world of man, and even though she wanted nothing more than to hold her wife, she forced her mind to stoically accept the present moment and filled herself with fearless rage.

"Come, Butcher! Come and taste my blades and know that you are not the most terrifying monster on Earth. I am!" Myriam screamed, her rasping voice a trophy proving that Hunters had every right to fear her.

Shira knew Myriam had spoken, but she couldn't discern anything over the raging brutality of her thoughts.

Die! Shira seethed as she envisioned the Hunter being torn ceaselessly to pieces by her blades. The wind shifted, slamming the group with a powerful gale that forced the women to brace themselves and sent Wesley tumbling several feet across the ground as if it were slick with ice.

Die! Shira boiled as she envisioned the Huntress' sinister neck ridge and the rest of her brain pierced up through the stem by Wintersbane.

Again, the wind shifted, this time slamming their backs as the atmosphere was violently sucked into the Hunter's vortexing vacuum despite being miles away.

Die! Shira churned as she envisioned Gambe's metal melting to glowing goop in some impossible heat she wished were real. The clouds above them dispersed in a wild flurry, and the pull of the wind forced Myriam forward a few steps. Wesley grabbed at a dead but hardy root in the exposed ground and held on for dear life.

Die! Shira raged as she envisioned Winters gasping and pleading for her mercy in his last moments. Her piercing rage and death-hunger could wait no longer, and she slammed both her fists against the Earth with gorilla might, shattering her unneeded fingers and knuckles with an audible crunch.

"Die!" Shira wailed viciously as she envisioned herself impaled on a giant stake in the middle of a desert, desolate and lifeless save the haunting, gnarling flesh trees of the death-rotten Earth.

Shira's eyes welled with blood full of quivering hate. She glanced at Myriam, but she no longer saw her lover, just another instrument of illustrious death.

Die! Die! Die! Shira commanded with inhuman savagery at the vortexing dust cloud, her organs and flesh crumbling with each passing second.

I'll kill them all! Everything! Everyone!

The real secret to battle is intelligence and deception. The story of David and Goliath that I was told as a child was not actually a parable about courage, but technology and surprise. In a "fair" fight, David loses every time to the enormous might of Goliath. Thus, one should never allow a fight to be fair. This is the real secret to victory.

If an enemy might find out your true motives, then you should appear driven by something unexpected. If an enemy knows your skills, develop new ones. If an enemy knows your weapons, devise a weapon they have never seen.

Pure strength is useless against the complexity of intelligent design. And yet, without initial strength, intelligence might never have a chance to flourish. The more intelligent being might be quashed by the mightier being before the former even has a chance to utilize his more powerful intellect.

And so, the greatest soldier is one who is both mighty and intelligent, strong and cunning, and most of all, unexpected. The moment a soldier no longer abides by the enemy's predictions is the very moment the enemy loses and the soldier tastes victory.

Intricate deception and boundless surprise—these will be my greatest weapons in my ceaseless battle to make this world my own. To those who would stand against me, I look forward to meeting you on the battlefield of life. I'm certain you will all serve to strengthen every part of me, especially my resolve.

From Mendel's Ladder: The Personal Journal of Denis Mendel, Written Circa 2033, Published June 2108 by Leif Mainstone, Federated Agency Publishing

Chapter 12
Battle Preparations

A solitary Nomad composed entirely of thick purple-hued muck loped and gushed across the ground, staring at Volya and Thompson as it curdled past them. Volya readied her leg to kick the living sludge out of curiosity at how its gushing body might reconstitute itself, but then she decided against it after seeing the Nomad squelch over a small boulder covered in bite moss. The Nomad's sludge melted the orange moss to a sickening black.

Volya picked up a rock and threw it at the mucky Nomad, and the projectile disappeared into the thick slime as the Nomad languidly but diligently continued on its way. It went on staring at Volya with a series of featureless humanoid faces embedded arbitrarily on the surface of the muck, like living rorschach blots ephemerally taking shape then just as quickly dissipating back into meaningless patterns.

Volya considered using her Hunter to explode the creepy, disgusting Nomad with a supersonic slap of his hands, but as she dipped herself into his mind, all she could do was shake her head in disappointment at Thompson's constant reminiscing of Anna's touch and the taste of her tongue and the vibrance of her verdant emerald eyes.

"Yuck!" Volya spat at her Hunter, more repulsed by him than the mucky Nomad. "Think about guts and gore or something, for Mendel's sake. Fuck! Watching your mind is like petting a three-legged kitten."

"Then stay out," Thompson scowled.

Volya chuckled beneath her breath. "You'd like that, wouldn't you, dog?"

I love you, little Hunter, Volya heard Anna's voice say within Thompson's mind, serving as a defensive vanguard quelling the ceaseless raring of his inner-rage.

"I love you, I love you, I love you," Volya mocked in an obnoxious tone. "Is that all you two ever said to each other the whole four months you were together?"

"You don't know love," Thompson told her pityingly.

"Damn right," Volya responded thankfully. "Love is just an idea—one that weakens and leaves the love-stricken vulnerable and stupid. It's a disease, ultimately."

"Sure," Thompson agreed flatly. "The only worthwhile disease in all of hell."

Volya laughed at her Hunter. "You're funny," she said, and then she took control of him and slammed him against the ground in annoyance.

"Sorry," she said with overt facetiousness. "My bad."

Thompson rose and consciously cleared the pain back to calming neutrality.

"What do you think the Eternal Hunt is, if not an idea—a story you believe in?" Thompson asked.

"The Eternal Hunt isn't an idea; it's an action. A movement upward. The ascension of Mendel's Ladder," Volya intoned.

"Do you even know what you're saying?" Thompson asked seriously.

"Do you?" Volya retorted easily.

Thompson shook his head, knowing it was useless to attempt to reason with a monster.

Even the worst monster can be redeemed, Anna reminded him, but Thompson couldn't help doubting her words in light of Volya. A pang of yearning filled Thompson's heart, and he couldn't help thinking back to the day the giant metal crafts descended from the sky—from Astrea—just as Anna said they would eventually.

Volya peered into her Hunter's mind and watched as the human woman didn't even put up a fight against her captors. Thompson was ready to turn the occupants of the crafts inside out, but Anna told him not to. Instead, Anna just forlornly walked up the extended ramp of the closest craft, and then she was gone forever as they ascended back to Astrea.

Thompson's rage bubbled, turning heinously inward in forlorn accusation of his own despicable failure to protect Anna.

Volya burst with laughter. "You...you just let her go?"

"You don't understand!" Thompson lashed, loathing himself even more than his own wicked captor invading his mind like an ax gouging the thick arteries of a flesh tree.

"You make me feel dirty, you know that? Your weakness is filth," Volya said, and she spat on the ground. "I know what'll make me feel better, though."

"Killing?" Thompson suggested tiredly.

"Killing," Volya confirmed with a devilish smile.

Both Hunter and Huntress turned at the sound of high-pitched chirping emanating from a solitary flesh tree full of something similar in appearance and smell to old world crab apples. The flesh tree was coated in thick ropes of fire vine, which only grew on certain, seemingly arbitrary flesh trees. If anyone, including Hunters or Huntresses, came within ten feet of the vine, it would combust its closest leaves and snap its stem at thunderous speeds, sending a spray of ravenous flames at unsuspecting victims. Volya and Thompson were both careful to keep their distance.

A fluttering of wings allowed Volya to pinpoint the source of the high-pitched chirping to a small blue bird perched on one of the flesh tree's wily branches as it painstakingly wrestled a small crab apple from a thick stem. The bird looked weak, its feathers falling out in painful-looking patches and one of its legs torn away with just a jagged stump remaining. Still, somehow, it found a way to survive the Nomadic world.

"A bird," Thompson said in awe and admiration, remembering the creature's distinct scent from childhood. "The last time I saw a bird was before I even met Anna. They used to fly over my birth-fire from time to time. I always envied them. I wanted to sprout wings and fly away. Funny. My skinsuit can easily do that for me with just a thought, and yet, here I am, still unable to fly away from my fate."

We make our own fate, little Hunter, Anna's voice responded, painfully reminding Thompson, once again, that people always had a choice. *As we invariably encounter forks on the path of life, we have no choice but to fork with it,* she said, and Thompson struggled against the terrible urge to weep as he reminded himself that Anna had not even put up a fight against her captors.

Why, Anna? Thompson pleaded with the same question that had plagued his more than three-decade long dream. *Why didn't you let me do exactly what I was born and bred and brutalized to do? I could have killed them all within a single beat of your beautiful heart. So, why did you tell me not to follow you?*

he thought, torturously remembering the soothing scent of her blood and the ataractic influence of her pulse on his violently unstable mind.

To Thompson's surprise, Volya didn't presently appear to be monitoring his thoughts like an obsessed, malevolent sentinel. Instead, she just stared at the small blue bird, her skin shifting absentmindedly through abstract patterns as she processed the tiny creature through the lens of the Eternal Hunt. She cocked her head in consideration, absorbing the old world creature with near-mystical wonder.

"There's barely any life out here," Volya said, her mind skeptically racing with statistics that told her this bird's presence was as unlikely to occur in the Butcher Wastelands as a human picnic. "What's the odds that this thing happens to be right here, just as we're passing? What's it doing? Why's it here? Right here?" Volya asked with a surge of wary curiosity and agitation.

"It's just living its sad life," Thompson offered with what he considered to be the most obvious answer. "It's just surprising to see. It must be the only old world animal in the whole area—I can't smell any others. Are there more animals outside my olfactory range?" Thompson asked.

"Not many," Volya said, knowing that when Thompson said animal, he was referring to the specific taxonomic phylum named by humans as chordata—most of which were vertebrates. She didn't bother asking the Marrow precisely how many still roamed the Earth. Volya only knew that it was very few, with no more than ten thousand or so individual chordates still grasping at life. Each year, a handful of animals would inevitably get trapped in a splicer bush, and soon after, they would begin the transformation into a brain-rotted, dangerous Mutant. Volya felt comforted in her confidence that eventually there would be no more animals, just as eventually there would be no more humans.

Without warning, Volya lifted a small rock from the ground and pitched it just slightly faster than the speed of sound, exploding the tiny bird's skull with a sonic boom. All that remained of the bird was a cascading flutter of feathers.

"It's better off dead," Volya concluded, her eyes peering through slits of distrusting suspicion.

Monsters can be redeemed, Thompson forced himself to mentally repeat as he mourned the loss of the fragile, tiny creature.

"For fuck's sake, fuck your redemption, Hunter. All your moping around and sympathy for life is seriously bringing me down. I'm only going to say this one more time: you better not give me a problem on the battlefield. You will obey me, or I will dispose of you," she said, pointing to the heap of feathers that had finally come to rest on the bitter Earth.

Thompson took a deep breath and was careful not to reveal the stinging fog that he kept ready at the edges of his mind.

"Okay," he said uncharacteristically, not fighting back even in his tone.

"Okay?" Volya checked.

"Okay, you win," Thompson told her, and though she could sense dishonesty in the deepest layers of his mind, she didn't bring it up. There was no need. Her control was absolute. Even if he tried to block her mind with the stinging fog again, she had already proved that she could get around it after just a few seconds. It was no more than an inconvenience, but it was still one she wished to avoid. She knew from the memories of thousands of other Pairs that doing battle with Wintersvilla Women was not something to underestimate.

But my Hunter and his skinsuit are beyond any Hunter or Huntress that has ever hunted, Volya thought with a rapacious delight for bloodshed. *Maybe there's even a way to destroy their metal craft,* she considered, though she wasn't sure how it would be possible to inflict damage on something that wasn't even fermionic in nature—something beyond all known matter on Earth or the rest of the known universe.

It might not be a living thing by definition, but if it exists, if I can perceive it and it is tangible, then I will find a way to destroy it, Volya resolved.

Like cracking a whip, Volya mentally spurred Thompson's legs to bend and kick forward, then break into a quickly accelerating run. She was happy to see that he did not fight back, just as he had agreed.

There is still resistance deep inside his mind, but I will break him. It is only a matter of time, Volya assured herself as she stood and watched her Hunter rocket toward the distant horizon.

Thompson ran at a casual pace of four hundred miles per hour, kicking up dirt, dust, and scant plant life in his wake. Volya felt him unintentionally rejoice at the liberating feeling of running across the Earth's expansive surface. He tried to hide the feeling behind his self-torment, but she could still feel it seeping out of his mental constraints like piercing sunlight.

That's right, Volya thought. *Find joy in the power of your body, Thompson. Remember what it means to be a Hunter.*

Volya flipped to her mental partition containing the live video feed of the Earth, and she was astonished to see that the platinum craft's vector was altering course away from Downver's main entrance. It was heading directly for the three impact craters—monuments of glorious power left behind by old world humanity's greatest weapons.

"Wait," Volya said in his mind from several miles behind him. There was no distance the mental tether connecting her mind to his skinsuit could not reach.

Thompson skidded to a halt, and he thought for a moment that she was just politely letting a large pack of skittering tangle grass pass him undisturbed.

"No, don't stop running," she lashed, and Thompson kicked once more at the ground, pulverizing a row of tangle grass and unintentionally exploding through a small grove of squat, flaxen-hued Nomads anchored deep into the ground that Thompson mistook as plant life. He reached a sustained four hundred miles per hour again in less than ten seconds, and as he peered back at the Nomads, he saw them erupt into a grove of flesh trees nearly identical in size and shape to their original Nomadic forms, though now they shone brightly with rainbow variation in color from one flesh tree to the next.

"The group of humans—they just entered that strange cylinder thing." Volya relayed with the excited edge of a predator seeing its prey break into a desperate run for survival. "And now it's moving at a steady sixty miles per hour. Its vector is pointed toward the three craters." Volya's heart skipped a beat in anticipation. "Our prey is officially on the run, and I'll be damned if we're going to let them get away. You need to run faster, Thompson."

At her command, Thompson felt himself flex and swell, and his muscles doubled in size, allowing him to run at just over 800 miles per hour. His ear drums exploded in the wake of his own sonic boom as he passed the sound barrier, but the skinsuit was quick to rebuild new ear drums that could easily withstand a direct blast of supersonic air.

I said faster, dog! Volya shouted in his mind, seeming even more anxious suddenly. *Faster!*

Thompson felt his control fully slip away as Volya seized every cell of his body, pushing it far past a normal Hunter's limits. Scalding heat exploded from his pores as waste, but the skinsuit had no difficulty keeping up with Volya's demands as it altered Thompson's body, raising the specific heat of every one of his cells so that they would not boil. A soft membrane grew across his ears, muting the roaring winds and funnel clouds generated from his heat mixing with the temperate atmosphere. His muscles quadrupled in size, crushing his bones as the skinsuit instantly rebuilt them harder, more malleable, more tensile.

Faster! Volya ordered, demanding even greater speed. Agonizing pain gushed through him as he fell forward, his spine cracking and bending as it reconfigured his skeletal system to be quadrupedal. Thompson ran on all fours, and he felt his fingers shorten and his toes lengthen as his feet became lupine. His ribs contracted, allowing his legs even more room to rotate, and his lungs reformed so that they ran the length of his spine, expanding vertically to match his new rib structure. Gaping slits slick with fresh blood ripped open the flesh of his neck and chest, allowing him to absorb even more oxygen from the atmosphere. The mitochondria of his cells were twisted and reformed so that they could feed his rapidly replicating cells with lightning speed and efficiency.

Faster, dog, faster! came Volya's wicked, lashing voice, and his body obeyed, tearing more oxygen-absorbing slits across his back and reforming his mouth into baleen-like partitions that filtered and further ionized the already electronegative oxygen, energizing Thompson's cells with the overwhelming force of a nuclear factory powering a single light bulb.

At just under 2000 miles per hour and the Hunter's body teetering on the very edge of breakdown, Volya was finally satisfied.

You're going to kill those little girls first, along with their Hybrid protector, Volya said, going over their battle plans. *And then you rip apart the half-dead Wintersvilla Woman, and then the other one.*

And the strange craft? Thompson asked, surprising Volya by still going along with her plans.

Maybe I'm successfully breaking him after all, Volya considered.

155

Ignore the craft for now, Volya told him simply, and Thompson didn't push the issue. He wanted her to feel comfortable. To let down her guard. He would only have one chance to effectively use the full strength of the stinging fog against her. Now that he knew it was effective, he could go all out with it. His timing had to be perfect, and until the precise second he unleashed it, he had to follow along so that he could retain the element of surprise.

He's planning something in that half-baked little brain of his, Volya knew, but such was to be expected from such a pitiful, unruly Hunter. At least his power made up for his disobedience. It was certainly better than having a loyal but weak weapon.

Satisfied with his speed and vector, Volya detached slightly from Thompson's mind. She spotted a patch of razor bushes and carefully plucked a few out of the ground by the base of their stems, easily gripping them with subtle placements of her fingers that would ensure she would avoid the bushes' flesh shearing blades.

As the Eternal Hunt dictated, she cupped her hands and used her own powerful arms to dig a small den in the dirt. She knew exactly what to do, as these were the typical baseline strategies of all Pairs, and a cursory glance at historic battle data revealed that the digging of a den afforded a Huntress both safety and heightened thermal regulation.

As she dug, shooters, little worms that turned at sudden ninety-degree angles every other second, filled the local soil, indicating that something had recently died here.

A good omen, Volya rejoiced, looking fondly at the little creatures shooting away from her in a flurry of unpredictable movement. *The Eternal Hunt demands death, and it is I, Volya, who will dutifully answer Mendel's divine call toward Ascension.*

Shimmying herself into the tight hole, she couldn't help the surging excitement of finally hunting. After covering her entire body, head and all, with dirt, she set a partition of her subconscious into sentry mode, ready to alert her if anything larger than a small bird came within 500 feet of her buried body. Finally, she fully detached her mind from her own body and observed the world solely from the perspective of Thompson and the thousands of satellites in orbit around the Earth, at least half of which were still operational. In response to her heightened mental state, her body and brain gushed out thermal waste, but being buried beneath the cold earth helped to keep her temperature just below the threshold of causing permanent damage.

The nightmarish dust storm churned by Thompson's heat and speed raged so violently that it altered the weather behind Thompson, whipping flesh trees and other plant life out of the ground as ultra-powerful gales slammed against the world at wind speeds double those generated by the nuclear bombs of old world humanity.

The fiery blasts of wind alone will kill them all, regardless of what he's planning, Volya thought with glee. *It's time to do what I was born for. Time to fulfill my purpose. It's time to kill.*

As the Nomads grow in population, so too do their own stories and religions. Their overarching culture and goals remain ubiquitous across the globe, but the little harmless details are left to their own limited discretion.

One of the stories of the future that all Nomads know is the coming of the Mirror-Man. It is a term I embedded into the Nomads' very genetic structure, and it is a word I continue to whisper into their network to this day.

There is only one other they will labor for besides me. One other whose command they will heed. It is the words and will of the Mirror-Man from Astrea that the Nomads will not only listen to, but also respect, for he will be honest, righteous, and selfless. Just like the Nomads. His coming will herald a shift in Nomadic activity spanning the entirety of the Earth. The day he sets foot upon the surface, nothing will ever be the same again.

From Mendel's Ladder: The Personal Journal of Denis Mendel, Recorded Circa 2065, Published June 2108 by Leif Mainstone, Federated Agency Publishing

Chapter 13
A Fall from Heaven

High Commander Roland pushed Samuel again, forcing him up a slight incline further into the enveloping darkness.

"My family, please, Roland," Samuel tried again, dropping Roland's title.

"Quiet. It's for your own good. And theirs. Besides, the darkness is cleansing. Embrace it," the High Commander answered ominously.

Samuel did not feel cleansed, and after at least ten minutes of Roland pushing him forward as he stumbled through the dark with his arms held nervously in front of him, Samuel thought the darkness might never end, until finally he saw dim rays of light in the distance. As they approached the light, their destination finally came into view, and for the first time in his life, Samuel laid his eyes on the Luxury Quarters.

This place is like the Foundation, except it's even more beautiful...entrancingly beautiful, Samuel thought in horror, for the beauty surrounding him was woven into the same place that all Foundationers eventually went to die. Like the Foundation, the Luxury Quarters was also formed by curved, rotating, gravity-inducing walls. It was smaller than the Foundation, with no more than a third of its circumference and an even smaller fraction of its length. Despite just exiting the cramped, pitch-black hallway, Samuel felt slightly claustrophobic being able to see so much detail across the entirety of its, at most, six-mile length.

This place is so tiny compared to the Foundation, Samuel gawked, amazed that people could stomach living in such a cramped amount of space. *They must live right next to the recyclers, neighbors with factories of death. How?* Samuel gasped, seeing the Luxury Quarters citizens as something utterly alien to him—like a whole other species.

Despite the differences in size between the Luxury Quarters and Foundation, Samuel was surprised by the number of similarities. Glowglobes floated here and there, but there were far fewer, and they all shone radiant shades of gold, creating a brilliant yet dim, golden-hued environment full of shadows and unseen corners. It was like a perpetual, foreboding golden hour. Like the Foundation, it was full of winding rivers, intersecting grass roads, small collections of quaint houses, and multiple districts brimming with exotic plant-life, some of which Samuel had only seen on his children's telescreens.

Margot would love it here, Samuel winced, breathing heavier at the mental image of his daughter. *And Nathan would complain about how dark it is. And Sandra would just be happy we were all together. Goddamnit!* Samuel seethed as he continued painfully absorbing this environment that had been here all this time, just a thick wall away. Rather than the familiar twin peaks of Mount Mendel, four colossal pearl-white towers jutted every ninety degrees from the outside walls, aligning with the doors leading back into the Foundation. A part of Samuel's racing mind couldn't help marveling at the ornate columns composed of an unknown sparkling white material supporting the mass of each tower, all of which met in the middle of the curved Luxury Quarters like spokes of a wheel. Impressive but ominous windows of stained glass depicting major historical events from the old world beckoned Samuel's attention from the walls of the structure: the nuclear bombs, the rise of the Changed People, the launching of Astrea, the Hunters raining down from space, and many others that Samuel could only guess at with his limited knowledge of history.

In front of each of the four ornately carved towers spanning the Luxury Quarters' circumference, a tiny, gray cube-shaped building with one door and no windows waited like a silent reaper ready to harvest death. Like the ornate towers, these cube-shaped buildings were perfectly aligned with each of the four doorways leading back to the Foundation.

The recyclers, Samuel gasped, comparing the drab buildings to the infamous descriptions and seeing no other buildings that might constitute their sharp angles. Samuel could barely believe that he had viewed the prospect of being recycled as honorable and necessary only a handful of minutes earlier, but that still didn't assuage the deep feeling that he deserved the recycler for murdering the Queensguard, no matter the circumstances.

The colorless, spartan simplicity of the recycler buildings contrasted starkly with the grandeur of the illustrious towers exuding the very extravagance that made the name of the Luxury Quarters perfectly apt. However, it was like an oil painting made by a machine pretending to understand human art and life. Every adornment and intricate detail coating the surface of the luxurious grandeur sickened Samuel, and for the first time, rather than obedience and acceptance, he felt only loathing for recyclers and the Luxury Quarters and everyone who had ever looked upon any aspect of Astrea in a favorable light, including himself.

"This place is…this fucking place…" Samuel said, unable to fully form his thoughts out loud through his debilitating disgust. Though Roland remained silent, he didn't outright disagree with Samuel's tone. He just kept up his indelible gait, pushing Samuel forward as they continued invariably toward the recycler. The path curved, making a wide bend around a grove of fruit trees brimming with vibrant apples and pears and oranges and numerous other fruits that were not available in the Foundation.

These trees and the extravagance of this place…why does this even exist? Samuel pondered angrily for not the first time, though now he did not cut his thoughts off with the rationalization that the Luxury Quarters citizens deserved their lavishness.

As they passed the grove of fruit trees, Samuel considered breaking away and running back to the Foundation to search for his family, but he decided this was not the right time. Roland would easily stop him. He had to let the man think he was still going along with his plans, and at the right moment, he would break free somehow.

I have to find them. I can't fail my family, Samuel repeated internally like a self-inflicted wound, hating himself for not doing more to protect them. *But if I try to run now, Roland will probably kill me, and I can't save them if I'm dead. For now I'll keep walking, but I have to take the first opportunity I get.*

The recycler and the rest of the Luxury Quarters' foreboding, golden landscape came back into view from behind the trees. The four white towers had beckoned Samuel's initial attention with tangible demand, but now he peered beyond them, to the far wall. Rather than being covered in lush ivy, its untextured golden surface appeared uniformly uninterrupted across its entire surface area. The golden wall contained no obvious doorways or passages. It was just an endcap, like the Space Wall at the far end of the Foundation, revealing that Albatross and Damian and his father and all the rest had to be wrong about the Paradise Quarters lying beyond the Luxury Quarters. It all just led back to outer space.

Goddamn fools, Samuel thought, with himself at the very top of the list. He felt surging remorse for all the young hackers who had thrown their lives away over a light at the end of the tunnel that didn't even exist. He envisioned countless dead Foundationers strewn across their homes, all of them dead over a figment of their imagination. *This is all your fault,* Samuel couldn't help thinking as he imagined his dad seeing the same golden wall in equal horror. Or maybe his father had felt even more horror, if he was capable of fully understanding all the pain and suffering he had caused with his hapless and destructive desire for a dreamland— a place that existed solely in his mind. *You're not my father,* Samuel accused the figure he saw in his thoughts as they reached the open doorway leading to the recycler building's interior. *You're just a goddamn revolutionary rat, the worst of them all,* Samuel told his father torturously, seeing himself in the exact same light, regardless of his own intentions.

"Paradise is a goddamn fiction," Samuel concluded with forlorn regret as they entered the building.

"Wrong," Roland responded levelly, surprising Samuel with an actual answer. "The Paradise Quarters are perfectly real. They are just beyond the Golden Wall," Roland continued bleakly, lacking all of the hope and excitement that filled the voices of the conspiracy theorists when they spoke about paradise.

Samuel gasped in horror. *Dad was right?* he thought painfully in a sudden flurry of existential disorientation. But he still felt intense hate for his father, blaming him for the wanton death caused by both the past and present revolution.

"It's…it's real?" Samuel stammered, his disbelief doing little to ward off the feeling of going insane. The High Commander returned to ignoring Samuel and continued pushing him forward through the building's single empty hallway, ending in a T-intersection and reminding Samuel of Madeira's advice about forks in roads.

Obviously I didn't listen well enough, Samuel concluded grimly. *Obviously I chose the wrong path.*

The building's spartan exterior was reflected in its interior, with the walls and ceiling painted a bare beige and the design a series of striking ninety-degree angles. It was a startling contrast to the rest of the Foundation and Luxury Quarters.

Hearing what sounded like war drums, Samuel peered anxiously over his shoulder, and he went wide-eyed at the snaking, sepulchral procession of countless Queensguards emerging single file from the pitch-dark passage leading back to the Foundation. One after another, they walked the path winding around the fruit trees and leading directly to the recycler building. Each of them carried armfuls of dead Foundationers. A few of the Queensguards worked together to carry the armored bodies of their traitorous brethren.

Just like that, the revolution is quelled, Samuel thought, his eyes welling with tears at his inability to do anything but walk to his death and wait helplessly for a window of opportunity.

They arrived at the T-intersection. Samuel looked left and apprehensively observed another short hallway leading to a lonely transparent tube and nothing else. The tube was large enough to fit a handful of people or a pair of Queensguards, armor and all. The top of the tube led into the ceiling, where a large, flat piece of metal attached to a giant metal arm hovered above a section of ground pitted with holes, leading to what Samuel assumed was the machinery responsible for converting people and materials back into atmosphere and rivers and soil and nutrients—back into the very fabric of Astrea.

That has to be it, Samuel knew with a horrible, churning pit of repulsion in his stomach. *The recycler.*

"You crush us to death?" Samuel gawked in horror as he envisioned his family being mashed to a pulp by the metal arm and squeezed into pressurized streams of warm fluid.

"It's quick," the High Commander offered simply as they turned right and continued down another hallway leading to a doorless room at its terminus. "Extremely quick. The press pushes down on the body with 250,000 PSI in just under one–thousandth of a second. If you prefer, I can execute you first the old-fashioned way, with my gauntlet. But just between us, the recycler is the quicker and more humane option. It is also the most noble, for not an atom is wasted. A concerning amount of blood and bowels will have already been spilled through battle and execution. It risks the very balance of Astrea."

Samuel was surprised that the man was talking so readily all of a sudden, and for a moment he thought he might be able to get through to him. That is, until they turned right at the intersection and entered a single room at the end of the hall. In the center sat a solitary chair with old, dried blood all around it.

"You torture people?" Samuel asked with abject horror, not out of fear of pain, but because it was unthinkable that any part of the supposedly just, righteous city of Astrea would contain a torture room. "This place really is hell then," Samuel nearly whispered as the High Commander pushed him onto the spartan wooden chair, still damp and sticky with the room's previous victim.

Not yet, Samuel told himself as he quickly scanned the room for some implement to incapacitate Roland. However, the room was empty, not even containing instruments of torture.

Roland shut the door, then turned around and gazed sullenly at Samuel with a mix of exhaustion and disappointment.

"It's a goddamn shame you couldn't just stay away from those goddamn Sons and Daughters, Samuel Kaminski," Roland said. Samuel started to protest, but the large man went on. "It's a shame you had to follow in your father's footsteps, rather than your mother's. She was a truly remarkable woman. There was no one else like her in all of Astrea. In all the world. In all of heaven or hell."

His accent and the way he speaks, Samuel realized with scant hope that there might be a way to survive this ordeal. *He sounds just like mom and dad.*

Distant childhood memories flooded Samuel's mind. "You were friends with them. I remember you from when I was a boy. I remember you," Samuel said in an attempt to strike a thread of emotion in the High Commander. "Are you going to torture me, Uncle Roland?" Samuel asked directly.

Roland slowly shook his head no and continued to gaze at Samuel with disappointed eyes. "Not me. The Queen's Servant will, I assume. He has tortured others before, but sometimes he just talks. He'll be here soon."

Samuel shook his head in confusion.

"Queen?" he checked, and it was only then that he realized the implication of the title *Queensguard.*

Roland must have seen the realization spread across Samuel's face, because he nodded sadly and said, "You take the word for granted. You grew up with Queensguards. But there was a time before the Queensguards, Samuel. A time before the Queen."

"The Queen?" Samuel probed, caught off guard by these new revelations, but Roland just shook his head, biting his lower lip as he paced with avalanching, sordid memories coursing through his every feature.

"Roland," Samuel pressed. The golden-armored Queensguard stopped pacing and let his eyes fall on Samuel's pleading stare.

He's afraid of something, Samuel saw in the man's eyes. *He isn't just a hulking metal robot. He's wrestling with something terrible. Something unspeakable. I might get through to this man. I might make it out of here alive.*

"Yes. The Queen," Roland said in defeat, his voice like shattered rubble suddenly. "The Queen, Samuel. Astrea itself. I still remember it like a vivid fever dream," Roland practically whispered, his eyes looking right through Samuel now as he appeared to relive his past. "A…a particular old Foundationer told me something strange one day," Roland bewilderedly said with a furrowed, pain-stricken brow. "Something about forking paths. It was so strange. And later that day, David, I mean, your father, he lit the first flames of revolution, even though your mother and I tried over and over again to talk him out of it."

Roland began breathing more heavily, his eyes wandering forlornly as flashbacks streamed across his vision.

Forking paths, Samuel wondered disconcertedly at Roland's words. *Old Man Madeira talked about forking paths earlier.*

"Your dad never stood a chance, boy," Roland continued, breaking Samuel from his thoughts. "There were no Queensguards to stop the revolution. They weren't needed. It was the other Foundationers that stopped your dad and the other revolutionaries. No one wanted revolution back then, Samuel. It was just a handful of people along with your father that wanted it. All of us were from Earth, of course, and the Earth had been turned to hell. No one was willing to risk going back, no matter what the revolution might promise." The High Commander gulped hard, struggling with his next words. "All the Foundationers came together and dragged the revolutionaries to the Luxury Quarters, to the recyclers. Your mom and I, we pleaded for them to stop, Samuel. We did. I was big back then too, and it took ten other men to stop me from getting to your father and escaping with him back home to the Foundation. I tried, Samuel. I tried to save him."

Samuel could barely believe what he was hearing, but Roland was pouring out his emotions in a way that told him everything he was saying had to be the truth.

"My father, he threw away what could have been heaven. He did it out of greed. He—"

"No," Roland interrupted with cutthroat finality. "Your father was a good man, Samuel. And smart. Too smart. He was the first hacker, the one to give rise to the hacker movement we see today. He hacked into the system and found pictures of Astrea's early days, when the orbiting city was still being constructed. He was the one who first learned that there was something beyond the Golden Wall that the Luxury Quarters residents always spoke about with an air of mysticism. Even they didn't know about the Paradise Quarters—about paradise itself."

"What is it?" Samuel demanded, still unable to fully change his view on what he perceived to be his father's greed. "What do the pictures show that could possibly warrant throwing heaven away?"

Not heaven, Samuel lashed correctively in his mind, but he did not reveal his thoughts to Roland. It was better to let him continue speaking. Samuel couldn't help his curiosity surrounding this information that had been hidden from him his whole life, but more importantly, he felt like Roland was growing closer to him with every passing second.

I can convince him to let me go. Just a little longer. Just a little more.

Roland shook his head distressingly, looking tiny suddenly in his astonishing golden armor.

"Tell me what you saw," Samuel urged, feeling like every death, every minute of confusion, every moment of suffering, everything, hinged on Roland's answer.

"The old world," Roland said, his voice one of pure disbelief despite clearly seeing it with vivid lucidity in his head. "Earth, Samuel. Before it was transformed into hell."

"Earth?" Samuel questioned with sudden skepticism. "What are you talking about? Astrea is in space."

"I know, boy. I'm well aware," Roland said with a level of agitation. "I don't know what else to say. The old world is behind those walls, Samuel. A whole universe."

168

"Roland," Samuel urged. "Listen to yourself. That doesn't make sense. Are you hearing yourself? The pictures could have been doctored. Isn't that an easier explanation than there being a whole other universe on the other side of the door?"

His mind is corroded by Astrea, bent and warped from living as a demon in hell all these years. But he's breaking, Samuel reasoned. *I'm getting through to him— showing him the absurdity of his position. Any second now, and he'll be fully on my side. This is the only way I might see my family again.*

Roland nodded at Samuel's reasonable skepticism, then said, "Yes, of course the pictures could be fakes. Of course. That's exactly what Mona and I told David," he recounted with terrible regret. Shocks traveled down Samuel's spine after hearing his mother's name aloud for the first time in so long.

"But I saw it," Roland said, his voice cracking unbecomingly for someone who only ever exuded strength and stoicism. "The day they killed your father, the Golden Wall irised open, like a divine flower unfurling the entrance to actual paradise. We all saw it. All the men and women that day. But…but David died before he could lay eyes on it."

"Roland!" Samuel pleaded. "What did you see?"

"Another world, Samuel," Roland answered suddenly, his eyes and voice full of hellish horror. "Another universe. An endless expanse. Solid ground full of old world trees and shrubs beneath a starlit sky that went on forever. And then," Roland said, shaking suddenly as tears welled in his eyes. "And then we saw her, Samuel. The Queen. Something terrible. Eldritch. A creature violently plumbed from the collective nightmares of humanity itself," Roland said, sounding like a scared little boy. "She descended from the night sky of that other world, electric cables and braided wires extending from the back of her head of raven hair and up into the infinite black space of her own personal universe. She…she looked like a Huntress, Samuel. Identical to a Huntress. But worse. Her skull was open at the back to accommodate those thick black wires that went on forever. It looked like a nightmarish crown atop her gaping head. Fresh blood flowed from her piercing emerald eyes, and her mouth was like an abyssal maw, as if she were screaming at the height of agony forever without end. She was in pain, Samuel, a pain worse than you or I can possibly imagine," Roland cried as he appeared to fully revisit his sordid past for the first time in decades. "She continued screaming silently and crying blood, seeming to

169

not even notice us. But then she spoke into each of our minds. She knew us. Each of us. She...showed us things, Samuel. Impossible things. And then...and then she looked about the room...her body still an unmoving statue in a state of eternal agony. But the wires in her head— they moved her around, Samuel, as if they were her body, and she was just a sensory organ attached to them." Roland shook his head in defeat, allowed himself a few breaths, then said, "She killed most of the room with just her eyes. It happened so fast. People just dropped dead. My neighbors and friends. Just gone like that. A handful of us stood there in shock, waiting for our own deaths, but instead, her head cables undulated, and all of a sudden armor began growing over our bodies, entombing us. Enslaving us," Roland explained, gawking at his armor with implacable revulsion. "Except for your mother and the Queen's Servant. Her servant was the only man in the room who wasn't forced into this infernal armor. And your mother was the only woman left alive. The Queen let her live, Samuel. That devil spared her own servant and your mother, and she subjugated the rest of us with this demonic metal," he finished, gaping in horror at his gauntlets.

"My mom never told me any of this," Samuel said breathlessly, shaking his head as his mind reeled and conjured lucid visions of Roland's ghastly descriptions. "Not a word."

"We all agreed. The Queensguards and your mother and the Queen's Servant too. We all agreed to never say a word. It was...it was too much. The Queen is proof that this place is hell, for she must be the devil, Samuel. What else?"

He thinks this place is hell. That's it. He'll help me, Samuel reasoned with tangible hope for the first time since the revolution began. *But I have to know more. I have to understand what the hell is going on if I want to keep Sandra and the kids alive longer than a day. I have to take on the immeasurable weight of all of Astrea, and I have to make things right, and that means I have to understand who...and what the Queen is.*

"Why did the Queen spare my mom?" Samuel implored, barely able to contain himself in his drive to finally pivot the conversation and convince Roland to help him find his family and keep them safe until he could figure out his next move, whatever that might be.

Roland shrugged in despair. "I don't know, Samuel. I don't know. But I...I thought that your mother and I would finally..." Roland stammered despondently, "with your dad's death, even though he was always my best friend…I thought that…your mother, Samuel, she…I loved her…I…even before Astrea. I loved Mona more than life itself…I…" Roland appeared to lose himself for a moment, then collected himself with a shake of his horror-stricken face.

"The Queen, Samuel. She effortlessly killed hundreds with just her stare, and she instituted the Queensguard in response to the last revolt. Do you understand what that means?"

"That we must destroy the Queen somehow," Samuel said, certain that this was the moment Roland would agree and tell Samuel they should work together to save the others and kill the Queen. "We need to destroy her and take Paradise for ourselves. How else can we possibly keep everyone safe, Roland?" he finished, hearing his dad's own words spoken through him.

But it's true, even though I'm saying all this to get Roland on my side. It's still true that the Queen is everyone's enemy. If what Roland says is true, then the Queen is the reason that heaven is hell.

"No!" Roland scolded. "It means she will come back. She will institute something worse. She is a god, Samuel. You understand? It is the height of foolishness to test a god's might."

Samuel gawked in disbelief at Roland's animal fear.

He's full of all this fear deep down inside because he's been alone all this time, Samuel reasoned. *But not anymore. We can work together.*

"Roland, you said it yourself. She looked like a Huntress. Huntresses can be killed, can't they?"

Roland did not seem to even take notice of Samuel's point. He turned and looked at the doorway with nervous apprehension, then turned back to Samuel.

"The armor heightens my senses. I can hear his footsteps, Samuel. The Queen's Servant is here. The one who lives among us and works directly on her behalf."

Shit, Samuel cursed himself, realizing he was going to miss his chance to convince Roland to help him.

"Roland, I'm begging you. Help me get out of here. Help me save my family," Samuel pleaded. If he couldn't convince him to help, then he was prepared to charge at Roland unexpectedly, hoping the element of surprise might be effective in toppling him to the ground.

"No, Samuel. It's too late for that. That'll only make things worse," Roland explained in defeat.

"My family is in danger," Samuel cried. "Please, Roland! If you loved my mother, then help me. Help Mona's son. Help her grandchildren. Help me!"

Roland was about to speak, but then the door opened, and the oldest man in Astrea entered, followed by his gargantuan, misshapen son.

"Old Man Madeira?" Samuel gawked in utter confusion.

"Yes, my boy, yes, it is me," Madeira said in his typical cheerful and grateful tone. He seemed to take pleasure in Samuel using his *Old Man* title out loud, even though it was something people only said in private out of courtesy.

Turning to Roland, Madeira said, "You've done well, High Commander. I'm sure the Queen would agree."

Roland simply nodded, then turned away from Samuel as if in shame.

"What's going on, Mr. Madeira?" Samuel asked, hopeful now that this man whom he knew and loved and had labored on behalf of for nearly his whole life was here, even if it was true that he served some deadly woman with wires coming out of her head from what people believed was a different universe. "Roland said you're—"

"That's right," Madeira interrupted. "I'm the Queen's Servant," he explained with a gentle smile.

"But...but..." Samuel stammered as countless memories of Madeira raising him like a distant grandfather filled his mind.

"Not to worry, my boy. I'll explain as much as I can. Come now, come with me. High Commander, again, I thank you for your service to Astrea, to the Queen, to me, and most of all to humanity."

High Commander Roland bowed nervously to the old man, and Samuel stared in disbelief as everyone and everything he knew was flipped upside down.

What the hell is going on? Samuel thought, shaking in confusion. *Madeira has been my enemy all this time? This sweet old man?*

Samuel looked down at the blood surrounding the chair.

"You...torture people?" Samuel asked, unable to imagine the old man hurting a plant, much less another human being.

"Come," Madeira said jovially, ignoring his dismay. "We are on a strict schedule now that things are in motion."

The old man's confident and gentle tone alongside Norman's severe look forced Samuel out of the chair. Everything seemed hazy and heavy, as if he were in a dream.

Is everything I've ever known a lie? Samuel considered, horror-struck as he reluctantly followed the old man. A part of him was in shock, but another part of him was still ready to break away from this madness and search for his family, no matter the risk to his own life.

"Samuel," Roland bellowed as Samuel passed through the door's threshold and into the hallway. He looked like his old self now—stoic and impenetrable. "I will do my best to protect your family…if I can find them."

Yes, Samuel rejoiced and nearly sobbed. *I knew it. I knew he would help.*

Samuel stopped and turned to face Roland, but Roland shook his head.

"You have to go with him, Samuel. If you want any chance of keeping your family safe, then do what he says. You understand me?"

Is it possible this is just a front? Samuel considered carefully, his family's life on the line. *Is he just saying this to stop me from fighting back?*

"There's no more time for talking with the High Commander, my boy," Madeira stated. "And timing is particularly important for this part of the plan."

Samuel shook his head, uncertain what to do, but Roland moved forward and pushed Samuel toward the old man and his strange, gargantuan son.

"Go," Roland said. "I will find them, Samuel. I will not allow Mona's grandchildren to die. I will protect them with my life," Roland issued, his voice like a blade through flesh.

Samuel clenched his fists, contracted his colossal musculature in helpless hatred for his inability to alter the course of events, and said through his own sharpened tone, "You fucking better, Roland."

Peering deep into Roland's eyes, the only conclusion Samuel could come to was that he really was telling the truth.

Goddamnit, Samuel scolded himself as he forced his legs to turn around and follow Madeira through the hall. *There's nothing I can do at the moment. If I run, Roland might be forced to intercept me. He's clearly got his hands tied with Madeira. He's a puppet attached to his own strings, but I could see it in his eyes: he isn't a bad man. My best option right now is to do what he says, at least for the time being. I'll know the right moment when it comes. For now, I have to trust Roland's eyes and believe him when he said my best bet to keep Sandra and the kids safe is to follow Madeira. For now, at least.*

Samuel scanned the old man and knew that he could break him with ease. He could likely even take down Norman since the large man had grown so weak in his old age.

I can't fully trust Roland. Not with my family. But I need to make it seem like I trust him. Just for now. Besides, with how old they both are, I have a better chance of escaping Madeira and Norman. For all I know, that's exactly what Roland is expecting me to do.

Straight ahead, a Queensguard deposited four dead bodies into the recycler, then stepped back and pressed a small button on the wall, sealing the tube and launching the recycler's metal arm. Without a sound, the pile of bodies was instantly squeezed into liquid through the tiny holes in the ground. Samuel winced, but the Queensguard looked unfazed, as though it were just another day.

Old Man Madeira hobbled along on his cane, and Norman followed alongside him. As they exited the recycler, Samuel saw that the procession of Queensguards was still emerging from the dark passage leading back to the Foundation. He twisted at the neck and saw an identical looking procession of Queensguards trudging to each recycler—four snaking lines of hulking metal carrying the corpses of Samuel's friends and neighbors and fellow citizens no matter where he turned his head.

And maybe my family too, Samuel thought in horror.

"Mr. Madeira," Samuel began, "my family, they—"

"Come on then, Samuel. Norman will pick me up. We must walk faster," Madeira explained as Norman lifted the old man into his arms, surprising Samuel with his strength since Madeira had said that his son was no longer capable of working. "It's important that only Queensguards see us here, and not any of the other citizens from the Luxury Quarters. And it is essential that we make it to our destination on time. I always thought that far too much of the plan hinged on getting this timing right, but I'm not going to argue with my better half."

"The Queen, you mean?" Samuel asked in disgust that Madeira could be so compliant and docile toward a lethal tyrant.

"Yes, the one they named the Queen. It was in response to that title that I began using the term Queensguard to refer to those she bestowed with the gift of the electric armor."

He calls it a gift, Samuel considered, weighing the terrible implications of Madeira's tone of joy concerning the Queen and her enslaved subjects.

"Who are you, Mr. Madeira? And who is the Queen? And…and what is going on? I feel like I'm going crazy here," Samuel pleaded, desperate for answers, any answers. All the while, he readied himself to either immediately run, or to knock out Norman with a fist to the skull and then run—whichever seemed like the best option at the moment.

"Can you please just take me to my family?" Samuel asked before throwing away all attempts at reason.

"I cannot," Madeira answered with seeming genuine regret. "I can, however, tell you who I am. Who I really am."

The way Madeira spoke made Samuel feel entranced, as if hearing the old man's true identity might elucidate some semblance of rationality concerning everything he had learned thus far.

"My full name is…Andre Madeira," the old man explained, pronouncing his full name with elongated, unfamiliar rolls of his tongue. "It's not a name that history remembers, and yet, I am the orchestrator of history as you know it. I am the founder of Astrea."

How is that possible? Samuel thought as he glanced over his shoulder and saw that they were approaching an area full of shadows—a perfect place to make his escape.

"But Mendel," Samuel protested, almost curious to hear Madeira's story. "Denis Mendel. Is he not real?"

"Oh," the old man said with a smile. "Mendel is real. Very real. He is also the founder."

"You are cofounders, then?"

"Something like that," Madeira answered cryptically.

"And the Queen?" Samuel asked, uncertain how much he could believe the words of this ancient man he had spent his entire life viewing as a distant grandfather.

But that doesn't matter. Just keep talking. Keep thinking I'm the docile fool you helped raise.

"She is part of my plans, and I am part of hers," Madeira answered as if it explained everything.

"You're the one who turned the world to hell, then? Is that what you're claiming?"

"Yes, my boy. I did."

Samuel shook his head, unable to accept that Old Man Madeira had worked alongside Mendel as cofounder of Astrea and creator of hell. He might be the Queen's Servant, but there was no way he was one of the architects of Astrea. All the while, Norman continued walking directly toward the area of dense shadows, exactly as Samuel hoped he would. It was out of sight from the processions of Queensguards as well.

"Why are you telling me this?" Samuel asked. "If it's all true, then why are you telling me?"

"Because just like the Queen," Madeira answered easily, as if expecting this exact question, "you, my boy, are central to my plans."

"Me?"

"Yes, you, Samuel. You see, I was beginning to think that I would never receive the signal. I was starting to think that the Queen had somehow broken free of my influence and made her own plans that didn't involve me. But that's not the case. The plans just took longer than I expected they would, and without direct contact with the Queen, I had to just wait all those years for a sign. And this morning I got it."

Finally, they arrived at the area of dense shadows. Norman carefully placed his father on the ground and helped him find his footing. Then, Madeira removed a small syringe from the pocket of his tunic and presented it to Samuel as if it were the most precious object that had ever existed. The syringe reflected the dim light of the closest glowglobe, revealing its contents to be a swirling, perfectly reflective substance.

I need to run now, Samuel thought, but he felt transfixed by what appeared to be a liquid mirror inside the syringe. Glints of dancing light whisked Samuel's awareness to a state of painful awe, devouring thoughts of his family with glimmering betrayal.

"What is it?" Samuel asked through a mystified whisper. It felt as though he were being drawn toward the substance. As if it were beckoning him to never look away.

176

"I found this on my bedside table. It's the sign I've been waiting for, Samuel. The sign that my plans are finally moving forward. It even came with a note that had a time written on it, down to the second." Madeira removed a small gold pocket watch that Samuel had never seen him with before. "We have exactly five minutes and eighteen seconds."

"Until?" Samuel asked, his mind overrun by a deep, inexplicable confusion and dread.

"Until the beginning finally comes to an end, my boy, and the next phase begins. It is time for the Earth and its people to ascend to the next rung of my ladder."

"Mendel's Ladder," Samuel said in shock. "So, you are Mendel, then?"

"No," Madeira said sincerely with a tinge of melancholy. "It's more complicated than that Samuel, and we don't have much time left for explanations."

The mention of time nearly running out struck Samuel like a sledgehammer to his spine, explosively convincing him that there was only one thing that mattered.

"My family," Samuel pleaded as a last ditch effort before resorting to sucker punching Norman and Madeira and running back to the Foundation and killing anything that might stand in the way of him and his family. "You have to help me. If you control this whole place, then you have to help me find my family and make sure they're safe."

"Oh no," Madeira corrected hastily. "I don't control Astrea. I am one of its citizens, Samuel. That much is true. Another me…a different me…he controls Astrea. The Queen controls Astrea. My original plans control Astrea. But not me. Not anymore."

"What does that mean?" Samuel demanded angrily, taking the old man by the arm and squeezing with furious rage. "I labored a lifetime for you, you old bastard."

Norman grabbed Samuel's hand and twisted it, breaking it without effort. Samuel stifled his screaming and gritted his teeth to endure the pulsing pain.

"That was too much, Norman," Madeira scolded gently. "But I suppose it doesn't matter, does it?"

Norman nodded in agreement.

"My family. Please," Samuel begged once more, knowing it would be better to enlist Madeira's help than to run wild and hope he could find his family before the Queensguards did. "Can't you just help my family. After everything I did for you? And for your son? He could have done his own labor, clearly, carrying you and breaking my hand with such ease. I'm just asking you to protect my family. Is that so much to ask?"

"Make no mistake, Samuel," Madeira corrected. "I have been crafting you. Forging you. Day after day. Year after year. Your labor was not meaningless. It has made you into who you are, and you are a truly good man, Samuel Kaminski. Honest, righteous, and most of all, selfless beyond any other. But I cannot do what I cannot do, my boy. And I cannot protect your family just as much as I will no longer be able to protect myself without Norman. He will be going with you. He has waited all these years for this moment. His moment. I am proud of you, Norman," Madeira said, patting the large man on the same hand he had just used to snap Samuel's bones.

"Going where?" Samuel asked, his heart suddenly beating quicker.

Madeira checked his golden pocket watch again, then turned to Norman and said, "It is time."

Norman unbuttoned his shirt, and Samuel reeled in horror at what he saw. Norman's chest and abdomen were covered in a sticky, yellow fungus-looking substance, which undulated across his body like disturbed water.

Samuel instinctively fell a few terrified steps back, gawking at the men as if they were aliens.

Run! Samuel urged his legs, but it was too late. He was only able to frantically turn himself around before the slimy yellow substance shot from the large man's chest in a volley of gooping strings that wrapped about Samuel's torso and pulled him tight against the large man's body.

"What the hell is this?" Samuel demanded as the substance grew and slithered over his limbs, chin, and forehead, constricting and squeezing so hard that he could barely even flex his muscles.

"That yellow substance is a variant of a particularly intelligent old world slime mold. Norman is not my son, Samuel. He's a Hybrid Nomad."

"A Nomad?" Samuel gasped, still trying desperately with all his might to muscle through the seemingly unbreakable slime.

"Yes, what your parents and the other Astreans came to refer to as the Changed People. They are my creation," Madeira responded proudly. "Well, technically the creation of Tomasz and Ruben, but I was the one who came up with the idea in the first place. So, my vision."

Madeira is mad, Samuel concluded wildly as he continued flexing and futilely struggling to break free of Norman's hold. *Or this is a nightmare. Norman can't be a monster from Earth. And Madeira isn't the creator of Earth's monsters. That isn't possible. None of this is possible.*

Madeira held the syringe to his eyes, admiring the substance as if it were manna from heaven, then in a single, swift movement, he injected it into Samuel's left shoulder.

"What have you done?" Samuel lashed, feeling a tingling at the injection site.

"A minute-twenty, Norman, get ready. It'll be quick. Very quick," Madeira stated calmly.

"What's happening? Tell me what you're doing," Samuel pleaded, madly flexing his mountainous musculature but still unable to move even an inch.

Madeira scanned Samuel and Norman's feet, inspecting them from several angles.

"Yes, this is the exact spot. It will be very quick," Madeira said, more to himself than Samuel or Norman. "That's what she said to me some thirty-four years ago—the last time I spoke directly to her—the last time anyone spoke directly to her. The Golden Wall has been sealed ever since the last revolution. She'll be opening that Golden Wall again soon enough. I'm sure of it," Madeira continued, rambling to himself as the slow beat of the Queensguards' footsteps ceaselessly resounded in the distance.

Samuel squirmed with every bit of strength his selfless labor had ever provided, but it was useless against Norman's slime—as if all those years of pain and self-torture at the power stations had been for nothing. All the while, Madeira went on rambling.

"This old brain still remembers the major parts of my plan, at least. Like this part with you, Samuel. It's a shame I'll miss seeing her again. She was always special—even more so than the others. I'm glad it was her in the end, at least."

I slaved away my life for this madman and a creature of hell, Samuel thought, deriding himself for being such a foolish failure of a man. The tingling in his arm began expanding, moving into his fingers and across his back. Samuel lifted his arm and gasped, going wide-eyed as he stared into his own reflection. Then his vision adjusted, and he realized that his arm was coated in the mirror substance, which was rapidly spreading across his entire body.

"What the hell is this?" Samuel nearly screamed, and Norman grunted and wobbled at Samuel's sudden, desperate burst of strength. Samuel tried to break free of Norman's slime again, but it was gripping him with inhuman strength.

"You are him, Samuel Kaminski. I knew you were him since you were a young boy. I knew it, Samuel, and the fact that you didn't die from that injection proves it. You're a perfect match. You're him, my boy. The Mirror-Man. The one who will command the Nomads and change everything."

"Mirror-Man?" Samuel gasped in grisly dread.

What is this lunatic doing to me? What the fuck is going on? Samuel's mind spiraled madly at the absurdity of being transformed into a mirror. *What the fuck does that even mean?*

Madeira checked his watch one last time, raised his head as if in exultant thanks, then stepped forward, just inches away from Samuel and Norman.

"I'm proud of you, Samuel Kaminski. I know you will do what's necessary. Thank you, my boy. For everything so far. And everything still to come." Andre Madeira took a deep breath, looked to the Golden Wall, smiled with tears in his eyes and said, "You can do it, my Queen. I know you can. Whatever or whoever it is you find out there—burn them down. Make them pay."

The mirror substance expanded over the whole of Samuel's body, and then everything changed. One second Samuel was transfixed by the mirror substance seeping without feeling toward his mouth and eyes, the sparkling white towers and Golden Wall of the Luxury Quarters reflected behind him, and the next second he was in outer space, sucked out of Astrea through a sudden opening in the ground that opened and closed again in a single heartbeat, leaving the three of them in free fall over the blazing blue Earth. The force of being blasted into the void

180

obliterated Andre Madeira's old, fragile body, shattering him into a collection of flittering pieces of rapidly crystallizing blood and guts.

Sandra! Samuel pleaded, screaming without sound. Every moment was an extra thousand feet of nothingness separating him from his loved ones.

How am I not dead? Samuel gawked in disbelief as he tumbled with bone crushing g-force. The right side of his body was numb, crystallized, and bloated, while the left side felt perfectly fine as it undulated as a reflective liquid. The substance continued spreading, returning feeling back to his right side and finally his entire body.

Transformed into a fucking mirror! You fool, Samuel Kaminski. You fucking fool! You're better off dead, you goddamn fool, because you'll never see your family again. Not now. Not ever.

Though Norman had not been shattered like the old man, he was also no longer the same being that Samuel had always known. Samuel could see in the reflection of his flailing mirror-limbs that Norman had burst into a giant tree made entirely of the yellow slime mold. Still, the slime clung to Samuel, refusing to let go.

The planet's gravity had them now, and as they tumbled in free fall toward the treacherous Earth, Samuel couldn't help feeling that he was falling from heaven, even though he knew that Astrea and Earth were both hell.

But my family is in Astrea, Samuel seethed within as he screamed soundlessly into the void. *Heaven is family,* Samuel knew, his mind racing in excruciating anguish. *And I just lost heaven forever.*

He wanted to die rather than live another moment knowing he would never see his family again, but the mirror substance wouldn't let him. From one hell to the next, Samuel Kaminski was cast down to Earth.

Violence is as natural to humanity as respiration. It is unavoidable in our current form. As long as we depend on natural evolution, we will always succumb to savagery. Our genetics are written in the language of cruelty and suffering. Our dexterous hands did not initially evolve to make tools. First, they evolved to punch and beat and strike. Our astonishing endurance was not forged for the sake of helping others. The original purpose was to chase and outlast every other form of life so that we may strip their exhausted flesh from their bones. Our creative intellect did not emerge through the lenses of compassion and empathy. Its genesis lies in exploitation and callousness.

Humanity in its current form is a reflection of nature, and nature is unforgiving, dispassionate, and heartless, for it cares only to continue and nothing else.

People call me violent, but my violence ends violence. This may seem hypocritical, illogical even, but as stated, violence is presently unavoidable. Our viciousness must be redirected and used for a higher purpose, or else we will never be rid of it, and we will be robbed of our myriad potential futures while still in the cradle.

Humanity is currently living through an era I have made overtly barbaric so that one day our natural inclination to beat our fists against one another may be transcended.

Until then, violence will continue, and as old powers give rise to new powers, the intensity of violence will naturally crescendo before humanity hears the final closing notes of the symphony I've been orchestrating since birth, the same orchestral tapestry the universe has been unfurling since the beginning of time.

From Mendel's Ladder: The Personal Journal of Denis Mendel, Recorded Circa 2063, Published June 2108 by Leif Mainstone, Federated Agency Publishing

Chapter 14
Old Powers and New

Time slowed, and Myriam went wide-eyed with equal horror and pride as she viewed Shira standing near the edge of the crater in Overdrive. Her lover was already dead, replaced by some terrible beast of unrestrained power.

Like a goddamn Hunter, she thought with glorious awe as she witnessed the full unleashing of Wintersvilla's infamous general, Shira Arcadia, Wielder of Wintersbane.

Wintersbane ejected from Shira's wrist, and Myriam saw that Shira's hands were totally shattered from slamming them impatiently against the ground.

It was probably her exo that did that intentionally, Myriam figured, as now the bones and ruptured flesh would be easier to break down and utilize in exchange for more time and explosive energy. Shira didn't need her hands anymore, just her blades, her spine, and her brain, which didn't even technically need to be alive. The exo could operate a corpse, if necessary, as long as it had flesh to convert to energy.

The winds grew progressively stronger as the hurricane wall and flaming vortex at its center rocketed faster than a bullet to their location. Shira let out another impatient battle cry, and Myriam knew that she would have already charged forward if her suit thought she had enough energy for such a maneuver.

She was already on the brink of death when she activated Overdrive, and since her very life is the exo's energy now, it must be saving what little life she has left for the blades rather than allowing her to charge forward, Myriam reasoned, knowing that an exo, despite being a thoughtless machine, was more cunning and quicker than any warrior that had ever lived.

Myriam zoomed in on the Hunter and was stunned by the complexity and strangeness of his adaptations. Its body was a horrifying, chimeric assortment of grotesque mutations, but its eyes were still the typical unaltered Hunter's eyes, those pale-yellow pupils behind vertical slits that Myriam dreamed of permanently closing each and every night.

"I will make you my second slayed Hunter, foul Butcher of the Wastes," Myriam threatened over the wild winds, and she felt her body tingle and flush orgasmically at the prospect of this battle's profound glory. Win or lose, to meet the Butcher on the battlefield would surely earn both her and Shira their rightful place in the Afterworld, where they would wage illustrious war forever in a dazzling, eternal free-for-all between the greatest female warriors who had ever lived. It didn't matter that Shira didn't believe in the Afterworld. Myriam was certain that within the next five minutes, they would both earn the indelible right to taste glory after death.

All of a sudden, faster than should be possible, the Hunter's wolf-like feet elongated and widened into thin, webbed pads. His thighs bulged to quintuple their current size, and he launched himself a hundred, then five hundred, then a thousand feet into the air in a quarter of a second, making it difficult for Myriam to visually track him. As the Hunter ascended into the sky, the rapidity of his adaptations did not falter, and he sprouted thick, heavy wings while the rest of his body smoothed itself for aerodynamic efficiency. Finally, he dive bombed at a 45-degree angle with the Earth and changed his body again in another quarter second, his hands stretching into giant claws and his face elongating into a sharp, beak-like cone. The Earth's rocky innards spewed into the air as the Hunter bored violently into the ground, burrowing beneath the women and Gambe with earthquake tremors.

Myriam gasped in utter disbelief at the terrifying speed of the Hunter's adaptations. In less than a second, the Hunter had undergone a series of biological transformations that any other Hunter would have required a full twenty seconds to complete.

By the time Myriam realized that the Hunter's diving vector was aligned precisely with the hidden entrance at the bottom of the crater, a whole additional second had passed, and she heard the upturning of gravel and sand as the Hunter blasted out of the crater wall. Myriam turned and saw that Shira had already launched herself over the edge and into the crater's depths.

"The girls!" Myriam screamed at Gambe over the still increasing 130 mph winds. Gambe nonchalantly waved his glimmering hand at her, brushing off her words unconcernedly.

Wesley finally lost his grip on the thick, dried out roots in the ground he was still clinging to. He tumbled across the ground and over the edge of one of the other craters. Although Myriam found Shira's compassion for the old slave adorable if not admirable, there was no time to help him. She bent at the knees and launched, slamming Summit Splitter against the ground to gain extra speed as she sailed over the crater's edge to intercept the Hunter alongside Shira.

As she shot through the tumultuous winds and fell into the crater's depths, she was forced to steel herself against her surging dismay at what she saw. The eight-foot entrance to the Downver tunnels was blocked by a colossal boulder that could only have been put there intentionally. There was no getting into Downver this way. The crater was a dead end. A trap.

It can't be! Myriam thought as she frantically scanned every inch of the crater to find that the girls were nowhere in sight. Off to one side of the boulder blocking the hidden entrance, a copy of Gambe stood over the exploded remains of Rooli's wooden flesh, which was scattered in gruesome chunks around the Hunter. The Hunter lay in a bloody mess on the ground as if paralyzed.

His dive must have shattered Rooli and vaporized the girls, Myriam concluded grimly, but she did not allow sadness to break her adamantine battle-focus. Instead, she let her rage and fury course and churn through her veins with the insatiable drive for vengeance.

We will avenge you, girls, if it's the last thing we do, she promised them, saving the bittersweet tears she would shed for them and the Hybrid and for Shira most of all until after the battle.

Already at the bottom of the crater, Shira wasted no time with thought or caution. In a supersonic flash, she pounced on the Hunter, her blades gouging and whirling and slashing and spinning at hypersonic speeds, shredding and dicing the Hunter and his wicked body-membrane as she heaved sprays of blood from her chest and mouth with every one of her grating, rapid breaths. A battle with a Hunter was always one of attrition. Without his body-membrane, the Hunter was no more lethal than Wesley, but the body-membrane wasn't just something a Hunter wore like an exo or clothing. It was truly a part of him—a thoroughly symbiotic relationship extending through every cell. The membrane couldn't just be ripped off the Hunter—it had to be worn down until it could no longer heal itself and the Hunter. At the swing rate of Shira's rampage, Myriam estimated that the Hunter's membrane was probably already nearly dead.

Why didn't the Butcher fight back? Myriam wondered nervously as she slammed against the ground nearly at terminal velocity, her exo exhausting the kinetic energy and absorbing the shock so that Myriam experienced no more than a gentle bump. The Hunter still just lay stupidly on the ground as Shira chopped it to pieces, and Myriam couldn't help feeling on edge at the possibility that this was some strange and unexpected strategy the Pair had devised before the battle.

Shira screamed, spraying her own blood into the liquified pool of remains that she continued hacking at with wild abandon, spattering the mix of her and the Hunter's innards into a haze of crimson fog.

It's dead, Myriam knew, nearly laughing in disbelief. *We did it. We killed the Butcher. Was that really all he had?* She couldn't help seeing the Hunter in aspects of Shira and herself, its body-membrane analogous to their exos, except that their exos had not failed them, nor were they totally useless without them. And yet, as Shira's exo refused to falter in its unstoppable brutality, Myriam felt less and less impressed by the exo's power.

We are bound to our exos through battle and blood, like the Hunter chained to his membrane and Huntress. Seeing the metal bars of her own exo and Shira's agonizing thrashing in the distance, Myriam suddenly felt sick, and she longed desperately to eject from the exo and feel her lover in her arms one last time.

I have to get out of this fucking exo, Myriam thought for the first time in her life, feeling self-loathing for thinking in such a weak manner.

The bullet-speed storm finally reached them, raging on the surface six hundred feet above and forcing the winds at the bottom of the canyon into a flurry of wild gusts. Standing on the edge of the crater, the thick dust cloud swallowed Gambe, who appeared unfazed by the unearthly winds before they finally occluded him fully from view. The copy of Gambe at the bottom of the crater just stood and excitedly watched Shira go on mindlessly massacring the pool of blood that was the Hunter's remains. The tumultuous dust cloud continued precipitating toward them like waves of heavy rain, funneling through whirlwinds of temperature differentials as it descended.

Though it had always felt like a natural part of her body, like an additional limb, now Myriam's exo felt like it was constricting her, squeezing the life out of her, and just as she was about to eject from it, the impossible happened.

With an explosive crack, the dilapidated mess of blood and guts and bones and brains resolidified in the blink of an eye, blasting Shira's already broken body into the air with a sanguine shockwave. The Hunter was but a two-dimensional sheet of flesh spread against the ground with a flat face at its center. His vacuous, open mouth turned red, then orange, then white-hot, and before Myriam could react, the flattened Hunter discharged a sun-hot beam of superheated atmosphere from its mouth, piercing Shira's metal sternum with ease and passing right on through her back, leaving a gaping, four inch diameter hole through the middle of her chest that Myriam could see right through. The beam pierced the dust clouds above, revealing Gambe still standing and observing them enthusiastically from the crater's edge before the churning dust cloud enveloped him once more.

How is the Butcher still alive? Myriam seethed as she dove toward Shira, desperate to taste the sweetness of battle despite each of her ports yearning to be freed from the exo.

Not now! she spat at this sudden tumorous growth of weakness in her mind.

The Hunter, somehow fully healed, reformed into the bipedal, humanoid shape of its birth. Then, his eyes rolled back in his head, and he looked about the crater with frantic urgency.

"My Huntress is distracted!" the Butcher growled with his rumbling guttural voice, teeth flashing menacingly. "Just run away! Please!"

Shira was already charging at the Hunter before he finished his words. Her mammary glands and pectoral muscles were consumed by the exo all at once, deflating her breasts to useless sacks of skin. Not bothering to fully repair the death-yawning hole in her chest, her body built strings of pulsing veins and arteries using the material stolen from her breasts, haphazardly stretching ropes of slick, pulsing viscera across the hole. Her skin was an endless series of open blisters exposing stringy, black necrotic flesh, leaving Myriam in awe that Shira was somehow still conscious, screaming savagely as her exo plunged her back into battle.

The Butcher pleading for them to run away actually stopped Myriam in her tracks. His tone was one of genuine sorrow and regret, something Myriam knew wasn't possible for Hunters to experience. But Myriam blinked and the despair and pleading in his face was no more. He was once again a beast who thirsted for violent retribution against every human being who still drew breath upon the Earth.

Shira's ten blades made contact with the Hunter's healed flesh all at once, but his skin turned to heavy iron scales at the last second, deflecting the onslaught. In another blink of an eye, his bones jutted with capricious spikes from his chasming flesh, branching again and again into endless curved barbs before thrusting them at Shira, who deflected each hypersonic lunge with ease and dove back at the Hunter, aiming for unscaled areas of his constantly transforming body.

Myriam ran forward, but at the speed and ferocity of their battle, she knew she would just be getting in Shira's way.

I have to do something though! Myriam demanded her body and exo. *Something! The warriors in the Afterworld surely watch us even as we speak. I cannot fail. Not now during the most glorious moment of my life.*

The winds above the canyon were slowing down, but they still raged with deafening gales. Thick, howling dust continued to precipitate, nearly upon them now. Myriam eyed the copy of Gambe at the bottom of the crater, still just standing and observing Shira's blood-drenched, feral skirmish with the Hunter rather than lifting a finger to help. Myriam glanced something at Gambe's feet; it was Aliana and Aurelia's backpacks, perfectly clean and not caked in their obliterated bodies. Then she saw it—a small hole between the ground and the boulder. It was just large enough for two thirteen-year-old girls to slip through.

They're not dead! Myriam rejoiced momentarily, regaining and steeling herself now that she knew there was even more at stake than glory.

The Hunter's mouth broke at the jaws and snapped unnaturally wide open as he contorted his spine at ninety degrees and fell flat to the ground, launching himself at Shira with his unhinged mouth full of razors. Shira dove and deflected, rapaciously parried and slashed, the metal of her exo glowing orange and beginning to buckle in some places. Her right calf imploded in offering to her exo, allowing her to match the Hunter's burst of speed. However, she only had so much flesh left to sacrifice, and most of what was left was black and fully dead already, significantly decreasing the energy it could provide.

Shira only has a minute left at most, Myriam considered, stilling her mind to a state of time-forged calm. *And after she's dead, the Butcher will go for the girls. Surely he can smell them even now. It would be simple for this Hunter to turn to a liquid and seep through that hole, then reform and mutilate the girls with sickening ease.*

The Hunter morphed through a series of wildly unpredictable forms and attack patterns, but he could not break the General of Wintersvilla, who responded with each of his attacks with her own in kind.

I don't have a choice, Myriam concluded finally, seeing no other way. *Life or death makes no difference. Only Glory. Shira will lead whole armies in the Afterworld, and I will be at her side always and forever. For glory, my gorgeous general! Strength and glory!*

Myriam took one last breath, held Shira's time-worn yet beautiful face in her mind, then entered her manual override command, activating Overdrive just as the precipitating, raging dust cloud fell across her vision, obscuring Shira and the Hunter's superhuman savagery. But that made no difference now. Her muscles bulged and veins inflated, exploding vessels in her eyes and nose. The unquenchable thirst for savage violence filled her, flooding her body with god-like strength. Myriam's exo was one of a kind. While Shira's standard issue exo was mostly titanium within a carbon-silicon matrix akin to chitin, Myriam's exo was enhanced with an iridium and zirconium alloy core and plating, along with staggeringly more intricate programming and biological compatibility. She was the benefactor of Wintersvilla's technological pinnacle, estimated to be at least ten times the power, speed, and intelligence of Shira's standard exo, and its full strength was about to be unleashed for the first and last time.

Myriam's exo translated every subtle sound and tremor into enhanced vision, illuminating the world in hyper detail. Time slowed to a crawl, and the lightning strikes exchanged between Shira and the Hunter became dream-like slow motion blows through water.

Die! she seethed at the repulsive, foul creature as Overdrive reconfigured her neurons into instruments of scalding hate. Summit Splitter felt as light as a twig, and she shifted her grip, holding it easily now in one hand despite its ten-foot length and seven-hundred-pound weight.

Die! Venomous animosity overwhelmed her mind as she felt herself slip away. Her final thought was a scene of herself and Shira and Rooli and the girls and even the slaves, all of them standing on the edge of a cliff, overlooking an endless expanse of old world pine trees, the same type that grew in the Wintersvilla arboretum where she loved to play and practice battle when she was still a child.

"Die, Butcher!" Myriam screamed, her mouth gaping with mindless rage as her lips and the corners of her mouth were ripped open. And then Myriam was no more. Overdrive took over completely. Myriam's exo launched with bone-shattering velocity across the floor of the crater, snapping her collarbones and dislodging both her shoulders from their sockets.

The exos recognized each other's presence, and they synced, allowing the women to fight in perfect unison, as if they were composed of a single body. Myriam's left hand gouged with her claws, and her right hand swung Summit Splitter in a furious barrage, slicing it through the solid walls and ground of the crater with each swing against the Hunter as if the Earth were suddenly made of soft animal fat. Despite the speed of both women's blades, their synced exos made them move like a single organism, each of their swings a response to the other's. The Hunter adapted in endless ways, his body-membrane utilizing genetic sequencing and patterns from every species that had ever existed, even long dead extinct monsters from millions of years in the past. An infinite database of life and all its varied evolutionary strategies was at the Hunter's disposal. Every one of the Hunter's subtle movements gave way to an unpredictable alteration. It parried with mace-shaped bones as hard as diamond and riposted with its barbed tongue like a whip and defended with forearms turned to unbreakable shells and countered with jet sprays of acid so corrosive that it could bend metal and melt bone. But the Women of Wintersvilla fought like demons, and if Hunters could experience nightmares, it was these blood-wild women who would strike fear into their hearts and make them wish they did not have to wake up.

Summit Splitter cleaved as more than a dozen blades sliced and gouged and pierced, and for a moment, it seemed like the Hunter was slowing down, his adaptations becoming more patterned and predictable with every second.

Shira looked as though she were in the late stages of some full body flesh-eating disease, and she faltered for only one painful moment, but it must have been exactly what the Hunter was waiting for. He had apparently been fighting his own war of attrition against the women, probably betting that their sleek metal suits would run out of juice long before his body-membrane did. The Hunter dove at the weakened Shira suddenly, leaving himself fully open to Summit Splitter's cleaving blow. Myriam arced the giant blade over her head and severed the Hunter in two, but just as quickly, the Hunter, with only the upper half of his body, tore Shira's right arm out of her torso, ripping away a whole section of her exo with it.

The Hunter slammed his fists against Shira's torn body and rocketed himself back to his legs, dodging two consecutive cleaves from Summit Splitter. His body reconnected, and as his arms morphed into mantis-like blades, he dove again at Shira. In response, Myriam's exo sprayed the explosive gel across the whole of Summit Splitter and ignited a concoction prepared for extreme rates of thermal release rather than a kinetic blast. Summit Splitter erupted with fervid heat, turning the metal white-hot and boiling the air around them. Myriam swung and deflected the Hunter's attack against Shira, strewing molten sparks across all three of their bodies as she sliced the lava-hot blade through the air and through the earth with ferocious swings faster than sound. She swung again and again and again, each time with greater ferocity. The Hunter's flesh melted against the blade, then reformed, bubbling and blistering, then flattening again to a state of perfect vitality. The intense radiation blinded both women, but their eyes were unneeded, so their suits consumed them and converted them into explosions of energy. Both women dove at the Hunter, but Shira was far too slow now, and the Hunter once again allowed Myriam to hit him. This time he sacrificed one of his legs in exchange for slamming against Shira and growing an additional arm in order to rip away her three remaining limbs with a single explosive tug, sending Shira's torso flying in a splattering of her dwindling vital fluids. In another flash, his body turned mushroom shaped, and he launched like a spore back to his leg, reattaching it in an instantaneous movement.

The veins around Myriam's ports began turning purple black, but she didn't take notice of her ports nor even Shira, who still somehow clung to life as the remaining sections of her exo forced her back into the battle by rolling and dragging her body along the ground with her mouth.

Myriam dove and gouged the Hunter with titanous swings from her blazing blade, and it seemed like an eternity passed as they exchanged blows, but all it took was a fraction of a second, and the Hunter found his opening and headbutted Myriam's left leg with a skull of thick iron. The endoskeleton and exoskeleton of her leg shattered as the rest of her body was whipped across the ground by the force of the Hunter's head-on collision. Summit Splitter went flying in the opposite direction, scalding the Earth as it finally came to a sizzling rest hundreds of feet away.

Myriam wasn't even close to being finished. She flipped herself onto her arms and bent her single leg over her head like a striking appendage. Then she scurried forward on her hands, looking like a scorpion as she extended the heel blade from her remaining foot. Her exo haphazardly patched the stump of her lost leg, quelling further blood loss so that it would have more of Myriam to consume in its unceasing pursuit to kill.

"That's enough," came the carefree voice of Gambe.

The Hunter's body elongated in a serpentine fashion, and he dove at Myriam, slithering across the ground, his body covered in pincers and blades and a multitude of hungry mouths full of sharpened teeth. Myriam readied her heel-blade, but a second before the Hunter landed his strike against the strongest Woman of Wintersvilla, Gambe appeared like lightning and grabbed the Hunter with just one hand, subduing his advance by some unknown means. The Hunter's body went limp in Gambe's grip, and he slowly began morphing back into his birth form.

Myriam lunged at the defenseless Hunter, and with just a word, Gambe did the unthinkable.

"Stop," he issued to Myriam, and though it should be impossible, he somehow deactivated her state of Overdrive, plunging her full awareness back into her broken body. Her skin roared with stinging pain, black and blistered with third degree burns from Summit Splitter's blazing heat. With her eyeballs consumed completely, Myriam's exo utilized the vibrations of the environment to generate a visual representation of her surroundings in her racing mind. She peered down and saw that her right hand and forearm were fully melted away, leaving only charred bone. Fragments of bone crumbled as she lifted the useless but painless hand, and she forced herself to steel her mind against the hideous sight.

Gambe waved his open hand, effortlessly clearing the dust and settling the winds to an eerie silence.

To Myriam's left, just a few feet away, the handful of self-contained metal beams that remained of Shira's exo still dragged her body forward by her now broken teeth as blood poured freely from every surface of her body. Even her ears bled profusely, the inner cavities ruptured by the battle's hypersonic booms as her nearly destroyed exo gave up on applying the inner pressure and stabilization needed to keep her inner ear intact. She was blind, deaf, maimed, burnt, broken and torn to pieces, but still the insatiable hunger for carnage did not abate. It should have been a glorious sight, but it was the most horrific thing Myriam had ever seen.

"Shira!" Myriam screamed, suddenly abandoning all thoughts of glory and violence. "My gorgeous general! My love! My love!"

The agony of seeing Shira's mindless, charred, oozing torso still desperately demanding battle was too much for Myriam. Gambe didn't stop her as she crawled with the help of her now constricting exo on her two functional limbs to her already dead love, as Shira's movements were more like post-death muscle spasms than actual willful acts.

Myriam did not hesitate to apply the thermal gel to the still firing mind of war within the few remaining scored and warped metal bars of Shira's exo. And then she ignited them, severing their connection from Shira's spine once and for all. Shira's blood-curdling panting turned to gentle silence, and her body finally gave up.

This world did not deserve you, Shira. And neither does the Afterworld. You will be a goddess on those illustrious battlefields spanning eternity. I can already see it, my love, Myriam said within, visions of the Afterworld filling her mind like a bridge to the promised land of warriors.

Gambe stared at the Hunter, cocking his head as if trying to solve a puzzle. The Hunter was fully paralyzed and unable to speak in the metal man's grasp. Myriam saw that Gambe's metal had penetrated directly into the body-membrane rather than the Hunter's actual body. The metal tendrilled and spread, appearing like a neurological network across the Hunter's skin.

He could have stopped the Hunter at any time, Myriam realized with sordid dismay as she stared at the smoldering remains of her wife. *There was no need for any of this. The bastard could have ended all of this with a wave of his hand. He may be metal, and the Butcher may not be human, but they still look like men. And they sound like men. And they act like men. I despise this world of men,* Myriam seethed within.

"I'm sorry," Myriam gushed to Shira, and she ejected from her exo, her ports aflame with the black, splintering veins of oncoming death. Blinded and without the aid of her exo, Myriam felt for Shira by touch, found her, then pulled her corpse to her chest and embraced her love, not caring that she was holding a charred, bloody husk of a human being. This was Shira. Her general. Her wife. Her love. Her very soul. Tears of blood filled with both sorrow and joy streamed from Myriam's mangled, empty eye sockets. She had fought valiantly and selflessly in battle alongside Shira, and now the Afterworld was a guarantee for them.

"I want to die with you," Myriam told Shira. "We did what we could for the girls. We took them all this way, my love. I want to die now with you and do battle in the Afterworld at your side." She hugged her closer and said, "You still owe me a proper honeymoon, damnit, and I can't imagine anything more perfect."

"Would ya please be quiet, woman?" Gambe asked with surprising gentleness. "I ain't done with ya, ya feel me? I got plans for ya. I ain't ready to see ya die yet."

Myriam ignored the metal man and went on caressing Shira's shattered skull. She was pleased to feel the stump of her leg rip back open, the lackluster repair from Overdrive failing and leaving her quickly bleeding out.

Good, she thought, her smile wide with satisfaction and fulfillment. *Let me drain out and go to my love's side.*

Gambe shrugged and left Myriam to gush blood for the time being.

"Ya in there, Huntress? I got some questions for ya," Gambe stated like a friend at a neighbor's door. Tendrils of Gambe's metal snaked out of the Butcher's despairing, forlorn eyes and brain. The pale yellow of his eyes fluttered to the back of his head, and then they returned, glaring murder at Gambe.

"There she is," Gambe marveled. "'Sup with your Hunter, eh? He all sad and...weird, ya feel me?"

"His brain was corrupted by a human, and now he is stupid like the rest of you," the Huntress growled with Thompson's horrifying voice, like a tortured demon stuck in a cycle of agonizing, unceasing death throes.

Gambe chuckled at the Huntress' verbal attack and nodded in satisfaction.

"You Huntresses are vile as they come. It's always fun makin' one of your acquaintance, always an interestin' conversation or battle or both, ya feel me?" Gambe threatened lackadaisically.

"How many of us have you killed?"

"I lost count," Gambe admitted with a hoot of laughter, "but I ain't one for numbers either, so that ain't a boast, ya feel me? But it's been enough of ya to know that I can flatten ya like a gravestone inside that den ya dug like a goddamn ol' world badger. I can see ya, Huntress, as if ya were right in front of me. And there ain't nowhere you can hide where I ain't gonna find ya, ya feel me? So just answer my questions. What's the deal with your Hunter and that body-membrane?"

"Body-membrane?" the Huntress spat, clearly spiteful that she was being forced to talk to this insolent machine man.

Myriam couldn't help but respect the Huntress' contempt for the man, machine or not. The uncomfortable thought that she and the Huntress were far too alike crossed her mind like an arrow through mist, and she let it pass, savoring her final moments with images of fucking Shira in back-arching ecstasy and decimating the Hunter in glorious battle.

"You mean the skinsuit?" the Huntress checked. "I don't fucking know either. You know how frustrating that is? I had a fucking skinsuit ready for him, and he already fucking had one. It's fucking ridiculous. That's not how the Eternal Hunt works."

"He supposed to come find ya and view ya as a merciful goddess who cured his pain," Gambe recited.

"Fucking right," the Huntress simmered. "But that skinsuit is special somehow, as you had the privilege of observing. What the fuck are you anyway, huh? You're non-fermionic, I can see that. But Marrow says you're something pure. So, what the fuck are you made of?"

"Beats me," Gambe stated simply, and Myriam couldn't help furrowing at the strangeness of these blood-thirsty, merciless titans, standing here discussing their states of being.

"Mom would know. Prolly Julian too. Oh, and Harald, he's the Sixth. He knows everything, and he's even more ruthless than you. I bet ya you would like him, Huntress. It's a shame, but—"

"You don't know what you are?" the Huntress interrupted with childish condescension. "You really are stupid like a human. But you're not weak, I'll give you that."

"I never said I ain't stupid, Huntress. I ain't know shit about shit, ya feel me? But that ain't matter to me. I'm a pathway of neoevolution that your pathetic Mendel could never even fathom. Mom was always better than him, ya feel me?"

"Do you live with your mom, or what? Like an old world teenager? What the fuck are you, damnit? Who are you?"

"You don't know?" Gambe asked with genuine shock. "I am Gambe, the Fourth Prodigal Son of the Agency. It's a pleasure, Huntress."

"I can't say the same, Gambe. And—" the Huntress said, stopping suddenly mid speech. The Butcher's eyes rolled back in his vertical slits, and then he was once again full of torment and contrition.

"Hurry!" the Butcher said urgently. "Just run! All of you!"

Gambe cocked his head, then burst out in laughter, his bass voice wailing across the canyon of mangled entrails and crimson dunes of dust.

"What in the actual fuck is up with ya?" Gambe asked. "This just an impressive act?"

"Please! No one has to die today," the Butcher begged in such a pathetic tone that Myriam almost felt sorry for the wicked creature, before reminding herself that it had to be a trick.

Again, the Butcher's eyes rolled with torturous fluttering, and then the Huntress took back control.

"You know what you are, Gambe?"

Gambe looked caught off guard, and he nodded at the Huntress, telling her to go on.

"A misstep. An abomination. An affront to Ascension."

Gambe chuckled and shrugged. "And yet, I'm the one holdin' ya here. I'm the apex predator, and you the endangered and soon to be extinct animal, ya feel me? You the old power. I'm the new. But I ain't gonna kill any of ya, though. Y'all made me lose those girls, but it ain't no thing. Julian will pick 'em up and bring 'em to Mom. They walkin' into a spider web, ya feel me? But since I lost those girls, I gotta make up for it somehow. And that means I'm goin' to come collect ya and take ya and the Hunter and this Wintersvilla Woman with me to the Agency. I bet Mom'll want to do some experiments. That's kind of her thing, ya feel me?"

A pang of terror sprang through Myriam as she imagined herself chained to some laboratory wall as metal freaks tortured her for all of time.

No, I refuse that fate. Her blood continued flowing from her severed limb, and though she felt lightheaded and cold, she considered that it might not be enough—that Gambe might have a way to stifle the bleeding at the last minute and keep her alive long enough to steal her away to some grotesque society of beings who had long ago abandoned their humanity in favor of soul-deforming power.

Kill me! she demanded of her heart, entering the code for Overdrive over and over again in her mind even though her exo was a few feet away, standing erect like a monument to Wintersvilla's tenacious refusal to be wiped from history.

"That's fine," the Huntress agreed easily. "I'll go with you willingly to the Agency. You may be a misstep, but you are a powerful and worthwhile misstep. I see that now," the Huntress said candidly. "I bow to your power, Gambe."

Gambe allowed himself a few puffs of satisfactory laughter then said, "I knew Huntresses were intelligent, but not this much. Smart move, Huntress. Maybe Mom'll even make ya the first Prodigal Daughter, ya feel me?"

"It would be a dream come true," the Huntress purred.

Myriam placed her claws against her neck, hoping that her ancestors and Shira and those watching from the Afterworld would understand that she was not killing herself out of weakness. She could not let the Agency use her, not after seeing what they had become. Gambe and his people were soulless, seeing everyone around them as a tool or resource to be extracted and understood. The Huntress could go with them and undergo some terrible transformation. Myriam refused to be a part of that madness.

She applied pressure, and the three blades sank a centimeter into her neck then stopped suddenly, her body fully paralyzed.

Gambe said, "Enough, Wintersvilla Woman. You belong to the Agency now. Mom gonna be happy, I know it."

How? Myriam gasped. *It isn't just my Overdrive. He can control my whole body like a puppet.*

Myriam struggled against Gambe's hold, but she found that it was like attempting to move a whole flesh tree.

"Won't you do me a favor, Gambe, Fourth Prodigal Son of the Agency?" the Huntress entreated the metal monstrosity. "That copy of you near the blocked off hidden entrance—would you merge it back into this main body? I want to see such a feat in action. It would be a pleasure, my good sir."

Gambe heaved his shoulders in pleasant disbelief. "Well, certainly, Huntress. That's easy enough. I appreciate ya goin' along with me willingly, ya feel me? I ain't no villain, I just don't wanna piss off Mom, ya feel me? And I just wanna see her happy."

"Makes sense," the Huntress offered sweetly.

The copy of Gambe collapsed into a swarm and coated Gambe from head to toe, sinking into his body as if the swarm were pebbles dropped into water.

"You know, Gambe. You really are incredible. But you're surprisingly easy to probe and understand when I really think about it, you know that?"

"That so?" Gambe said with amusement.

"Yeah," the Huntress chuckled sweetly. "You see, Marrow could tell me that you're non-fermionic, but I can still see you. So, you're still interacting with photons. That means your subatomic structure still has a charge and a half-spin. Isn't that right?"

Gambe shook his head and shrugged. "I ain't know about all that. You can ask Mom all about it though when we get back to the Agency, ya feel me?"

"So that must mean your subatomic particles have a negative half-spin, implying that you're made of anti-fermions, or antimatter."

Like Gambe, Myriam wasn't sure what the Huntress was talking about. All that mattered was that she find a way to sink the blades another quarter inch into her flesh and drown to death on her blood so that she may continue basking in glory forever in the Afterworld with her love.

"I don't know for sure how you're stabilizing yourself," the Huntress continued. "I don't know how you're stopping the atmosphere and the ground from actually touching you. Some type of repulsive electromagnetic shield of some sort, or some other type of containment to keep you preserved in your own little vacuum, maybe?"

"Like I said, Huntress, I ain't know."

"Me neither. Not completely. But I don't have to have you fully figured out to know how to destroy you, Gambe," she threatened with a mercurial shift in her tone.

Gambe laughed unconcernedly at her open threat. "What ya gonna do, Huntress, sick another Hunter on my metal ass?"

"No," Volya laughed back through her Hunter's deep, abyssal voice. "Mendel has given me a new, unexpected weapon."

Gambe hesitated for a moment, then said, "What ya mean, Huntress? I'm a weapons expert. What kind of weapon we talkin'?" he asked, still not at all concerned for his safety.

"A peculiar weapon, Gambe. One intended for this very moment, it would seem."

Gambe chuckled excitedly.

"Show me," he said, as if placing a sword down his throat and offering her the hilt.

"Oh, I will, Gambe. The whole of the Wastelands is going to witness it. You stupid fuck. Your arrogance and lack of focus is your downfall," the Huntress spat, reverting back to her original wicked temperament.

Myriam rejoiced that their conversation was taking so long, for now she felt cold as ice, and though she no longer had eyes to see, she understood that the only reason she wasn't colder was that she was submerged in a warm pool of her and Shira's blood.

"Well? Where the weapon at?" Gambe asked impatiently.

I'll be dead in less than a minute, Myriam hoped, grateful that she would not have to take her own life and be forced to explain her actions to those legendary warriors of the Afterworld.

"You're anxious for death?" the Huntress asked Gambe, but the metal man just shrugged and looked around for the promised display of the so-called peculiar weapon.

I'm on my way, my gorgeous general, Myriam said as a gentle breeze, which she had not even noticed until now, caressed her mangled cheek. *Wait for me. Don't charge into the final battle without me, my love. We fought together in life, and we will fight together forever in death.*

"I really wasn't sure how I'd beat you, Gambe. I had resolved to dying today, and I was fine with it, for death on the Eternal Hunt is only right. But Mendel is truly a god, Gambe. He's planned for everything. Every little thing. Even you."

Gambe sensed something strange directly above them, and he lifted his head to see Astrea passing by, the city in the sky orbiting like a reflective, echoing tomb, perpetually reminding the survivors of Earth that the hell they endured was planned and executed by the same individual who escaped it all by seeking refuge in space away from the nightmare he forced the world to suffer.

"Do you know what happens when matter and antimatter meet, Gambe? Annihilation!" the Huntress spat, and her words called down a golden lance of radiant light like a spear from heaven. The atmosphere exploded, sending shockwaves across the vertical length of the exotic beam of rippling power. Faster than Gambe could react, the golden beam hit the center of his metal skull, piercing the strange, stabilizing shield around his body. The non-fermionic substance constituting his body made contact with the atmosphere, instantaneously annihilating the matter-antimatter mix in an ultrabright column of ravenous, radioactive power.

Myriam could not see the beautiful, blinding white light coaxing her to the Afterworld where she would fuck and fight alongside her lover for all eternity, but it still consumed her whole, washing away the world in a profound blaze of luminous glory.

My dream and the Earth's dream are one in the same. A dream of equanimity. Harmony. Balance.

The human mind depends on a neural network to exist. The Earth itself, a planetary being, is the same. Earth's singular mind has been unconscious since its genesis—a whole four billion years of sessility and stupidity, just waiting for the right life to grow and construct its neurology so that it may finally awaken unto itself. The Nomads are still building this network, but already the rudimentary mind of Earth speaks to me, and I to it.

The Earth and I have discovered that our plans align. My will and Earth's will are one in the same.

Soon I will enter a new state of being, abandoning the old. This new state of being is the precursor to another. And another after that.

Who knows how far the ladder ascends? All we can do is climb.

From Mendel's Ladder: The Personal Journal of Denis Mendel, Recorded Circa 2065, Published June 2108 by Leif Mainstone, Federated Agency Publishing

Chapter 15
His Foretold Future

S waying Goldenrod slinked across the ground, following her dwindling pack to the outskirts of the Three Scars, where a great cataclysm of hypersonic explosions raged at the bottom of the Scar containing the blocked off entrance to the human city. She and the rest of her pack had dragged the boulder across the sacred Butcher Wastelands for many moons, but Swaying Goldenrod didn't concern herself with keeping track of time. That was Funneled Chanterelle's job, and he had already transitioned the previous night, bursting into resplendent, fanning woodland mushrooms reaching vertically toward the clouds and funneling back down through the Earth to feed on the soil's nutrients. A few additional chuting roots of the flesh tree that had been Funneled Chanterelle were undoubtedly attached directly to the global mycelial network, providing access to the senses of all other connected life around the world, and also bearing their own senses for the taking.

The carnage taking place in the closest Scar finally ended, and the hurricane dust clouds raging above slowly cleared, turning everything silent as if the world had suddenly stopped spinning.

Almost time for transition, Swaying Goldenrod told herself, listening for His voice to fill her patiently waiting aural organs with the ecstasy of being told her time had come. *I feel,* she thought excitedly, *almost time.*

Across the world, the People of the lands and seas and skies labored with love, moving to the music of His orchestration as they constructed Earth's new organs and expanded its infantile mind.

Swaying Goldenrod could not tap into the network yet—her form did not allow for it until she transitioned. But she glided her shallow roots through the soil, tilling it lovingly as she relinquished her tangle grass companions back to Earth and rooted herself fatefully beside the others. A small patch of slapping ferns tore through the flesh of a handful of her thousand skinny antennae, but they were just doing their fateful job. Swaying Goldenrod brushed away her dead antennae, feeding the soilies and shooters diligently collecting and distributing nutrients across Earth's face, then she directed her eyestrings to the sky above the Three Scars.

"It come now," Hulking Corpse Flower whispered using his flesh-rotting scent. The other nineteen People of Earth nodded in their own way, including Swaying Goldenrod, who swayed with excitement.

Several more minutes of silence passed, and Swaying Goldenrod cherished these final views of the Butcher Wastelands. Despite its desolation, the sacred area still exuded the beauty of Earth, and that was enough for Swaying Goldenrod. It was enough for all People of Earth.

Arching bands of colossal fungus nets lined the distant eastern horizon, some of them harvesting, some of them dispersing, all of them a symphonic extension of His divine plans.

The sky split in half suddenly as a beam of spectral golden light extended like a vertically grown vine from the stars to the Earth, lancing the Scar with the fabled Golden Stem, just as it was said in His Foretold Future. Then the beam exploded outward, instantly expanding into a pillar of blinding, snow-white light that ejected the Earth's breath and its numerous layers of gaseous skins into the void outside the planet, far beyond even City in the Sky.

Despite being miles away, the unnaturally bright light still blinded most of Swaying Goldenrod's eyestrings. She discarded them and pivoted her bushy body so that her rear eyestrings could see the rest of the foretold future playing out in real time.

Exactly as He planned, the shockwave from the Golden Stem slammed against the Mirror-Man's reflective body, sending him and a flesh tree of yellow slime mold sailing toward the great Western Waters, where the titanically expansive living ships fed on evaporated salts and swam through the sky in endless, globe-circling flights of fancy.

Tomasz Novak, Swaying Goldenrod thought, trying out the name from the unwavering past as if for flavor. *Sour, bitter, bad,* Swaying Goldenrod thought as she extinguished the name and the visions of Tomasz' multitudinous swarming body from her mind.

Now you transition, came His glorious voice, whispering the long-awaited ecstasy into Swaying Goldenrod's aural organs. *A life fulfilled. May second life restore, Swaying Goldenrod of the Butcher Wastelands,* the voice of Earth whispered into her mind in joyous celebration of her grueling but rewarding nine-Sol-revolution life, of which virtually every minute had been spent dragging the enormous boulder across the face of Earth alongside her pack.

Thank you, Earth, Swaying Goldenrod issued, and she knew the others had heard His voice as well, for the entire pack transitioned simultaneously, intertwining their branches and roots as they grew into an isolated but dense flesh tree grove. As their branches and flesh pods sprouted, their roots went on snaking through Earth's flesh, reaching far enough to merge their cells with those of the global mycelial network.

In her final moments of individual consciousness, Swaying Goldenrod peered through the senses of the flesh trees that had once been People of Earth called Inflated Puffball and Resilient Nightshade. They stood vigil in Hunter Dreaming, their flesh pods overflowing with the vitality of more People formed in direct response to Earth's glorious plans for Ascension. Swaying Goldenrod's awareness zoomed out, and among many of Earth's new organs, she saw the Great Honey Mushroom that towered thirty-six miles into the sky. It grew from the base of one of the Great Scars of the East, where shuffling masses of People formed packs numbering in the millions, ready and waiting for the Mirror-Man to command them and further His will. Now a new phase of His plans would begin, and the next rung of Mendel's Ladder would be ascended, fulfilling the very purpose of the universe and life itself.

Full of gratitude and awe, Swaying Goldenrod's consciousness faded completely, replacing her thoughts with unwavering compassion and care for her already sprouting flesh pods.

To Be Continued

Author's Note

If you have a few minutes, please take some time to leave a rating or review for this book.

AMAZON and GOODREADS

Thank you so much for your help!

– E. S. Fein

CONTINUE READING FOR A SNEAK PEAK OF BOOK 2!

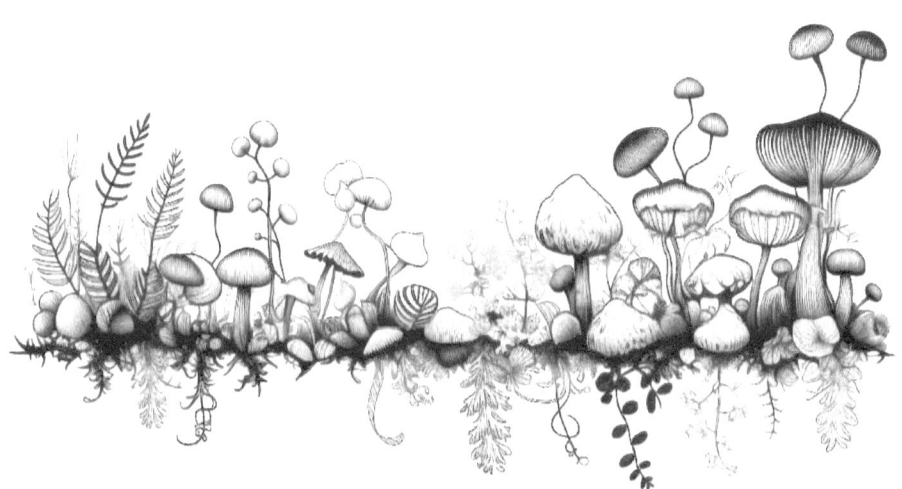

Volume 2

Winter's Remains

All of life and every individual exists on a spectrum of wickedness and selfishness. The elite of the world, the rich and powerful, are the most wicked and selfish among us. They are not noble. Neither are they righteous nor honest. They are the rot confining humanity to this singular cosmic speck of detritus. Even though I am one of them now—the very worst of them—they are still my enemy. They always have been. I was born as scum beneath their gilded boots—a sewer rat forced to fend for myself in the reckless and debaucherous remains left in the wake of the rich and powerful's global parading at the expense of the poor and meek. I have adopted their pretentious mannerisms. I have infiltrated their families and business partners. I have generated wealth beyond measure. I have become one of them—a Titan— but that doesn't change that they are my enemy, now and forever.

Of the ten Titans who agreed to my plan for the Earth and humanity, four will betray me outright. They will refuse to board Astrea, even though they will encourage their families to leave the Earth. They will not relinquish their power; they will choose instead to utilize their power and each of their families' respective scientific expertise to build their own empires of dirt. Of course, these betrayals are all part of my plan. Each betrayal is a rung of my ladder.

John Downver desires recognition, not power. He wants praise, not control. He is still as recklessly hedonistic as the rest of them. However, he is harmless compared to the others, and he will serve well as the architect and initial leader of Downver, until he dies of a heart attack a decade or so after Downver's founding. He won't know it, but I will aid him in Downver's construction.

Tomasz Novak desires security and superiority. He is a coward and a shortsighted academic. I will allow him to take refuge over the Pacific Ocean, pitifully hiding from my weapons and my

Nomads as he constructs his own biological counterattacks. He will believe himself safe and secure, and I will let him feel this way until the year 2099. Until then, he will continue working for me, even when he believes he's working against me.

Gladys Mainstone, my dear Gladys. She is the only one of the Titans I respect. Her vision is broad, and her ambitions lie far beyond material gain and ephemeral hedonism. And yet, she is still unable to let go of her own selfish desires. Regardless, her efforts against me will be crucial to my Ascension.

Craig Winters is the epitome of the filth constituting humanity's "upper" echelons. Vile, immoral, sadistic, proud. He is one of the very worst humans who has ever existed or will ever exist. He takes pleasure in the suffering of others, and he experiences pain at the pleasure of others. And yet, he still has a role in all this. His empire, Wintersvilla, which he will build atop the coming destruction of Vancouver, will eventually give rise to a great matriarchy of enhanced female warriors. The fall of this great matriarchy is part of my plan.

It's all part of my plan. I hold every string, including my own. I speak the very words of fate.

I am not selfish, and though I am wicked, it is only to combat the wickedness and selfishness still lingering in humanity's genetics like black mold. As my ladder is climbed, the divine light of Ascension will clear the mold away, and we will all be cleansed. Including me.

It's all part of my plan. Everything and everyone.

From Mendel's Ladder: The Personal Journal of Denis Mendel, Written Circa 2039, Published June 2108 by Leif Mainstone, Federated Agency Publishing

Chapter 1
The Fall of Wintersvilla

Year: 2098

A gentle breeze outside the Matriarch's throne room sighed like a lover's touch, filling Shira's wandering mind with pleasant thoughts of Myriam. The permanently blue daytime sky was filled with puffy white clouds that cast colossal shadows across the handful of old world steel towers constituting Wintersvilla's Central Command District. Shira could still remember a time when onslaughts of ink-black typhoons collided with the city on a weekly basis, year-round, making the steel of the hundred-year-old buildings wail as they resisted the cataclysmic winds caused by old world humanity's careless and wanton destruction of the entire planet's climate. Imagining such atmospheric chaos almost seemed like a distant dream now, for the Nomads had fully tamed Earth's climate over a decade ago. There were no more typhoons, but neither was there rain. There were no more blizzards, but neither was there snow. There weren't even any strong gusts of wind. The sky remained blue, the sun shined brightly, and the cotton white clouds drifted aimlessly, day and night.

Wintersvilla managed without precipitation by desalinating seawater, thereby using the ocean to irrigate their old world crops and provide water to its millions of citizens. Shira wasn't sure how the rest of the world and life in general could survive without rain or weather variation, but of course, the world and its people weren't the same anymore. It was their world   the Nomads, and Shira wondered what it might look like in a hundred more years. There was a time she thought that Wintersvilla might actually have a chance at expanding far beyond its current borders—at making the whole world a Matriarchy, like Nomusa always dreamed. But Shira knew those dreams were over, destroyed by the reality of waking life.

This world belongs to the Nomads. It's only a matter of time, Shira thought uneasily. *South Wintersvilla or North Wintersvilla or the farms and fisheries outside the city's walls—it doesn't matter where. It all belongs to them. They choose not to take it—that's the only reason we have any of it. It's only a matter of time before every inch of Wintersvilla is turned to soil and flesh trees. And with the Rover King at our border, we might already be out of time.*

Shira envisioned Nomusa's throne room as seen from above, an anachronistic metal yurt surrounded by the sprawling metal metropolis constituting North Wintersvilla's Command District. She imagined the thick crimson smoke pouring out of the yurt's several chimneys, telling the citizens of the Wintersvilla Matriarchy that an Inner Circle meeting was in session, and that the meeting was not to be disrupted.

The best possible thing that could happen for Wintersvilla is for this meeting to be disrupted. The city's citizens should be pouring in here and demanding that Nomusa take heed of the danger standing right outside our walls. But they won't do that. None of them will. So that leaves me.

All seven members of the Matriarchy's Inner Circle sat around the throne room's round black walnut table. The six chiefs of Wintersvilla waited silently as Nomusa finished reading the morning's reports. Her obsidian complexion and intricately woven dreadlocks radiated both striking beauty and an aura of meticulously crafted and maintained power. She wasn't as bulky as Shira, but her natural height and consistent daily training ensured that her bare, toned musculature demanded attention from even the most impressive warriors, whether friend or foe. Nomusa, by her own decree as Matriarch, was the only individual allowed to wear an exo outside of battle or labor. She was already naturally taller than all the others, but in her exo, she towered over the rest of the women like a true queen lording over her subjects.

As the Chief of Logistics and General of War, Shira observed the other women, considering each one carefully as she weighed how to convince them of the terrible truth they all needed to accept if they hoped to survive the coming days.

Shira turned to her left and scanned the length of the table. Mei, the Chief of Science and Trade, pored over a bevy of her own reports concerning domestic trade between the city's many districts. There was a time when she also oversaw imports and exports to various known human settlements and the only other major human cities on the planet: Downver and Vida. However, Downver and Vida had grown self-sufficient over the years so that they no longer required the protection of Wintersvilla Warriors. This translated to a severe decrease in the number of men being traded like currency with Wintersvilla and forced into slavery. Nowadays, Mei mostly concerned herself with domestic matters, so she was undoubtedly aware of Wintersvilla's quickly crumbling foundations.

Mei's braided black hair and meticulous makeup reflected the precision and flawlessness of her work. She was the only woman in the room without ports or a metal endoskeleton. Wearing loose magenta robes, she was also the only chief with most of her body covered for the sake of comfort and convenience. For Mei, glory was found on the battlefield of knowledge and negotiation, and on that battlefield she was a ruthless goddess of war. She might not have any ports, but she was the only reason, along with the Agency, that Shira and the others had theirs.

I can convince Mei. She's always been reasonable and fair, even when it came to Aliana and Aurelia and the agreement with the Nomads, Shira considered carefully, recollecting the time when, twelve years earlier, Rooli, who was only called Enduring Ironwood at the time, walked right up to the looming, austere Northern Wall of Wintersvilla and asked to speak to Queen Nomusa on behalf of the Nomads worldwide. *Mei was the one who finally convinced Nomusa to take the deal in the end,* Shira reminded herself, bolstering her confidence that Mei would see reason during this meeting that would decide the fate of all their lives.

Nomusa continued silently reading Shira's report, and Shira turned to scrutinize Lain, the young Chief of Reconnaissance and Expedition. The unfettered warrior effortlessly picked at one of her forearm ports and hummed a simple melody to herself, traversing some distant horizon in her mind. Spending her entire childhood on expeditions beyond Wintersvilla's walls, Lain felt most comfortable away from home. She was only back in the city by coincidence, having returned to repair a malfunctioning section of her exo just a few nights earlier. Lain had been born to a renownedly beautiful and naturally athletic birthing mother named Jude just after the forming of the Matriarchy. As a particularly fit and clever newborn, she was subsequently raised by the previous Chief of Reconnaissance and Expedition, the ruthlessly intelligent and brutally effective Nichole Adamich, who was called the Serenading Slayer, for she was known to sing with joy as she effortlessly slaughtered her enemies on the battlefield. Shira grimaced as she filled her head with images of Nichole, her closest childhood friend after Nomusa. Nichole had stolen an exo and gone rogue sixteen years earlier, when Lain was only eight years old. Shira still couldn't help clinging to a distant hope that Nichole was happy somewhere, though she was likely dead.

I wish you could have met Aliana and Aurelia, Shira thought remorsefully, knowing that Nichole would have fallen in love with them even more than Shira had. Shira knew it must have been hard for Lain to lose Nichole, but Lain had never expressed any pain over her second mother's traitorous departure. The same day they discovered that Nichole had stolen Wintersvilla property and abandoned the Matriarchy, they told Lain the truth. She responded simply, "Nichole does as she pleases. She's stronger and smarter than all of Wintersvilla combined. I say good for her for attempting to survive alone, as a true warrior should." Even now, Lain still didn't seem affected by Nichole's absence, though it was impossible to know if she was just adept at disguising her despair. She kept to herself, and she seemed to genuinely prefer her own company.

Lain will remain neutral as usual, Shira concluded, recognizing that the girl was not necessarily a friend nor an enemy, but rather a fellow warrior whom she deeply respected and admired. *The wilds of the Nomadic world are her true home. At the very least, she won't stand against me,* Shira determined with a reserve of caution, for Lain was by far the most unpredictable and hardest to read of all the chiefs.

Nomusa cleared her throat, prompting everyone in the room to turn and face her, but she just went on reading the reports, taking her time to scrutinize Shira's data and proposals. Shira turned back to analyze the other chiefs, and this time she glanced at Greta, the Chief of Slavery and Birthing. The battle-scarred and gruff woman twisted her thick neck and stretched at the shoulders impatiently, flexing her bulky and only slightly sagging warrior muscles as if in agitation. Despite their shared glory in the past, the bond between Shira and Greta was a tenuous knot of tragedy and trauma, culminating in a deep, begrudging distrust. Shira knew a part of Greta loved her for killing Craig Winters and freeing Mei, Nomusa, Nichole, Shira and herself, the five founders of Wintersvilla, from slavery. However, Shira also knew that Greta equally loathed her for killing Winters on her own. The perverted, foul old man had raped and tortured the founders of the Matriarchy in this very room when they were still just children. The other four, but especially Greta, viewed Shira killing Winters by herself as a betrayal rather than the act of love

Shira intended it to be, and for the last twenty-seven years, Greta's resentment toward Shira had grown to a violent head. Shira reasoned that Greta's hatred for Aliana, Aurelia, and Rooli was just collateral damage in her bitterness toward Shira. Shira had concluded many times in the past that it was only a matter of time before Greta made an attempt on her life, as Greta openly and vocally desired Shira's position as general, believing it to hold greater prestige and benefit than her own role as the city's premier slave driver. As was the Wintersvilla custom, it was Greta's right to duel Shira to the death, but Greta was clever enough to know that she would die in a heartbeat in a duel with Shira.

Greta is a great warrior, but I am greater, Shira concluded with what she considered to be fairness and modesty. Regardless, were it not for Nomusa's demand that Shira remain general, she would have let Greta take the position. *I didn't choose this life. It chose me,* Shira ruminated. *Greta won't help me. She will undoubtedly stand against me, along with Nomusa's young bodyguards.*

While Mei wore her robes, the other women in the room wore light strips of silk undergarments for convenience and sanitation, except for Nomusa's personal bodyguards, the nineteen-year-old twins Sophie and Lina, the Joint Chiefs of Protection, who were naked at all times. Their constant nudity was seen as one of the marks of a true Wintersvilla Warrior; like an old world animal, a truly vicious and effective being had no use for the comfort and safety of clothing. It was a custom originally started by Nomusa in the early days of the Matriarchy's founding. Nomusa's original intention in being nude as often as possible was a statement to the world of men that women could now openly bare their bodies as much as they pleased without fear of molestation or rape. However, over time, as warriors mimicked the actions of their queen, the nudity custom took on new meaning, and warriors, including Shira, took it as a challenge to remain as bare as possible during battle and leisure.

As the twins sat silently beside Nomusa, they stared daggers at Shira, refusing to take their eyes off her from the moment Shira had entered the room.

They hate me, Shira knew. *Even more than men. They think I've grown weak. They think my caution and carefulness is an affront to Wintersvilla's might. All the young warriors see the old timers as weak, it seems.*

Shira visualized the tens of thousands of Wintersvilla Women who had died in battle over the years, and she marveled at the glory of their sacrifices. *These young girls are so eager for death and battle despite never having tasted the real thing. The greatest danger they know are duels to the death with their fellow sisters. They don't know what it means to hunt and be hunted by a Hunter. But I guess that's my fault, after all. I've made this world a safer place, and in turn, I've deprived these young warriors of their promised glory. They can't help but despise me.*

Shira let her stare fall away from Sophie's and Lina's rabid glares, and then she ran her hand across the wooden table. It was the same table Winters had once used to dine and formulate his sordid plans for world domination. A stream of terrible memories coursed through Shira whenever the Inner Circle met, reminding her of all the times Winters had violated her atop the very same wooden table. She could still vividly smell his suffocating cologne and taste the bitterness of his rotten skin. Shira had begged Nomusa to destroy the table when they were still kids, but Nomusa always refused, claiming that it was important to be reminded where they came from and that it was men who were their true enemy—the enemy of all women. It was the same reason she never changed the name of Wintersvilla. It was like a trophy to her, but to Shira it was just a terrible nightmare that she wished she could drain of life and leave in the dirt.

"Something the matter, Sister?" Nomusa asked Shira. She had finished with Shira's reports and had been watching Shira stare at the crimson stain on the far edge of the table for an unknown amount of time. The stain was a mix of Shira's and Winter's blood from when Shira had gutted the disgusting old man with his own prototype weapon, which remained embedded into her endoskeleton the old way—direct into the flesh without the use of ports.

"No, Musa. I'm fine," Shira stated, flattening her wandering mind and nodding for Nomusa to start the meeting.

"Come on then, Shira. Let's hear what you have to say," Mei offered, gentle but to the point.

"Is there something wrong with the table?" Nomusa issued with a twinge of impatience, revealing a surge of the cold distance she'd actively built between herself and Shira, especially over the last couple years.

"It's nothing, Musa," Shira said once more, knowing that Nomusa was perfectly aware that the table made Shira uneasy to the point of feeling nauseas.

It's like she's starting to hate me just as much as Greta, Shira thought. *It's the girls. And it's Rooli. That much is obvious. She was never the same after we made the truce with the Nomads, allowing Rooli to live within our walls and never leave the girls' side. She still sees it as a shameful bending of the knee since the Nomads agreed to allow Wintersvilla to stand, implying that they would destroy Nomusa's Matriarchy if she didn't comply with Rooli's presence in her queendom. And she blames me most of all, for I was the one who argued most heavily to take the deal.*

Shira sighed deeply, unsure how to begin.

"Cut the troutshit, Shira," Greta lashed with an impatient roll of her eyes. "You're the one who convinced Nomusa to call this so-called war council in the first place. I've a city to run, you understand, General? I don't have the pleasure of spending all my time raising little lab-grown girls."

Shira held her tongue, not allowing Greta's bristling indignation to pierce her facade of calm stoicism. Technically, with all Hunters and Huntresses extinguished from the Earth, Shira's job as General of Wintersvilla had been completed nearly a decade earlier. Shira knew that Greta detested her for completing her appointed duty in a way that Greta, as Chief of Slavery and Birthing, never could. There would always be more births and more projects for slaves to complete, always something grander to build in Nomusa's name. But Greta's ill will toward Shira went far deeper. Despite Shira barely speaking to Nomusa about anything except Matriarchy affairs since the girls were born over a decade ago, Greta was still jealous of Shira's childhood closeness with Nomusa and also envious of Shira's legendary status as the slayer of the most Hunters and Huntresses of any Woman of Wintersvilla who had ever lived. But worst of all, Greta coveted Shira's title as the destroyer of the worst monster that had ever breathed: Craig Winters.

Greta eyed Nomusa, goading her to make Shira speak so that she could go back to taking out her envy and ire on hordes of enslaved men and boys who far outnumbered the women. Nomusa looked to Shira and nodded in turn, requesting that Shira explain the reason she had called for this meeting.

"Fine," Shira issued, accepting that there was no perfect way to address these women that might leave them all in agreement.

But I still have to try to convince them. They'll hate me for this, but I have to try. I don't have a choice. This is the only way to keep the girls safe and give Wintersvilla any chance of surviving through the week.

Shira took one last deep breath, then said, "War is upon us, sisters. You all know that. But what you all refuse to accept is that this entire city will fall to the Rovers and Biofreaks. We are doomed if we don't parley and attempt to negotiate an armistice and eventually a lasting truce, like we did with the Nomads over a decade ago."

Nomusa glared at Shira as if Shira had just challenged her to a duel for the right to rule as Matriarch. Mei didn't bother looking up from her reports. Lain looked as though she hadn't even heard Shira. Greta and the twin bodyguards looked at one another, then burst out laughing.

"Is this really the General of Wintersvilla's recommendation?" Sophie asked with obnoxious, condescending laughter.

"A parley with the pathetic little boys our Matriarchy threw away?" Lina added, smiling as she shook her head in disappointment.

"Did I ask either of you to speak?" Nomusa lashed without altering her inflection or averting her eyes from Shira.

Sophie and Lina obediently lowered their heads but not their condescending smiles.

Shira nodded, having already predicted exactly how each woman would react. The young bodyguards were kept in check by Nomusa, but Greta was another matter entirely.

"Are you intentionally attempting to insult us, General?" Greta asked as she allowed herself a few final chuckles at Shira's expense. "Maybe we should let the Rovers take turns enjoying Wintersvilla Mothers too? Would that satisfy the general?"

Shira ignored Greta's disgusting suggestion and kept her eyes locked with Nomusa.

"Musa," Shira said, her tone that of a friend rather than the Queen's general. "You read my reports, right? You understand what they mean, Sister?"

Nomusa sighed deeply then finally broke her stare from Shira and scanned the other women with an unflinching gaze.

"Have all of you read Shira's reports?"

Sophie and Lina remained still, their eyes still downcast from being scolded earlier. Mei and Lain nodded absentmindedly while Greta shook her head in disapproval.

"I skimmed it. It was troutshit," Greta scowled. "Waste of my time. I had a fatherfucking little boy bite my ankle this morning in the reclaimed part of the Metro District. The kid is lucky he isn't a runt, or I'd suggest using him as cannon fodder tonight against the Rovers." Greta turned and smiled at Shira with overt facetiousness. "But that wouldn't do any good, would it, General? The Biofreaks are, what did you say in your report? Unstoppable?"

Nomusa growled beneath her breath at the suggestion that the Biofreaks could possibly have the upper hand against her Matriarchy, but she otherwise did not break her silence.

"Musa," Shira continued with controlled calm as she ignored Greta, "the Biofreaks and Rovers assembled just beyond our lands aren't like the ones we're used to. The majority of the Rovers follow a king now, and he organized an army of Rovers who have unprecedentedly deep connections with their Biofreaks. These Rovers communicate with their Biofreaks like Wintersvilla Warriors with their exos. And their king, BigBilly, he—"

"What do we care about a goddamn Rover king, General? Or about Biofreaks, no matter how organized they might be?" Greta chastised, her voice like the slaving-whip gripped in her thick hands. She rose from her chair, her muscles twitching in agitation. "Enough of this. We are nearly finished renovating one of the largest towers in the Metro District. And after I'm done with that, I will be overseeing the securing of the Northern Wall. And I still need to punish that little biter!"

"You will sit, Greta," Nomusa issued, and Shira was caught off guard at the sight of Sophie nodding to Greta then quickly glancing at Lina before returning her simmering stare back to Shira. Shira had known these women long enough to realize that something was going on between them.

What the hell are they up to? she considered carefully.

"We all know the skin of a Biofreak is impenetrable," Nomusa stated, stealing Shira's attention from the twins' death glares. "But their eyes aren't. We stab their gaping eyes, and the Biofreaks fall. A handful of

Wintersvilla Women can dispatch a whole legion of Biofreak mounted Rovers. You disagree, General?"

Shira heaved a deep sigh and restrained herself from challenging Greta with a stinging stare before answering. "Normally I would agree with you, but things are different now, Nomusa. This Rover King, BigBilly he calls himself—he has trained a platoon of Biofreaks to fight like an organized army. They aren't detached or stupid like the others. They are cunning and focused, as if fueled by some unquenchable hatred."

"A hatred for Wintersvilla, yes, General? For me, you mean?" Nomusa offered with a proud chuckle, then added. "I should have killed them all. It was compassion to throw them over the walls. I should have just suffocated the little runt slaves the moment we cut their umbilical cords, and then all this could have been avoided. You see? This is where compassion leads, sisters."

"Nomusa—" Shira began uneasily, hearing Winters in Nomusa's words and tone.

"No matter, General," Nomusa interrupted, her voice booming through the echoing chamber of her throne room. "I made this mess, and I will clean it up. I was going to do it alone, but I will defer to your caution as our esteemed general. The six of us," she said, pointing to everyone except Mei, "will take our exos into battle alongside seven of our best warriors, your wife included, Shira. We will utilize all thirteen of the exos presently stationed in the city, including the new one your wife synced to. Thirteen of the finest Wintersvilla Warriors will meet this Biofreak legion in battle, and we will exterminate them in a single night. Okay, General? Let Major Myriam know that she should get some rest before tonight's battle. I've no doubt she's training Tomasz' girls as we speak," Nomusa finished placatingly, and it stung that not only had Nomusa referenced the girls pejoratively, but she had also totally disregarded Shira's warnings with the same hollow placations that one might offer an overly concerned spouse.

"Nomusa, we've never battled Biofreaks like this," Shira warned with only partial restraint as she rose from her chair. "These aren't the Biofreaks we've all encountered in the northern and eastern wilds. This is an army. They'll kill us all. Even Overdrive won't be enough, Musa," she said, softening her tone to one of sisterly love. "Have I ever steered us wrong, Musa? These aren't wild Biofreaks, Sister. These are—"

"I am Matriarch of Wintersvilla," Nomusa announced with a room-shaking bellow, extending the knees of her exo into a fully upright standing position so that she towered even higher over Shira and the others. "Shira Arcadia is my general, not my queen. Is that understood?" Nomusa said with smoldering condescension. The twins and Greta smiled with tangible satisfaction at Shira being publicly scolded.

"Yes, Sister. You're right," Shira nodded, scolding herself inwardly for trying to sway the most stubborn woman who had ever lived. If the pictures and information in Shira's report from a week earlier didn't convince her that the Rovers had the upper hand, then of course her words wouldn't either.

But I had to try, Shira reasoned. *At least I can say I tried. So now I have no choice. The decision is made for me.*

"Of course she's right," Greta hissed, and she pushed from the table and stormed out of the room.

"Enjoy the rest of the afternoon, sisters," Nomusa said as she turned to ascend the staircase leading back to her private quarters. "Tonight, fatherfucking glory is ours."

From the third story balcony of her penthouse apartment, Shira slowed her breathing to a controlled state of focus. Her direct view of the training fields filled the recesses of her troubled mind with scant enjoyment as the rest of her mind incessantly and repeatedly went over her reckless but unavoidable plans for the night. Myriam and the girls were down in the training fields now, clanging blunted but still heavy steel training swords together as Myriam tirelessly parried the ceaseless blows of a two-on-one onslaught. A dozen paces away from the sparring trio, Rooli stood and watched with unblinking eyes. The girls didn't hold back, and though they were unable to land a single blow, there were numerous instances when Myriam had to retreat a step or two in her maneuvers, which was impressive on its own.

My little warriors, Shira beamed, and she imagined the pain that any man would suffer were they to dare cross paths with the seemingly weak and fragile Aliana and Aurelia. Shira trained them to utilize their perceived weakness against their opponents—to do battle with their minds first and their bodies second. As she watched the girls work together, she marveled at their ability to read each other's subtlest movements. Aliana deflected in the same moment Aurelia charged and swung, then Aurelia parried exactly as Aliana pivoted and deflected. They fought as though they were wearing fully synced exos, but of course, that was something they would never be able to utilize without metal endoskeletons and ports.

But that doesn't matter, Shira reminded herself. *They are meant for something far greater than warriorhood. Something beyond anything I or anyone can imagine,* Shira told herself, though in truth, no one had even the faintest clue what their fate might entail.

A Virus and Cure—that's all Tomasz could ever offer, and even then, Tomasz is just an instrument of some higher power. I'm certain of it.

Thinking of Tomasz reminded Shira that he could have helped them escape Wintersvilla, but he had refused all of Shira's attempts at communication over the past several months, ever since Shira realized with terrible certainty that Wintersvilla's end was near.

There are no more than 100,000 women in the whole city at any given time, including the suburbs. And there are at least 1,500,000 slaves, Shira considered grimly, seeing the disparity in those numbers as the killing blow to Wintersvilla rather than the Nomads or Rovers. She had warned Nomusa about the gradual decline in the female population of Wintersvilla on several distinct occasions over the years. Even Mei and Greta, to Shira's surprise, echoed her concern. But Nomusa always contended that the slow decline was manageable and temporary—the result of Wintersvilla Warriors being sold to Vida, Downver, and numerous other settlements and pockets of civilization that had dwindled and mostly disappeared over the last few years.

The truth is that most women just leave, Shira brooded somberly. *They use their training as a means of survival, and even without an exo, they choose the wilds of the Earth over the constraints of Wintersvilla.*

Particularly loud clangs of metal broke Shira's thoughts and directed her mind back to the training fields. The girls dove at Myriam in unison, and Myriam deflected hard, leaving the girls tumbling across the field. They lifted themselves and laughed along with Myriam, not even noticing the scrapes and cuts from raking their exposed skin across the rough sand of the training fields.

All I know is that we must leave this place. We should have left weeks ago, but I thought we had more time. The Rovers gathered at our borders so suddenly. Regardless, I will do what has to be done for them, for they are meant for something more than all of this, and nothing will stand in their way. Whoever tries to stop them will have to come through me and Myriam first. And Rooli too, Shira thought. However, she had never seen the Hybrid do battle, and Rooli had spoken no more than a handful of words and the occasional incomplete sentence in the last twelve years that Rooli had lived in Wintersvilla. She was never more than a handful of paces away from either girl, who she demanded remain together at all times. Luckily for the girls, they preferred to be inseparable, even if they were at each other's throats most of the time.

But that's just how siblings are when they're young, Shira told herself. It was just another behavior that made the girls perfectly human in her eyes, regardless of their nonhuman genetic makeup. *They're more human than a whole lot of humans I know,* Shira concluded, seeing Winters with terrible clarity in her mind. From Winters, Shira's mind turned to Nomusa and the rest of the Inner Circle. *They've left me no choice,* she concluded as she watched the girls dive back in for a coordinated attack. *I will watch this city burn before I let anything happen to you girls,* Shira seethed, and she felt only anger, not sadness, as she visualized the entire city and its people being ransacked by unstoppable brutes. Suddenly the Biofreaks she was visualizing transformed into the old world mercenary armies who had raped her and killed her family and her neighbors out of fear that if they did not obey the command of Craig Winters, then the nightmare Hunters released by Mendel would torture them and their families in even worse ways.

Everyone's the fucking same, Shira lamented, wishing desperately that the girls could live in a world that knew only peace and equanimity…and love.

Shira winced at the thought of love, and she suddenly ached to hold Myriam and make love to her. She let her mind slip under the covers with her beautiful wife, but then suddenly she was nine years old again, bent over the wooden table of Winters' throne room, crying and pleading for someone to save her. Anyone.

Shira gritted her teeth and forced the memory to change. Suddenly she had Wintersbane, and she screamed and pounced on Winters, plunging his own blade into his throat and chest and gut and groin over and over and over. Shira yelped out loud and realized her breathing was shallow and rapid. She inhaled a deep breath into her lungs and held it, and as she exhaled, so too did the thoughts diminish in intensity, becoming stinging wisps of fog in the periphery of her mind.

Everyone's a fucking monster, because the world forces us to be that way. There's no way out of it. You become a monster, or you get used and eaten up by monsters. The girls' smiles beamed beneath the sunlight, and Shira's eyes widened at the intensity of emotion she felt for these girls—a severe and savage selflessness that she never fathomed was possible.

I am a monster, Shira accepted painfully, something she punishingly reminded herself again and again through the years. *But you two are mine, and I will protect you from every other monster of this world, no matter how ferocious or terrible. I will be worse, because I love you both. I will destroy myself if it means giving you even a day longer to live. I am a monster. But I am yours just as you are mine.*

Tears streamed from Shira's eyes, and she considered doing a round of pushups when three loud knocks resounded at her door.

Must be a courier, Shira thought as she considered what she had ordered and apparently forgotten about. She wiped her eyes and envisioned a lithe, muscular courier standing outside her door—a breed of slave born and bred to deliver packages around the city with incredible speed and endurance.

She opened the door and felt the hair on the back of her neck rise upon seeing the dual, contemptuous smiling faces of Sophie and Lina. They wore chest-binders and undergarments meant for battle, and Shira realized it was the first time she had ever seen the Chiefs of Protection wear any type of clothing. Glints of light directed Shira's eyes to their hands, and it was only then that she realized the women were each wielding twin tri-blades, elongated daggers with their blades sharpened in a triangular fashion to make wounds harder to heal and more likely to cause infection.

One part of Shira's mind reeled in disbelief, but another part had been ready for this moment ever since Nomusa had, just a few years earlier, created new chief positions out of thin air and appointed these lethal twins as her personal bodyguards. The surprised part of her mind wanted to reason with them, but the battle-hardened part of her mind was already ejecting Wintersbane from her wrist and thrusting it forward in a perfectly timed deflection of all four blades.

Shira jumped backward, but the women were as quick and ruthless as Hunters and pounced on her, slashing at Shira with unrestrained viciousness. Shira kicked her squat coffee table at Sophie, distracting her for a few seconds so that she could focus on Lina.

Wicked little thing, Shira thought, and she swung upward then downward, forcing Lina to subconsciously anticipate Shira's next attack coming from below, but instead, Shira pivoted her hips and roundhouse kicked Lina in the head, missing her temple by mere centimeters. Sophie dove back into the fray and swung for Shira's liver with one blade and her knee with the other. Shira deflected the liver shot, but Sophie managed to slice an inch gouge just above Shira's right knee due to Lina presently recovering and hurling herself at Shira with wild abandon. Wishing she had an exo, Shira bent at the knees and dove backward with a grunt of force, deflecting several rapid blows as she deftly grabbed the old world relic of a sword that had sat over her fireplace mantel for ten years collecting dust. Shira wasn't sure if the blade would be able to withstand the repeated strikes of two of Wintersvilla's most vicious warriors. The twins swung, and though the old world sword chipped against their blows, it did not shatter.

Shira's two blades kept up with their four for a few more seconds, but out of nowhere Lina landed a sweeping kick, slamming Shira against the window and shattering the glass before she recovered and jumped back to her feet. Her battle reflexes deflected multiple blows without conscious input, allowing Shira to notice in a flash that Sophie's mouth was slack with exhaustion. Despite Lina's head already swelling and bruising from Shira's powerful kick, she appeared unfazed, and she lunged at Shira, clearly impatient to strike her down. Taking advantage of the young woman's eagerness, Shira anticipated her lunge and deflected then parried, aiming for Lina's left kidney with Wintersbane as she passed. Lina twisted, forcing the blade to nick her shoulder instead.

Shira readied for another pounce, but as the twins rose, their labored breathing revealed that they had reached their limit and needed a few seconds to recover. Shira was grateful they lacked her much larger musculature and time-forged endurance.

Blood trickled from Shira's arm, and she glanced down to see thin lines of blood streaming slowly from several shards of window glass protruding from her scarred flesh. Even more of her blood covered the wall and ground.

I need to end this before I lose too much blood, Shira resolved, and though she felt an urge to pull the shards out, she knew it was better to leave them and let them serve as crude plugs to stifle the bleeding.

"We've dreamed of this day, Shira Arcadia," Lina said as she slowly prowled to Shira's right.

"To do battle against the legendary General of Wintersvilla," Sophie marveled as she slipped to Shira's left.

"Did Greta put you up to this? Or was it Nomusa?" Shira demanded, gripping the old world blade in anger that an assassination attempt was being made on her life on the eve of battle. Every woman had a right to challenge another woman to a duel to the death, but such duels were regulated and observed. This was something else—a betrayal that Shira hated to admit she had seen coming, one way or another.

"It was me," Greta said as she entered the room and closed the door. Shira wondered if any of the other residents of the building might have heard the commotion, but everyone was likely already making their way to the outer walls to get a good view of the coming battle involving the Matriarch and Wintersvilla's founders. Rather than being afraid for their lives, the city was pulsating with excitement.

"You can't kill me yourself, so you get these two to do it for you, Greta?" Shira challenged, and she raised Wintersbane in preparation for a three-on-one battle to the death. "Or was it Nomusa? Is she behind all this?" Shira asked, feeling deep pain throb in the depths of her mind, for although she and Nomusa were now distant, there was a time they were more than sisters. Each served as the other's unyielding backbone through the worst days and years of existence. They were each other's saviors.

Greta smiled, and Shira prepared herself for the terrible answer.

"Nomusa has no idea," Greta stated with mocking amusement, and despite quickly losing blood and staring potential death in the face, Shira felt a great weight lift from her chest at Greta's words.

At least it wasn't you, Sister. I don't think I could stomach that.

"You're Nomusa's weakness. You realize that, Shira? Just like how those girls are your weakness," Greta said, shaking her head in disappointment. Lina removed her chest-binder and wrapped it around her shoulder to stifle the bleeding caused by Shira's blade, reminding Shira about her knee. Despite the shallowness of the cut, blood flowed far too quickly, and a small pool was already beginning to form at her foot.

Shira placed her hands against her casual silk strips and raised her eyebrows, wordlessly asking if they would let her stifle the wound before they attacked again. Greta offered a shallow nod, and Shira removed the strips from her chest and shoulders then tied them into a tourniquet around her right leg.

"I'm going to offer you a choice, General," Greta stated, her eyes slits of age-old spite.

"And if they had killed me before you got here, would I still have this choice?" Shira asked, glaring right back at Greta.

Sophie and Lina smiled, and Greta shrugged. "Don't take it so personally, Shira. You think I envy you. You think I want your position. But I don't, you high and mighty bitch. I am the true leader of this city. You're a glorified second mother, and Nomusa is as shortsighted as a man. The fact that these Rovers and Biofreaks are even alive proves that she is unfit to be Matriarch," Greta announced, and both Sophie and Lina raised their shoulders and stood as personal bodyguards at Greta's side.

"I'm just a steppingstone," Shira realized. "I'm just an obstacle to your true goal. You want control of the whole Matriarchy," Shira laughed at the audacity of staging a coup on the eve of being besieged, regardless of whether or not Greta viewed the siege as an actual threat.

"I want the whole world, damnit," Greta lashed. "And why not? The world used to be in the hands of men. It still is. We are still beholden to the Nomads of that goddamn fatherfucker Mendel. Someone has to be the leader, Shira, and Nomusa is unfit for it. You killed Winters. Nomusa led us to this point. Now I take over the rest," Greta said with perfect confidence in her ability to be leader of the entire world.

"Aren't you the one who got angry over a little slave bite this morning?" Shira goaded with a wrathful smile.

"Shut up, you dumb bitch," Greta lashed, speaking to Shira exactly as Shira imagined she always wanted. "Look at you. You don't even know your fate is already sealed. You're going to die in this room. This is where it all ends for you. And then we're going to kill Myriam and that disgusting Hybrid," Greta stated with rapacious indignation. Shira let her speak, allowing her words to fuel a torrent of boiling rage in every one of her cells.

"And then we kill Nomusa. And Mei and Lain if they don't obey," Greta finished with wicked satisfaction, as if this plan had plagued her mind for countless years.

"Is that it?" Shira stated simply, refusing to reveal the rage now bubbling and prickling every inch of her skin.

I'm going to slice you three traitors to fatherfucking pieces, Shira seethed within.

"Or," Greta continued, "you can take the girls and leave with your wife and the Hybrid. We won't try to follow you. We don't care about you, Shira. We just want what's right for Wintersvilla, and it isn't you or Nomusa. Nomusa will never relinquish her power. That's why we're going to kill her. But we will let you leave, Shira. I harbor no ill will toward you, despite what you might think. I just think you've always been an overrated brat. Doesn't mean I want to kill you though."

"Or," Shira began with a torturously controlled calm. "I can kill you three right here. Right now."

Shira lifted Wintersbane and the old world blade and bent at the knees.

"Wait!" Greta stated with her hand raised.

Blood still poured from her wounds, but Shira let the woman speak, hoping she might reveal more valuable information about her wicked plans.

"You kill us and your precious little girls will be on trophy spikes."

Greta's words paralyzed Shira, and though she kept her blades in battle-ready stance, she nodded for Greta to continue.

"Nomusa decided that she's going to use this battle to steal the girls right from under your nose. She assigned a whole platoon of slaves to kill the Hybrid, then kidnap the girls and bring them to an outpost. She's planning to chain them up and wait for puberty to hit. Whatever changes are going to happen, she wants to be in control. She wants to use them as a weapon."

Shira shook her head in disbelief. "A weapon for what?"

Greta shrugged at the obviousness of the answer. "The same thing anyone wants. Control. World control. Planetary power. She doesn't see them as little girls, Shira. She doesn't see them as human. None of us do, really. Just you. But one of these days they're going to change, and even you won't see them that way."

"You're wrong," Shira said. "They're the only ones I see as human."

Greta chuckled to herself. "Fine. Whatever, Shira. Then take them and leave. And don't come back. Wintersvilla is mine, you understand? The girls are yours. I don't want them. I don't trust them. So go now, and don't come back."

Shira weighed her options. She could take Greta's offer to leave with the girls and Myriam, but there was always the possibility she was lying. Greta might have her own terrible plans for the girls. On the other hand, if Greta was telling the truth, then even if she killed these three women, the girls would still be unsafe with Nomusa in control.

I know I'm right about the power of the Biofreaks, Shira considered, her mind firing more rapidly than she had ever experienced in her life. *They're going to tear this city and everyone in it to shreds. Thirteen exos just aren't enough. Maybe Greta's telling the truth. Maybe she's lying. But either way, she's not the one I need to come to an agreement with.*

"You're all dead tonight anyway. Whether it's me or the Biofreaks, you're all going to die. I can't trust you, Greta. And I can't leave here and let you live knowing you might show up one day and kill me and the girls in our sleep. So, I'm going to kill you three, and then I'm going to parley with the Rovers like I suggested at the meeting."

Greta chuckled and shook her head while Sophie and Lina smiled with delight at the prospect of more fighting.

"So be it," Greta concluded with a flash of rage in her eyes. "Kill her."

Sophie and Lina hesitated for just a moment then pounced toward the General of Wintersvilla, the most formidable and revered warrior who had ever lived.

There was a time when Shira would have thought only of the glory each battle held, but now she fought for something truly meaningful. As Sophie and Lina charged forward, Shira held another set of twins in her mind, and she knew that nothing could possibly hurt Aliana or Aurelia for as long as she drew breath.

That's why I can't die here, Shira knew. *Fuck glory. My girls are all that matter—in life and in death. I'll kill you all to protect them. Every single one of you.*

Shira had never felt such overwhelming confidence in her abilities, and she marveled at the power of selfless love.

My love for those girls is the deadliest instrument of war I've ever known, Shira thought as Sophie and Lina finally closed the gap. *Now, come and taste my love's unforgiving edge.*

What the others can never understand is that I don't strive and labor for myself. I am not climbing Mendel's Ladder for my own sake. I do not aim to ascend to godhood to save myself. All that I do is in the service of humanity, the universe, and the Great Beyond. I strive for the beyond laid before us—a destination unknown by any human mind until now. There are seemingly infinite paths to the Great Beyond. The one that I have chosen for the Earth and its people is one of many, but they all lead to the same destination.

At the crux of this particular path lie a handful of unique individuals who will bring my rightful Ascension to fruition. Of these individuals, the two that cannot be allowed to deviate in the slightest from their course will also be the most vulnerable and feeble. I will tell Tomasz to design them and birth them this way—as seemingly weak and frail little girls. It is from this place of feebleness that they will learn what it means to be strong, and it is from their vulnerability that they will learn to value calculation and poise. All of this is necessary for what fate has ordained them to become.

I do not know their names—I will leave that up to those who raise them. Their names don't matter, for their eventual domains lie in namelessness. A virus and a cure. A poison and an antidote. A weapon and a shield.

They are the key to my design, and my design is the key to the ineffable beyond.

From Mendel's Ladder: The Personal Journal of Denis Mendel, Recorded Circa 2065, Published June 2108 by Leif Mainstone, Federated Agency Publishing

Chapter 2
Little Smooth Talker

Year: 2099, Present Day

It all happened in a single breath-stealing moment. Shira's eyes shot open with adrenaline fueled alertness, and then she was suddenly an inch from Aliana's face. Just as quickly, Aliana found herself in free fall with the bottom of the crater racing toward her and her stomach lurching into her throat.

Holy Muto we're going to fucking die! Aliana screamed within. A giant boulder at the bottom of the crater rapidly grew in size as she raced toward it, her mouth open in shock at being thrown out of the window of Gambe's body by the woman who had raised her and her sister since their birth on one of Tomasz' many living ships. Time slowed to a supernatural crawl, and in her wildly racing mind, she was suddenly back on the training fields on the night of Wintersvilla's destruction, coordinating with Aurelia to try landing even a single blow on Myriam. The memory was so vivid that she could still hear the shatter of glass as Shira's arm burst through her penthouse window while fighting for her life against Nomusa's sadistic bodyguards. Aliana fully detached from the fear of falling for just a second longer and became totally absorbed in the memory as she marveled at the swiftness of Rooli telling Myriam to go and save Shira, then grabbing the girls and running at full speed toward the Eastern Wall of the city.

Rooli, Aliana thought urgently as time returned to normal and she was jarred back to the present, submerged suddenly in the tumultuous ocean of fear coursing through her body at seeing the ground and sudden death only a few seconds from her face.

"Rooli!" she screamed desperately just as she felt something tighten around her waist. The tip of Aliana's nose skimmed the crater's bottom as the rest of her body was thrown in a wide arc and ejected upward by some unknown means. A gunshot blast resonated from below, and Aliana peered down to see that Rooli was standing in her own shallow

239

crater, the result of her heavy landing. Two vine-like arms extended fifty feet into the air on either side of Rooli's body, and as Aliana's ascent slowed to a halt, she traced one of the vining arms back to herself and the other to her sister, who was suspended a dozen or so feet away.

Rooli whipped at the shoulders and hastily retracted her arms, sloughing away her excess tissue with painful groans as she reeled the girls in.

Rooli, Aliana rejoiced with tears in her wide eyes. *You'll never let anything bad happen to us. Like Shira and Myriam and even the men.*

Placing her boots back on solid ground, Aliana glanced at her sister to make sure she was okay. In typical Aurelia fashion, she appeared unfazed by the plunge into the crater, as if she had already anticipated exactly how everything would transpire.

She always has to act so tough, Aliana thought before reminding herself that it was her sister's very existence that had forced her to become tougher than anyone could imagine. The horrific, flesh-rending black scars permanently cleaving the skin of her face were more obvious than ever, tendriling beyond her torn and tattered face mask, nearly reaching her eyes now. Not a single person other than Aliana, Rooli, Myriam, and Shira could bear to look at Aurelia without flinching. Even those who claimed otherwise were just lying to her—both girls were perfectly aware of that.

But that doesn't mean she has to be such an emotionless bitch all the time, Aliana grumbled, and she turned to look back at the ridge from where they had been tossed.

Please don't die, Shira, Aliana pleaded inwardly in terrible anguish despite knowing full well that her activation of Overdrive was a death sentence. *I don't care what Overdrive means. Find a way to live. Please, Shira. Please...Mom.* The word still didn't feel right to Aliana, even if Shira was technically her second mother. Thinking of her as mom just wasn't accurate. She was more than that. Mothers are naturally reckless with their love, unaware or unable to understand that untempered love can lead to unintentional weakness and dependence. Shira understood that, and she loved them in such a way that even her compassion and sympathy was controlled and measured to ensure that both girls would grow up with a precise mix of both independence and empathy, both self-assurance and self-actualization.

She made me who I am, and I love who I am. Just as Rooli helped make Aurelia who she needs to be.

"We need to go back," Aliana announced determinedly as the winds at the bottom of the crater began whining and tumbling dust into the air.

"Shut up," Aurelia signed. "Don't let their deaths be in vain. We need to find a way past that giant boulder."

"You shut up, Aurelia!" Aliana retorted, not caring about sounding clever.

How dare she say I'm letting them die in vain, or even that they're going to die! She doesn't know every little thing.

"They're not going to die, Aurelia. They're going to kill the Butcher. And Myriam will find a way to save Shira. They'll even find a way to take down Gambe!"

Rather than say something or stomp to break up their tiff, Rooli was already halfway to the boulder, inspecting every inch of it with her unblinking eyes.

"Whatever," Aurelia signed.

Whatever, Aliana signed back, but Aurelia was already running to catch up with Rooli and didn't see Aliana's hands.

She's right, though, Aliana forced herself to accept. *There's nothing we can do for them now. I have to just trust that they can win.* Aliana nodded to herself, injecting resolve into the deepest layers of her awareness just as Shira had always taught. *I have to move forward. I have to keep going. The strong don't stop. Ever. Even in death. I have to be strong. For Shira. For the whole world.*

The boulder towered over her by at least a full ten feet, and she wondered if it had always been there as part of the entrance or if the entrance had been intentionally sealed with the boulder at some point.

Who could have moved a boulder the size of a house? Aliana marveled as she reluctantly kept her anguish over Shira at bay. *It must have been dragged here by hordes of Downverians a long time ago to be used as a marker for the secret entrance,* she concluded reasonably.

Aliana ran forward toward Rooli and Aurelia, wiping away her tears and forcing herself not to look back toward the ridge.

"Not so fast," Gambe said as a swarm of tiny specks formed a funnel cloud suspended in the air, then solidified from the head down into his typical humanoid form. He stood before Aliana with his arms on his hips, blocking her path to Rooli and her sister.

"I'm takin' ya back to Mom. The Agency ain't so bad, you'll see. Mom ain't evil—not like the other old timers. Not like Andre and Mendel and all the rest."

"Out of my way, you lead-brained fatherfucker," Aliana demanded, and she strode toward him with her hand gripped around the hilt of the short sword sheathed at her waist.

"I said stop!" Gambe bellowed with an uncharacteristic measure of impatience, and he glanced up at the ridge as if in nervous apprehension.

Just try it, Aliana told him with her eyes, letting the winds and thoughts of Shira's impending death stir incredible rage deep within her very bones. *I might be afraid of falling to my death, but I'm not afraid of you. In fact, you're the one who looks afraid,* Aliana realized as she passed Gambe and continued walking toward Rooli and Aurelia. Gambe didn't presently try to stop her; he just continued staring at the ridge.

Since Rooli and Aurelia were already searching for the hidden entrance around the edges of the boulder, Aliana paused and allowed her mind a moment to satiate her unquenchable thirst for gaining knowledge against her enemies.

"What are you afraid of, Gambe? Do you fear the Butcher?" Aliana asked with a mix of challenge and curiosity, her grip tight on her short sword and her legs spread in battle-ready stance.

"Afraid?" Gambe said as if the word were gibberish. "I ain't got fear, little girl. I'm a weapon's expert. I'm just curious is all, ya feel me?"

Not afraid, Aliana thought, entranced by the very prospect of such power. *To be truly unafraid and secure—is that really what it's like to be him?* The winds intensified, and Aliana glanced at Rooli and Aurelia, who were searching the other side of the boulder now with a growing level of urgency. The winds struck a measure of fear in Aliana, but she knew she could offer the pair no extra help at the moment. The low howling winds whispering death, but this was her chance to understand something about Gambe and the Agency that she might never have the opportunity to elucidate ever again.

"You're not afraid of dying? Is it because you're not alive?" Aliana asked.

"I ain't afraid of nothing, Aliana. And I'm alive—more alive than ya think. More alive than you or your sister or that Hybrid even."

A glimmer of light directed Aliana's eyes to the edge of the crater, and she saw a copy of Gambe gazing at them from above, possibly even staring directly at her.

"What are you, Gambe? What are you, really?" Aliana marveled in both fear and awe. A sudden, strong gust tugged at her back, coaxing her body to move backward toward Rooli and Aurelia one step at a time without her even realizing it.

"The question is: what the hell are you and your sister, eh? I'm Agency hardware. A weapons expert and a means of transportation. Outside that, I'm a guy who likes to play games and make Mom happy, and Mom's all out of happiness, ya feel me? So mostly I just play games."

He's like a child, Aliana thought, shaking her head at the simplicity of Gambe's motivations. *I just need to placate him. And then maybe I can even convince him to let us go.* She glanced back at Rooli and her sister, who were rapidly signing to one another in the boulder's shadow. Their fingers were moving too fast to read, and both of their faces appeared stoic and emotionless, leaving Aliana unable to discern whether or not they could find the hidden entrance.

I'm more use here if I can convince Gambe. to just let us leave, Aliana knew, and she let Aurelia and Rooli continue handling the entrance while she handled their escape.

"I think it's cool you play games, Gambe. Games are an underappreciated medium," Aliana said craftily.

Gambe's arms fell from his hips, and he cocked his head in genuine surprise.

"You think?" he asked with childlike wonder.

"Yeah, obviously, you brainless metalloid. Games are what make life worthwhile," Aliana said playfully, reading Gambe now like a book.

Gambe nodded rapidly, and a faint smile formed on his otherwise featureless skull. He started laughing, then pointed excitedly at Aliana.

"I ain't ever met another person that loves games like I do!" Gambe said excitedly, like a kid realizing he had just met his best friend.

Too easy, Aliana chuckled to herself smugly, and at the same time she pitied Gambe, this toddler mind apparently forced to appease his mom, who he claimed was the Agency itself.

Aliana jumped in shock at something gripping her shoulder, but she caught herself after turning and seeing that it was just her sister.

"We have a problem," Aurelia signed with unnatural calm. "The entrance is behind the boulder. Rooli said the boulder isn't supposed to be here. Somebody did this. Somebody blocked our path."

The wind howled with a wild gust before returning to a state of relative calm. Distinct currents and eddies of pressurized air coalesced in the crater, feeding the roiling clouds above. The sight of chaotic storm clouds startled Aliana since she had never encountered any fluctuation in weather in her entire life. Blue skies and slow puffy clouds were all she and her sister had ever known.

Holy Muto, Aliana thought as her breathing quickened along with the wind.

"We have to get out of here," Aliana said, and she turned to Gambe, who was also marveling at the undulating, tumultuous clouds above. "Can you help us, metal head?"

To Be Continued

www.ingramcontent.com/pod-product-compliance
Lightning Source LLC
Chambersburg PA
CBHW020748250626
47155CB00003B/976